THE MYSTERY AT UNDERWOOD HOUSE

An Angela Marchmont Mystery Book 2

CLARA BENSON

MOUNT STREET PRESS

Mount Street Press

Copyright

ISBN: 978-1-913355-01-2

ClaraBenson.com

Cover design by Shayne Rutherford at
wickedgoodbookcovers.com

Interior Design & Typesetting by Ampersand Book Interiors
ampersandbookinteriors.com

PROLOGUE

THE LIGHTS BLAZED out from the house, casting a warm glow a few feet out onto the lawn. A man stood in the shadows just outside the pool of light, hunching his shoulders against the chill February air and glaring sulkily back towards the house. He was angry with everybody—but most of all himself. How stupid he had been to storm out on such a cold night wearing only a dinner jacket! Almost as soon as he had emerged into the garden his anger had dissipated and he had desired to return inside. But the door had locked itself behind him and now he would have to attract someone's attention if he wanted to fetch a coat, which would make him look even more of a snivelling fool than he already did. Why hadn't he done the sensible thing and stormed off to his room instead?

The windows stared back at him, seeming to mock him with their promise of warmth and comfort. Damn the house! He had always hated it, ugly thing that it was and harbourer of a lifetime of unhappy memories. He couldn't wait to get rid of it as soon as they'd let him. And damn the rest of them! He wanted none of them, money or no money. He would never be persuaded to come here again.

He fumbled in his pocket for a cigarette and lit it, turning away as he tried to determine what to do next. Of course he would have to abase himself sooner or later by begging to be let back in, but he judged that an hour or so outside would lessen his humiliation and enable him to maintain at least a modicum of dignity. At any rate, there was no use in skulking around miserably; he might as well take a brisk stroll to keep warm. With an impatient click of the tongue he set off in the direction of the lake. The sky was clear and there was a full moon, which lit his way forward.

He walked quickly, his footsteps making the only sound, although he was too absorbed in his own thoughts to notice. After a while he saw something glint through the trees, and shortly afterwards came out onto the shore of the lake, near a dilapidated wooden landing-stage. An old rowing-boat, its painter knotted and frayed in places, bobbed gently nearby. The water glimmered eerily in the cold half-light, and wisps of damp mist hung silently over it. The man walked to the end of the jetty and stood, hands in his pockets, gazing at the scene with a faint expression of distaste; he had had no love for the lake as a child, having a dislike of water in general, and had seen no reason to change his opinion as an adult. He had always felt that there was something desolate and unearthly about this place, something repellent, even. Why he had come this way he had no idea.

His blood was cooling rapidly now after the row, and he was beginning to feel rather an idiot. He wondered what the others were doing. Knowing his family, they had probably all returned to the drawing-room to pass the time in addressing each other with thinly-veiled contempt: that was the way things usually went during these affairs. Of course, two of them were absent today—queer, that, now he came to think about it. Very queer, in fact, that someone should have died at both of the last two gatherings. The first death hadn't been exactly a surprise; it had been the culmination of years of ill-health. But the second one, now; that had been something of a shock in its stark violence. He remembered, wincing, the sight of the broken, twisted body lying there, empty eyes staring at nothing. How had such an accident happened? It had really been most unfortunate. Why was the family dogged by bad luck? Who would be next? Suddenly and unexpectedly he was overwhelmed by the feeling that the woods and the darkness were closing in on him, pushing him gently yet inexorably towards the freezing lake and its unfathomable depths. He looked upwards, to where the trees hung over his head, and shivered. He had been here long enough; perhaps it was time to return to the house.

Lost in thought, the man did not hear the footsteps until they were very near. Only a creak as someone stepped onto the landing-stage behind him alerted him to the fact that someone was close by. He started and whirled round to see a figure approaching.

'Oh, it's you,' he said. 'Goodness, how you startled me!'

'I beg your pardon,' said the figure.

'How did you know where to find me?'

His companion smiled, but said nothing.

'I'm sorry about the row just now. We never did seem to be able to get along in company together. I don't know why on earth we should be forced to attend these gatherings. I think it must have been a joke on Father's part—although I can't say I find it very funny.'

'No?'

'You see things differently, I dare say. Well, I find it all a dreadful bore. I suppose they sent you to find me?'

'Not exactly.'

'Oh,' said the man, somewhat disconcerted. 'Well don't tell me you've come out for a walk at this hour. What time is it? It must be late.'

'It's twenty minutes to midnight,' replied the figure.

'Really? I've been out longer than I thought. I must be getting back to the house, or they will wonder where I have got to.'

'Just a minute,' said the other. 'I have something to say first.'

'Yes?' said the man impatiently.

'Do you know what day it is?'

The man stared.

'What do you mean? Of course I know what day it is. It's Wednesday. Or did you mean the date?'

His companion frowned, and in some undefinable way the man knew he had given the wrong answer. He was suddenly afraid.

'Another one. How soon people forget,' said the figure. 'Perhaps you will recognize this.'

The man took the thing that was offered and looked at it, uncomprehending.

'Why, yes, of course. That's my—but what does it mean?'

The figure began to speak. It spoke at length, the shadows of the trees closing in all the while, pushing them both towards the lake, and as he listened the man understood with a stab of fear that he would not be returning to the house again.

CHAPTER ONE

'OH, HOW CLUMSY I am!' exclaimed Mrs. Haynes, putting down the teapot with a clatter. 'No, don't move—I shall mop it up. I do hope it hasn't gone over your frock.'

'No, I don't think so. But don't use your nice, clean handkerchief. Here, have my napkin.'

Angela Marchmont sat back as her hostess flapped distractedly around a pool of tea that had begun to drip over the edge of the table and onto the rug.

'It's no good. I'm only making things worse. I shall have to ring the bell. Annie, I've made rather a mess here. Clear this up and bring us a fresh pot, please. You'd better take that cushion away too and see what you can do with it. What a good girl you are! I am sorry, Angela. We shall have to wait a little longer for our tea.'

'Are you quite all right, Louisa?' asked Angela. 'You seem a little out of sorts, if you don't mind my saying so.'

Louisa Haynes seemed to sag a little.

'Is it really that obvious?' she asked.

Mrs. Marchmont looked towards the damp stain on the rug with raised eyebrows and her friend smiled humorously.

'Silly of me. Well then, yes, I do have something on my mind now you mention it—' she let the sentence hang in the air, as though unsure whether to continue.

'Suppose you tell me about it,' suggested Angela. 'I have a feeling that you were going to anyway.'

She smiled and Louisa laughed, but there was a note of anxiety in her voice.

'Oh dear, I never was any good at deceiving people! And you were always so clever about that kind of thing. But you're right—I do have something I wanted to talk to you about. It's about John. And it's worrying me dreadfully.'

'Go on,' said Angela, cautiously, half-expecting to be asked to furnish a sympathetic ear and friendly advice in the matter of Louisa's husband and some bright young woman.

'Well, I say it's about John, but really it's about the Hayneses in general and old Philip who died a couple of years ago,' said Louisa. 'The dispute over the house really isn't helping and none of them like each other anyway and I do wonder sometimes if it wasn't deliberate, because he really was rather an old devil you know, although I don't like to use the word, but it was very odd of him to insist that his children meet twice a year if they wanted his money, and now Edward's dead and only John is left and we had the inquest and people are starting to talk. Do you see?'

'Not at all,' said Angela. 'Who is Edward? And why do his children have to meet twice a year?'

'Not Edward's children, Philip's,' said Mrs. Haynes. 'Because of the will.'

'Philip's will, or Edward's?'

'Philip's. I suppose the half of Edward's money that remains afterwards will go directly to Ursula and Robin.'

'I'm rather confused,' said Angela. 'Suppose we start at the beginning. By Philip do you mean Philip Haynes, John's father?'

'Yes.'

'And Philip died and left a will?'

'Yes, he left all his money to his four children in equal shares, with the proviso that they all dine together and spend the night here at Underwood House twice a year. In the will he said it was because he was sorry he had never succeeded in bringing up his children to love one another, and so he wanted them to meet regularly and attempt to get along better once he had gone. However, it's far more likely that he did it to make mischief. That was the kind of man he was.'

'Do none of the children get on? What about their mother?'

'She died about twenty years ago when John was quite a young man. I understand it was not a happy marriage. John doesn't like to talk about it much, but I gather the parents often used the children as pawns in their disputes, playing off one against the other and buying their loyalty with gifts and treats as it suited them. Poor things. It's no wonder they all grew up to mistrust each other.'

'John is the eldest, I seem to remember?'

'Yes. Then after him came Philippa, Winifred and Edward. I believe there was another girl, but she died many years ago.'

'So each child inherited a quarter of the money. What about the house?'

'He left that to them all between them, to do with as they wished. Of course, that caused problems immediately, as they couldn't agree *what* to do with it. John wanted to keep it, as he loves the old place, while Philippa and Edward wanted to sell it but disagreed on how to go about it and how much it was worth. Winifred, poor dear, who was always a little unworldly, wanted to give it away to a charitable institution for the education of orphaned girls. So nothing was ever decided.'

'I see. How difficult for them. But presumably it wasn't a pressing matter, since they had all inherited some money.'

'Yes, but even that wasn't as straightforward as it ought to have been. You see, Philip left them ten thousand pounds each, but only half of that sum was theirs to do as they liked with. The other five thousand was a life interest, so they received only the income from it and couldn't touch the capital.'

'And who was to inherit the capital after their deaths?'

'Well that's the queer thing. Under Philip's will, the money reverts absolutely to Mr. Faulkner, his lawyer.'

'Indeed? That seems a little unusual. Were they very good friends?'

'Oh, they were as thick as thieves,' said Louisa, 'but I shouldn't have called them *friends*, exactly. Old Philip didn't have friends. He had allies and he had enemies, and the one might become the other almost overnight, since you were either in favour or out of favour with him at any given moment. Mr. Faulkner is something of a character himself, and I believe there was a great deal of sympathy between the two of them. They used to spend hours shut in Philip's study, discussing who knows what.'

'Were the family surprised when they heard that Philip had left his solicitor the money?'

'I suppose they were. But they knew their father, you see—they were perfectly aware of how capricious and strange he was, and how useless it was to try and beat him in anything, so they accepted it with a kind of resignation, I think, and didn't examine it too closely. It was the same with the twice-yearly gatherings: none of them liked it but they went along with it, as they knew it was the only way to get their share of the inheritance.'

'I see,' said Angela. 'So where does Edward's death come in?'

'Well that's the thing,' said Mrs. Haynes. 'If it were only about him then I shouldn't be bothering you with all this. But it's all of them.'

'All of them?'

'Yes. They're all dead. First Philippa, then Winifred, and now Edward. Three meetings we've had since Philip's death. Three. And at each meeting one of Philip's children has died.'

'Good gracious!' said Angela.

Louisa nodded.

'Exactly,' she said. 'And it's starting to look rather suspicious.'

CHAPTER TWO

ANGELA, WHO UNTIL then had been perched on the edge of her seat in the manner of a formal visitor preparing to sup her afternoon tea politely and leave, settled herself firmly into the cushions.

'Tell me what happened, Louisa,' she said.

Mrs. Haynes, gratified that she had fully captured the attention of her audience just as she had hoped, adopted a more confidential tone.

'Well, it all started in February last year, at the first of the family dinners following Philip's death a few months earlier. You see, according to the terms of the will, Mr. Faulkner is responsible for summoning us all to these gatherings.'

'I beg your pardon, whom do you mean by "us"? It's not just Philip's children who attend, I take it.'

'Oh no. We all have to go. Of course, John and I have no choice in the matter since we live here, as did Philippa—she never married, you know. Then there's Winifred and her daughter

Susan, and Edward and his wife Ursula and their son Robin. A few weeks before the date, we all receive a letter from Mr. Faulkner reminding us terribly politely of the terms of the will, and inviting—or rather instructing us to dine together on a particular day.'

'Were any dates specified in the will?'

'Not as far as I know, but last year we all met in February and May, and this year so far we have met in February again.'

'On the same day as the meeting of last February?'

'Why, now you come to mention it, I believe it was. Let me think. This year we all spent the night of the 16th here, and—yes, of course: it was the same date last year too. I remember particularly because it was on the 17th that we heard that my god-daughter's baby had arrived early, and I was vexed because I hadn't finished knitting its hat and mittens. How odd.'

'Is there any significance attached to the 16th of February that you know of?' asked Angela.

'None that I can think of,' replied her friend, considering a moment.

'And what about the next family dinner? When will that be? In May again? It must be coming up soon, if so.'

'I have no idea. We haven't received anything from Mr. Faulkner yet. Is it important, do you think?'

'I don't know. I don't suppose so,' said Angela. 'Anyway, please go on.'

'Well, everybody duly turned up here as instructed, and we had dinner and were mostly civil to each other and a jolly miserable time was had by all, I should think. Then we all trotted off to bed and met for breakfast the next morning, but

Philippa didn't turn up, and when someone eventually went up to fetch her it was found that she had died in her sleep. Or so it was assumed, anyway. She'd had heart trouble for many years, so we were shocked but not exactly surprised when it happened.'

'Had she been well the evening before?'

'Yes, as far as I remember. I think she complained about the dinner. She was rather a complainer about things though. It was a little tiresome sometimes.'

'And was there any sign that her death was due to anything other than natural causes?'

'No, not at all. The doctor was quite happy to sign a death certificate, and she was buried and that was that. Or so we thought, at least. Then a couple of months later we got another letter from Mr. Faulkner asking us to gather here for dinner on the 27th of May, and that's when Winifred fell over the balustrade, poor thing.'

'Good gracious! How did it happen?'

'We don't know, as nobody was there at the time. It was in the afternoon, not long after most of the family had arrived—in fact I'm not even sure that everybody *had* arrived. People were scattered around the house, doing whatever it was they were doing, when suddenly there was the most awful shriek and a thud and everyone rushed out at once, but it was too late. She was lying there on the floor of the hall, quite dead.' Louisa paused. 'It was all rather upsetting,' she said unhappily.

'But how on earth did she manage to fall over?' asked Angela.

'There is a large chandelier that hangs nearby from the ceiling above. It was thought she must have overbalanced while leaning over the balustrade to dust the light with her handkerchief. She was rather a stickler for cleanliness. At any rate, there was a perfunctory inquest and her death was ruled as accidental, and again nobody had any reason to question that conclusion, although several people did remark that we seemed to be rather unlucky whenever we met as a family.'

Angela nodded sympathetically.

'Yes, I can imagine they did,' she said.

'Then we come to Edward,' went on Louisa rapidly, as though determined to get the story over and done with now she had begun. 'That's where all the trouble started. The talk, I mean. You see, there was a row after dinner. I think by this time everyone was getting rather sick of having to troop along here like good little boys and girls whenever they were summoned. And I imagine we were all somewhat on edge given what had happened to Philippa and Winifred.'

'What was the row about?'

'The house, as usual. It was always about the house. John started it. I was furious with him for doing it, but he never could resist needling Edward, who had no sense of humour at all.'

'What did he say?'

'Oh, the silly old fool made one or two jokes in very poor taste about how his sisters' deaths had removed two of the obstacles to his keeping Underwood House, and didn't Edward think that it was almost as though the house didn't *want* to be sold, and that perhaps he had better watch his step? Of course, Edward flared up at once and said some rather regrettable things, then lots of other people joined in, and it ended up with Edward's stalking out of the house in high dudgeon. He didn't come back that night, and by breakfast-time the next day Ursula was frantic with worry and insisted on having the grounds searched.'

She paused.

'They found his body in the lake that afternoon. It looked as though he'd gone out in a rowing-boat, fallen overboard and drowned.'

'I see. How terrible,' said Angela.

'Yes,' said Mrs. Haynes. 'It was, rather. Of course, it did look suspicious after what happened to Philippa and Winifred, but Ursula made things worse by kicking up an awful fuss. She kept on insisting that Edward hated water and would never have dreamed of going out in a boat by himself as he couldn't swim. And then she brought up the row of the night before and asked John what he had meant by his remarks, and before we knew it, she'd gone to the police and people in the village were saying that they'd all been murdered and that John was about to be arrested.'

'Oh, so it's a police matter, is it?'

'Yes, they came and asked us lots of questions and took a close look at the boat, but they didn't find anything conclusive.'

'Was there a post-mortem examination?'

'Yes, he drowned all right. There's no doubt about that. They found one or two bruises on his face and body, but they couldn't say whether those were caused by a struggle with someone or by the fall overboard.'

'But what was he doing to fall out of a rowing-boat? And why was he in the boat in the first place? It seems a strange thing to do if indeed he did hate water.'

'He was very angry when he left us,' said Mrs. Haynes. 'Perhaps he wanted to clear his head.'

'Perhaps. You said there was an inquest, I believe?'

'Yes. I was hoping they'd find it was an accident but in the end there was an open verdict, which of course set tongues wagging even more, as we're still none the wiser about what really happened. We've been the talk of the place for weeks now—thanks partly to Ursula, who refuses to be silenced. John is in the grumps and won't talk about it, but I want all the pointing and whispering to stop. I want your help, Angela.'

'But what can I do?' asked Mrs. Marchmont. 'I don't see how I can put an end to idle gossip.'

'That's just it. I'm not at all sure it is idle gossip.'

Angela's eyebrows rose again.

'Do you mean to say you think they *were* murdered?' she said.

'Yes—no. I don't know,' said Mrs. Haynes. 'But you must admit the deaths look very odd when taken together.'

'What do the police think?'

'I don't know. They can't arrest anybody, as there's no evidence. But if Ursula has been badgering them then they are probably keeping a close eye on us all and if anything turns up then they will act.'

'I still don't see what I can do.'

'Why, I want you to try and find out the truth,' said Louisa, then went on hurriedly as she saw her friend about to object.

'Do say you will, Angela. You're so terribly clever at that sort of thing. I don't know anybody else who could do it.'

'I? Why on earth do you want me? I am not an investigator.'

'No, but you do find out things. Your name was all over the papers after the case in Norfolk. "Mrs. Marchmont, the lady detective", they called you.'

Angela reddened.

'That was all rot,' she said crossly. 'But Louisa, if you really do suspect foul play then surely you ought to speak to the police about it yourself?'

'But I told you, they've already looked into it and found nothing to go on. And having them tramping all over the place again will just stir things up even more. I want somebody discreet.'

'But if it *was* murder then the police will have to be called in any case. You must see that. I should only muddy the waters even further by poking my nose in.'

'Oh dear, I suppose you're right,' said Louisa. 'But I did rather hope—'

She paused. Mrs. Marchmont gave her a searching look.

'I believe there's something you haven't told me,' she said. 'I believe you suspect someone in particular.'

'No-o,' said her friend. 'It's nothing, really.'

'Louisa!'

Mrs. Haynes relented.

'Well, it's just that Ursula has been so insistent on pointing the finger at John that I did wonder if she mightn't have something to hide herself.'

'Do you think she did it?'

'No, but perhaps—'

'Her son, Robin, then.'

Louisa looked half-ashamed.

'It's such a terrible thing to suspect one's own family of but really, I don't know what to think. My head is all of a muddle. Do please help me, Angela. We are all under suspicion at the moment and I simply don't know what to do.'

Angela was becoming increasingly alarmed at the turn the conversation had taken.

'But Louisa, I don't see what I can do that the police haven't already done. I should have to skulk about, asking impertinent questions and putting everyone's backs up. And what could I find out that they haven't discovered already?'

'Don't worry about asking questions. I shall see to it that everybody agrees to answer them. After all, if the police have come to a dead-end and Ursula really is as keen to find out the truth as she says, then she can't object, can she?'

Looking at her friend's hopeful face, Mrs. Marchmont said reluctantly:

'You must give me time to think about it, then.' She rose. 'I shall sleep on it and give you my answer tomorrow. I must go now or I shall miss my train.'

Mrs. Haynes rose too.

'Of course you must think about it. But I do hope you will say yes. I am relying on you, Angela.'

'I should far rather you didn't,' said Angela, smiling, and took her leave.

Chapter Three

THE TRAIN TO town was not busy and Angela had no difficulty in finding an empty first-class carriage. She took a seat by the window and prepared to spend the journey deliberating over the strange problem that had been put before her, hoping—if the truth be told—that a good excuse for refusing the task would somehow present itself.

But she had barely even had time to review the facts of the matter before her quiet solitude was interrupted by the entrance of another passenger into the carriage. Angela looked up, suppressing an irritated frown which immediately turned into an exclamation of recognition as she saw who it was.

'Why, it's Inspector Jameson,' she said.

'Hallo, Mrs. Marchmont,' said the inspector. 'You look as though you were deep in thought. I hope I'm not disturbing you.'

'Not at all,' said Angela. 'I have just been visiting an old friend and was thinking about something she told me, that's all.'

Inspector Jameson seated himself opposite her.

'So you are a friend of the Hayneses," he said.

Angela looked up in surprise.

'I saw you as you left the house,' he explained.

'Ah,' she said, suddenly understanding.

Jameson studied her for a moment.

'You are a very remarkable woman, Mrs. Marchmont,' he said. 'Anyone else would have immediately bombarded me with questions.'

'I should rather have thought that you had questions to ask *me* if you have been watching Underwood House,' replied Angela.

The inspector nodded in acknowledgment of the parry.

'I haven't been watching it,' he said. 'I was in Beningfleet this afternoon talking over one or two things with the local superintendent, including the Haynes case. I was passing the house on my way to the station when I saw you come out.'

'Well, I'm afraid I can't be of any help. I knew nothing of the matter until this afternoon.'

'I see.'

Mrs. Marchmont threw him a wary glance but said nothing. There was a short silence, then Jameson laughed.

'Yes, I see I shall get nothing out of you. You keep your counsel very well.'

'I have nothing to tell that you don't already know,' said Angela. 'I had tea with an old friend who told me about a number of unfortunate deaths in the family, but that is all.'

'Indeed? Forgive me, but I thought your friend might have asked you for advice.'

'Perhaps she did.'

'Perhaps she did, as you say. And perhaps she even asked you to investigate the mystery. Ah, I see I've startled you,' he went on. 'No, I wasn't hiding in a cupboard during tea. The simple fact of the matter is that a few days ago when I told Mr. Haynes that the police would not be investigating further unless some new evidence turned up, he growled something about his wife having a bee in her bonnet about calling in a friend of hers who was a detective. When I saw you, of course I put two and two together.'

Angela went scarlet.

'Oh!' she cried. 'How dreadful! I do hope you don't think that I go around telling people I'm a detective. It's all the fault of those horrid newspapers after what happened at Sissingham. Of course, I should never dream of setting myself up as a professional investigator. Louisa got hold of the wrong end of the stick, that's all, and I told her so.'

'Then you refused?'

'I said I should have to think about it, but that was more an excuse to get away than anything else. The last thing I want is to become involved in a family feud and create even more of a muddle than there is at present, and when you arrived I was just musing about how best to say no.'

'That's a pity,' said Jameson. 'I had thought that perhaps you could shed some light on the matter. Our hands are tied at present owing to a lack of evidence, but as a friend of the family acting informally, you might be able to unearth some new information that would clinch the thing one way or the other.'

'Do you think all three of them were killed deliberately, then? Or just Edward? Or none of them?'

'It's impossible to tell. We'd have to get exhumation orders from the Home Office for Philippa Haynes and Winifred Dennison in order to be certain, but we can't just do that on a whim. We need something to go on first. Vague suspicions and village gossip are not enough.'

Mrs. Marchmont pondered for a moment. 'I don't like this at all,' she said finally. 'Two people have now asked me to investigate this matter: you and Louisa. But one might almost say that the two of you are on opposite sides. What happens if I discover something that might be better kept hidden? What happens, in short, if I find out that one of the Hayneses is a murderer?'

'What does Mrs. Haynes say about that?'

'We didn't talk about the implications of her request, as I confess I was rather thrown into a panic by it and was anxious to get away as quickly as possible. But I'm afraid she doesn't realize that she may be opening up Pandora's box with this.'

'Perhaps you will find that there is no mystery.'

'You think I shall prove a negative?'

'I don't say that,' replied Jameson, 'but you may be able to find *positive* evidence that all three deaths were accidents.'

Angela was becoming interested despite herself.

'Tell me about Ursula Haynes,' she said.

Inspector Jameson scented victory.

'She is a most interesting woman,' he said, 'but I don't wish to prejudice you before you've met her so I won't say too much on that score, except that she is something of a tartar. It was she who first brought our attention to the affair.'

'I understand she refuses to accept the theory of an accident.'

'Yes, she has intimated as much to us.'

'And what about her son?'

Although there was nothing much in the question, Jameson was instantly alert.

'Robin Haynes? What did your friend tell you about him?'

'Nothing in particular, why?'

'I can't say too much, just that we have been interested in young Master Robin's dealings for some little time now.'

'Oh?'

'He works at Peake's, you know—the stockbroker's. There's nothing we can quite put the finger on, but there have been rumours coming out of the place lately which suggest that someone has been carrying out certain murky transactions there, and they have been traced back to his department. I gather from my informant that it may all blow up any day now.'

'I see,' said Angela thoughtfully. 'Does he benefit from his father's death?'

'Yes, he and his mother each inherit a half-share of five thousand pounds.'

'But if I remember correctly, they lose another five thousand pounds, which goes to the lawyer, Mr. Faulkner. Doesn't that strike you as strange?'

'Yes, it does rather,' replied Jameson. 'But I have seen much stranger in my line of work. Philip Haynes and Mr. Faulkner were close acquaintances, so it takes no great stretch of the imagination to accept that an eccentric old man might choose to express his gratitude to his solicitor through his will.'

'Who benefits from Philippa's death? I understand she was unmarried.'

'Yes. She had a wide circle of friends, to whom she left various sums. She also left money to servants and charities. The remainder went to her family, but I don't think anyone got more than five hundred pounds.'

'Hardly a motive for murder,' said Angela.

'That depends—a starving man might kill for a square meal.'

'True. And of course we mustn't forget the five thousand pounds for Mr. Faulkner. What about Winifred? Where did her money go?'

'Winifred Dennison was a widow with an enthusiasm for lost causes, and appears to have given most of her money to various organizations during her lifetime. As a result, her daughter Susan received little or nothing. You may have heard of the daughter—she is better-known in Bohemian circles as Euphrosyne Dennison.'

'Oh! The artist. Yes, I have seen her work. I believe she is meant to be quite the latest thing. Was she upset at the size of her bequest?'

'I have no idea. I didn't get much change out of her at all, I'm afraid. She rather looked down on me as a policeman and put me firmly in my place.'

Angela smiled at his rueful expression.

'Then it appears that only Mr. Faulkner has a motive for all three deaths,' she said.

'He is the only one with a purely financial motive, yes. But we have investigated his movements and found that he has alibis for the times when each of them occurred, so that's no go. There is another person who gains an advantage from all the deaths, however,' he went on cautiously.

Angela was nothing if not a realist.

'You are referring to John Haynes,' she said. 'I'd thought of that. With his sisters and brother out of the way it becomes far easier for him to claim Underwood House as his own. Unless Ursula or Robin or Susan had strong views about the house's fate, of course. I assume the shares of Edward and Winifred passed on to them.'

'Yes. John Haynes inherited the entirety of his sister Philippa's share when she died, so he now owns half the house. I have no idea whether he has reached any private arrangement with the remaining relatives to buy their shares.'

'From the impression I have gained of Ursula, I imagine that she would be unwilling to let John have all his own way.'

'She's certainly the type,' agreed the inspector.

The train was now arriving at Waterloo station.

'I do hope you will think about it,' said Jameson, as they prepared to alight.

'Oh, I shall think about it all right,' said Mrs. Marchmont.

The inspector lowered his voice.

'Officially, the police are maintaining a discreet distance, you understand, but I may be able to provide assistance if you need it—strictly unofficially, of course. You will always find me at Scotland Yard.'

They shook hands cordially, then Inspector Jameson strode off and disappeared into the throng. Angela gazed after him for a moment, then went in search of a taxi and returned to her Mount Street flat.

She had a dinner engagement that evening, and so for the next few hours was forced to put Louisa's problem out of her mind, but on the way home she was able to give the matter some thought.

'May I ask you rather an odd question, William?' she said to her driver.

'Certainly, ma'am,' replied the young man.

'If you suspected that someone you knew had done something wicked, would you try and find out the truth? Even if it meant his getting into trouble?'

William had spent his early career touring America with a vaudeville company and was a keen observer of human nature, which made him an invaluable sounding-board on occasion. He considered before replying.

'We-ell, if you have a particular instance in mind, I can't rightly say without knowing the details,' he said. 'But I do recollect one time, must've been back in Chicago, we had a lady who joined us to sing the opera. A real beautiful voice, she had. Why, the tears would come to your eyes just to listen to her. She brought along a husband who was by way of being her agent. There to look after her interests, she said. Anyhow, one day she came and raised an almighty ruckus, saying that one of us had stolen her precious pearl necklace, and which of us was it? Great store she always set by that necklace. It had once belonged to the Queen of Prussia, or some such personage. My, wasn't there a commotion! She wouldn't be satisfied until we all turned out our belongings so they could be searched, but nothing was found. As you may imagine, she made no friends that day but a lot of enemies.'

'Was the necklace ever recovered?' asked Angela.

'Why yes,' said William. 'It turned out that that no-good husband of hers was up to his eyes in debt to some card-sharps, and he'd pawned it. They went away soon after that. I guess she left wishing she'd kept her mouth shut.'

'I guess she did,' said Angela, by no means reassured.

CHAPTER FOUR

'I MUST SAY, I was rather surprised to find that it was Louisa Haynes who sent you,' said Mr. Faulkner, as he ushered Mrs. Marchmont with great politeness into his office. 'When my clerk told me that Mrs. Haynes was sending someone to look into these recent unfortunate events, I immediately assumed that he was referring to Mrs. *Ursula* Haynes. Please, do take a seat.'

Mr. Faulkner was a man of about sixty-five, and suited his name well, being tall, with a luxuriant head of hair which swept grandly away from his forehead like feathers, and a high, beaked nose. Despite his somewhat haughty air, he was the very model of old-fashioned courtesy.

'I'm afraid I hardly know where to begin,' said Angela. 'I agreed to do this rather against my inclination and now I find myself in the awkward position of having to ask pointed questions of people I have only just met.'

'Well then, suppose I give you a little assistance. I shall tell you everything I know—that is, everything I believe to be relevant to the story, and you shall ask me any questions that may occur to you as we go along.'

'Thank you,' said Angela.

Mr. Faulkner placed the tips of his fingers together and thought a moment.

'I think first of all you must understand something of the nature of the family with whom we are dealing, and Philip Haynes in particular, since he is the nucleus around whom they all—I almost said revolved, but it would be more accurate to say revolve, as his influence is felt to this day. You will no doubt have heard that he was a difficult character: capricious, mercurial and devious, and that he ruled his family by a combination of fear and manipulation. I was one of his closest associates, and even I cannot quarrel with such a description. Whether or not I approve of the way in which he brought up his children is immaterial; the fact is, they grew up under his guidance and turned out much as you might expect with such a father, with personality difficulties that manifested themselves in a variety of ways.'

'I see you are a student of psychology,' said Angela.

'One cannot practise law for over forty years without learning something of the human mind,' said the solicitor, smiling. 'At any rate, when old Philip died he left behind him a family beset by mistrust and rivalry—one might even say enmity in some cases: John and Edward disliked each other heartily, for example, and I believe the two sisters were hardly close.'

'The mother died many years ago, I understand.'

'Yes, and there was another girl who ran away from home and later died. Some might say she had a fortunate escape.'

'Philip Haynes seems to have been something of an eccentric, then,' said Angela. 'That must explain why he put such an odd clause into his will.'

'An odd clause? What do you mean?' said Mr. Faulkner, looking taken aback.

'I mean the condition that, in order to inherit, his children must meet at Underwood House twice a year.'

'Oh yes, of course, I see,' said Mr. Faulkner. 'Yes, that was in the nature of the man. He was malicious, you know, and very much the type to attempt to exert an influence even from beyond the grave. I'm afraid he would have taken great glee in the idea of forcing them to spend time with each other against their wishes.'

'You are the executor of his will. Did he leave specific instructions as to the dates on which these twice-yearly meetings were to take place? The first two were on the 16th of February and the 27th of May last year, while the last one was this year on the 16th of February again. Is the next one to take place on the 27th of May?'

'Yes, I believe it is, now you come to mention it. As a matter of fact, I was just preparing the invitations this morning.' He opened a drawer in his desk. 'Now, let me see—ah! Here they are,' he said, taking out a small sheaf of papers. He applied a pair of pince-nez to his eyes and frowned at the top page. From where she sat, Angela could see that he signed his name with a grand flourish. 'Yes,' he went on, 'the next date given is the 27th of May, 1927. How remiss of me not to notice the coincidence.'

'Is there any significance in the two dates?' asked Angela.

'Not that I know of,' said Mr. Faulkner. 'But I was not privy to all of Philip's secrets. I was merely instructed to send letters requesting attendance about two weeks before the date of the meeting itself.'

'Only two weeks! Isn't that very short notice?'

'Those were my instructions,' replied the solicitor.

'How did you make sure everyone attended as requested? I suppose you didn't go to Underwood House yourself?'

'No, as I told the police I was engaged elsewhere on each of those days. On the first two occasions I happened to be staying with Sir Maurice Upton, the Chief Constable of this district, and on the third I was the guest of Lord Willesden, the former Under-Secretary of State for the Home Department, and his wife, at their home in Somerset. No, I sent my clerk, Hawley, down to Beningfleet on the dates in question. He merely stayed until all the family had arrived then left. I did not think it necessary for him to continue there for the whole evening—whatever Philip had intended it was certainly not my objective to *force* them all to remain in company with each other. As far as I was concerned the Hayneses had fulfilled the conditions of the will by making the journey. Whether or not they chose to stay there once they had arrived was hardly my affair.'

'I see.'

'And besides,' he went on dryly, 'I knew them of old. Much as they disliked one another, it was unthinkable that any of them should show weakness and be the first to flee the field. They would far rather have stayed and fought to the death.' He caught himself. 'Dear me, that was a rather unfortunate choice of expression on my part,' he said.

'If you were not present at the time then I imagine you won't know much about how they all died,' said Mrs. Marchmont.

'Very little,' replied Mr. Faulkner. 'I know Philippa Haynes was thought to have died of heart failure, but that was hardly a surprise given the generally weak state of her health. And poor Winifred tripped and fell downstairs, I understand. Again, that doesn't seem unlikely. She spent much of her time drifting about in a day-dream and may easily have lost her footing.'

'She didn't fall downstairs exactly; she toppled over the balustrade,' said Angela.

'Ah yes, of course—I'd forgotten that.'

'Rather difficult to do that simply by losing one's footing, don't you think?'

'But now you mention it, wasn't there some talk of her leaning over to adjust a ceiling-light? Perhaps she was simply very unlucky.'

'Perhaps,' said Angela. 'Then we come to Edward, who drowned while out on the lake despite apparently hating water and boats.'

'Yes, it is difficult to see how that could have been an accident. But that doesn't mean it was murder.'

'Do you mean suicide? Did he have a reason to kill himself?' asked Angela. 'I don't recall its being mentioned as a possibility.'

'I do not know. For that you must ask Ursula Haynes—although in my experience, a wife is often the last person to know of her husband's unhappiness, so perhaps even that will be of little assistance.'

Angela reflected for a moment on what the solicitor had told her. It seemed to her that she had learned very little.

'There is also the question of motive,' she said cautiously. 'If all three of them were murdered, then it stands to reason that there must be someone who benefits from their deaths.'

Mr. Faulkner twinkled at her.

'Indeed, and I am fully aware that my name must be at the very top of the list of suspects as regards financial motive, but as I mentioned before, I was not myself present when any of them died. And money is not the only possible reason for desiring someone's death.'

'No,' agreed Angela. 'But it is the most obvious reason. It remains to be seen what other motives there might be in this case.'

'But it has yet to be proved that any of them *were* murdered. You are assuming that if Edward was killed deliberately, then Philippa and Winifred must have been killed deliberately too. Had it occurred to you that the first two deaths may have been entirely accidental?'

'Yes,' said Angela, 'but that doesn't make things any easier, I'm afraid.'

'I will admit I don't envy you your task,' said the lawyer, 'but perhaps you will find out something useful. You have a sympathetic face, Mrs. Marchmont, if you will pardon my saying so. You are the kind of person to whom people confide secrets. That is something of which you can take advantage if you wish.'

'Well, I shall try my best,' said Angela. 'Oh, I almost forgot. Louisa said you had Philip's will. Might I see it?'

'But of course,' said Mr. Faulkner. 'I have it here in my safe.'

He rose and crossed the room, then stopped. He patted his pocket in dismay.

'Ah, my mistake,' he said. 'I have just remembered that I took my safe keys out of my pocket at home yesterday evening and omitted to replace them this morning. I do beg your pardon. Perhaps another time.'

'No matter,' said Angela. 'I expect I have already heard the most important points.'

'Yes, I do not believe I have missed anything out that could be of use to you, but if there is anything else you wish to ask, I shall be more than happy to assist in any way I can.'

'Thank you. I believe my next step must be to find out more about the events of the three days in question. I shall speak to Louisa.'

'At least you have already eliminated one person from your inquiry. That ought to help you a little. And speaking quite frankly, it is a great relief to me,' said the solicitor.

'Yes,' replied Angela. 'You appear to have impeccable alibis. Nobody could possibly suspect a government minister and a chief constable of telling lies to protect someone.'

Their eyes met for a moment, then Mr. Faulkner smiled and bowed her out of his office.

CHAPTER FIVE

AS ANGELA APPROACHED the front door of Underwood House, it was flung open and a tall young man wearing a shabby Burberry and carrying a battered portmanteau emerged with a brow like thunder, and set off down the road at a great pace. Angela had the impression that she recognized him, but he was soon out of sight and she continued on into the house where she met Louisa Haynes in the hall.

'There you are, my dear,' said Louisa. 'Did you see Donald? I wanted to say goodbye but I'm afraid he was in rather a bad temper. Not to worry—he'll cool down in an hour or so as he always does. He's such a dear boy, but I rather think he's quarrelled with Stella. I saw her running upstairs a little while ago. I do hope they make it up. They have such flaming rows but they are so well-matched in every respect.'

'Was that really Donald?' said Angela. 'I don't believe I've seen him since he was quite a small boy.'

'Yes, hasn't he grown? He works at the Board of Trade. I don't quite know what he does but he travels abroad often and negotiates with foreign dignitaries and suchlike. He has gone off to catch his train, as he is attending an important conference in The Hague tomorrow, but I do wish he and Stella hadn't parted on bad terms.'

'Who is Stella?'

'Haven't you met her? She is my sister's eldest child, but she spends much of her time with us since her parents died. She works as a private nurse, looking after elderly patients. She is so kind to them—it quite warms one's heart to see it. She and Donald are engaged.'

'He is to marry his cousin? Oh, I quite forgot—Donald is not your own son, is he?'

'No,' said Louisa, 'we adopted him as a baby after his own parents died about twenty years ago. John knew the people and brought him home one day. It was very sad, but as we were not fortunate enough to have children of our own, it turned out to be a blessing in disguise for us.'

They were still standing in the hall of Underwood House. It was a handsome entrance, light and airy, with an oak parquet floor and an elegant staircase which curved up towards a galleried landing above. Light flowed through a high window and glinted off a large, old-fashioned chandelier that hung from the ceiling. Angela's attention was caught.

'This must be where Winifred died,' she said, gazing about her.

'Yes,' said Louisa. 'We found her on the floor just there with her handkerchief grasped in her hand. The poor thing fell from above, broke her neck and was killed instantly.'

'That was on the afternoon of the 27th of May last year. Do you remember at what time?'

'It was a little before four o'clock.'

'And you say no-one witnessed it?'

'No, we were all elsewhere.'

'All together?'

'No, I don't think so. Why do you ask?'

'It might be helpful in establishing alibis—or better, in proving that it was an accident.'

'I see what you mean. Well then, let me try and remember.' Mrs. Haynes reflected for a second. 'Most of the family had already arrived, I believe. Yes—as a matter of fact they must all have been there, since Mr. Faulkner's clerk had already paid his visit and left, after making sure we were all present. I was in the drawing-room to welcome the visitors, and Stella was there too. Oh, and Ursula and Edward. I don't remember where Robin and Susan were.'

'What about John?'

'John was in his study. He liked to leave it until as late as possible before showing himself. He said it was the only way he could survive these meetings without killing someone—oh dear! I didn't mean it in that way. How dreadful of me!'

Angela smiled understandingly.

'Is that everybody accounted for?' she asked. 'Where was Donald?'

Just then they were interrupted by the opening of the front door to admit a pleasant-looking young man of thirty or so who saluted Mrs. Haynes cheerfully.

'Hallo,' he said. 'It's awfully quiet here. Has Don left? I thought I saw him making for the station post-haste just now. I shouted but he didn't or wouldn't see me. What's the matter with him?'

'He's had another row with Stella,' said Louisa.

The young man grimaced.

'I say, bad show,' he said. 'Where is she?'

'In her room. I shall go up later and see that she's all right.'

'Poor thing. I do wish Don would rein it in sometimes. He's no right to go upsetting her like that.'

'Now, Guy, it's not fair to say that when we don't know what it was about,' said Louisa. 'Angela, let me introduce you to Guy Fisher. He has been running the Underwood estate since Philip was alive, and I simply don't know how we'd manage without him. Guy, this is my great friend Mrs. Angela Marchmont. She is the one I told you about, do you remember? She is trying to find out what happened to Philippa, Winifred and Edward.'

Guy Fisher regarded Angela with interest as he shook her hand.

'So Louisa has persuaded you to look into all this,' he said. 'Shall you succeed in unravelling the mystery, do you think?'

Angela laughed.

'I have no idea,' she said. 'Louisa seems to believe I may be able to shed some light on the affair. I am not sure I share her confidence, however.'

'Well, I shall be very happy to help if I can.'

'Were you here when Winifred Dennison fell over the balustrade?'

'No, I didn't arrive until some time after it happened,' said the young man. 'It was my mother's birthday and I'd been away visiting her. I returned to find the whole house in an uproar. Susan was hysterical, and no wonder.'

'Oh yes, poor thing,' said Mrs. Haynes.

'Who arrived on the scene first after Winifred fell?' asked Angela.

'Why, I couldn't say,' said Louisa. 'Let me think. Stella, Ursula, Edward and I must have all rushed out together, since we were all in the drawing-room at the time. But were we the first?' She screwed up her eyes. 'No—no, I remember now. The first thing I saw when I arrived was Robin bending over her. He looked up, terribly white in the face, and said, "She's dead." Just like that. Then I'm afraid he ran outside and was sick. And Donald was there too. I remember particularly because Stella cried, "Oh Don, not another one!" and ran over and clung to him. Then Susan emerged from her room, took one look at the scene and fainted on the landing. I had to rush upstairs and see to her. I don't remember when John turned up.'

Angela gazed around the hall, trying to picture the scene.

'How soon after you heard the scream did you rush out?' she asked.

'Oh, immediately,' replied Louisa. 'You couldn't ignore a sound like that. It quite pierced one to the bone.'

'Then there wouldn't have been much time for anybody to leave the scene. A murderer, I mean.'

'I suppose not.'

'May I?' Angela walked over to the stairs and ascended them slowly, looking about her as she did so. She reached the landing and stopped at the point from where Winifred must have fallen, then took out a handkerchief and leaned carefully over the balustrade as if to flick a speck of dust from the chandelier, which hung a little way away.

'Do be careful,' said Mrs. Haynes.

'She must have been leaning very far out to have fallen accidentally,' said Angela.

'Yes, she must. But the servants are rather remiss in dusting that chandelier, and she was always complaining about it.'

'Let's say she was pushed. Would there have been time for whomever did it to run down the stairs and perhaps appear with the rest of you, do you think?'

'Why don't we try it?' suggested Guy Fisher eagerly.

'Well—' began Angela, but he was already running upstairs to join her.

'Louisa, you go into the drawing-room,' he commanded. 'I shall yell out and then dash full pelt down the stairs. You run into the hall as soon as you hear me shout. Mrs. Marchmont, you shall stand at the bottom of the stairs and take notes.'

Angela could not help laughing at his youthful enthusiasm.

'Very well,' she said. 'Suppose we do as he says, Louisa.'

Louisa, looking a little surprised, agreed.

'All set?' said Guy, once Angela had reached the hall and Louisa had disappeared into the drawing-room. He lifted his head and gave a blood-curdling yell, then dashed down the stairs as fast as he could. He had just reached the bottom and was attempting to strike a nonchalant attitude when Mrs. Haynes arrived.

'There you have it,' he said.

'You only just managed it by the skin of your teeth,' said Angela. 'And you are a little breathless. Louisa, do you recall anybody's being out of breath when you found Winifred?'

'Why, I couldn't possibly remember anything like that,' replied her friend.

'What on earth was that frightful row?' demanded a voice from the top of the stairs.

'There you are, my dear,' said Louisa Haynes. 'I was just about to come up and find you.'

The new-comer was a self-possessed young woman, dressed pertly in the modern fashion, who had apparently just emerged from her room.

'Hallo, Stella,' said Guy. 'Sorry about the screeching. Did we wake you up?'

'I wasn't asleep, you ass,' said the girl without rancour. As she approached them, Angela could see that her eyes were red as though she had been crying.

'You must be Mrs. Marchmont,' she said, holding out her hand. 'I'm Stella Gillespie. Aunt Louisa says you are going to solve the mystery of Underwood House. Is that what all the shouting was about?'

'We were trying to find out whether someone could have pushed Winifred over the edge and then run downstairs and mingled with the throng before anybody was the wiser,' said Guy.

'I should have thought it was more likely that whoever it was would have run into one of the bedrooms nearest the top of the stairs,' said Stella.

'The only person upstairs at the time was Susan,' said Louisa. 'Everyone else was down here.'

'Robin and Don arrived on the scene before everybody else,' said Guy. 'We shall have to find out which of them got there first.'

'Yes,' murmured Angela.

Stella turned to Mrs. Marchmont.

'I must say it's jolly thrilling to meet a real detective,' she said, to Angela's private dismay. 'Have you decided which of us did it yet?'

'Isn't it always the most unlikely person who turns out to be the murderer?' said Guy Fisher. 'At least, that's what happens in the books I've read. That means it must be you, Stella. Or me. Or even Mrs. Marchmont.' He grinned slyly. 'You haven't told us where *you* were when they all died, Mrs. Marchmont. How clean is *your* conscience?'

'I'm quite sure my conscience is as grubby around the edges as anyone's,' said Angela lightly, 'but in this case I plead not guilty.'

'Let's have some tea,' said Mrs. Haynes as they entered the drawing-room. 'Ring the bell, Stella.'

'I should like to take a walk down to the lake afterwards,' said Angela.

'Certainly. I won't come myself, but Stella will go with you, won't you, my dear?'

'May I come too?' asked Guy. 'This is all tremendously exciting. I should love to do some investigating.'

'Of course,' said Angela politely.

She sipped her tea in silence as the others chattered gaily. She was by no means happy at the idea of turning what had been intended to be a discreet inquiry into a general free-for-all. In fact, the further she was drawn in, the more awkward her situation appeared.

'Assuming it *was* murder, how am I supposed to find out who did it if everyone is going to follow me about and demand to know my every thought on the matter?' she said to herself. 'And even if I *do* find out who did it, how can I stand there in front of everybody, point the finger and say, "It was *you*"? Angela, you idiot, why on earth did you allow yourself to be persuaded to do this? I don't like it at all.'

Chapter Six

'WE USED TO bathe here in the summer as children,' said Stella as they followed the path through the woods, ducking under branches and jumping over tree roots. 'All of us cousins, I mean. I'm not a blood relation of the Hayneses, of course, but I used to come and stay with Aunt Louisa during the holidays. Here we are.'

The trees fell away and they emerged into a little pebbled cove that sloped down to a small lake, completely surrounded by trees. Before them was an old landing-stage in a state of some disrepair, to which an equally dilapidated rowing-boat was attached by a frayed rope.

'Is that the boat?' asked Mrs. Marchmont.

'Yes,' said Stella.

'Then let us take a closer look.'

The three of them walked along the landing-stage.

'Not much to see, really,' said Guy as they stared down at the craft, which bobbed gently below them.

'No,' said Angela, 'and I imagine the police have already examined it closely for evidence—finger-prints and what-not.'

'Yes, they did,' said Stella.

'Did they find anything?'

'If they did, they didn't tell us.'

'I'm sure they would have said something if they had,' said Guy.

They returned to the shore.

'What happened that evening, exactly?' asked Angela.

Guy and Stella looked at each other.

'Nobody knows,' said Guy. 'But I do know it started with a big row between John and Edward after dinner.'

'But it wasn't just those two, was it?' said Stella. 'I mean, they started it, but then Ursula joined in, and Susan, and Don, and before we knew it they were all in the middle of the most terrific ding-dong.'

'Was that unusual?'

'They didn't generally get as heated, but I wouldn't say it was *unusual* as such.'

'No,' agreed Guy. 'The Hayneses have always been fond of a good, healthy falling-out.'

'And then Edward said he wasn't going to stand for it any longer, and stormed out,' continued Stella. 'We thought he'd gone to his room, but as it turned out he must have left the house.'

'I don't know what got into him,' said Guy. 'It was freezing cold that night.'

'He wasn't found until the next day, I understand,' said Angela.

'Yes,' said Stella. 'We had been searching all morning and found nothing. Then somebody spotted that the boat had somehow floated loose, so Uncle John got some of the men to drag the lake. That was when they discovered his body.'

'How long had he been dead?'

'The doctor couldn't tell exactly. "Somewhere between twelve and eighteen hours," was all he would say.

'Hmm. That's vague enough, anyhow,' said Angela. 'He could have died at any time after he went out or even during the night, presumably. Alibis won't be of much help in that case.'

'Yes, we were all coming and going that evening,' said Guy. 'I certainly couldn't tell you what anyone was doing at any particular time. Frankly, I'm not even sure what I was doing myself.'

'You were present at dinner, then?'

'Yes,' said Guy. 'I usually dine with the family.'

'Oh yes—we simply can't bear to be without him, you know,' said Stella mockingly. She sat down on a fallen tree trunk and pulled off her cap. The early May sunshine glinted off her golden hair as she stared absently out at the lake. Angela glanced towards Guy and caught him gazing intently at the girl. He saw her watching him and looked away, reddening.

They were all silent for a while, each lost in his own thoughts. Then Angela turned and looked at the boat.

'If I wanted to drown someone deliberately in the lake, how would I go about it?' she asked.

They all considered the question. Guy was the first to speak.

'If it were I, I should catch him unawares in the shallows and hold him under,' he said.

'But then how did he end up in the middle of the lake?'

'Perhaps, knowing Edward couldn't swim, the killer simply took him out in the boat and pushed him overboard,' suggested Stella.

Angela shook her head.

'Rather a dangerous approach on the part of a murderer, don't you think, to rely on his victim's incompetence?' she said. 'What if it turned out that Edward could swim a little after all? At least, well enough to get back to the shore? And besides, if it *was* true that he loathed the water, then he would never have gone out onto the lake willingly. There would have been a struggle.'

'That's true,' conceded Stella. 'Well then, he must have been dead or at least unconscious when he was put in the boat. But why did the killer take him out into the middle of the lake?'

'To make it look like an accident, of course,' said Guy. 'Don't you agree, Mrs. Marchmont?'

'Yes, that seems the most likely answer,' replied Angela. 'Assuming all three deaths are connected, then whoever was responsible has taken some care to make them look accidental.' She walked slowly back towards the jetty, trying to imagine the scene. 'Very well, let's say he was drowned here by the shore, and that whoever killed him then bundled him into the boat, rowed him out into the middle of the lake and threw him overboard,' she said. 'How did the murderer return to shore?'

'Must he necessarily have gone out in the boat with Edward?' asked Stella. 'Perhaps he merely put the body in the boat and set it loose.' She shook her head and laughed. 'Oh! How silly of me—someone had to be there to throw him overboard, of course.'

'Yes,' agreed Angela. 'If it *was* murder, then someone went out on the lake with him, alive or dead.'

'He must have swum back to shore,' said Guy. 'Or perhaps there was another boat.'

'*Are* there any other boats hereabouts?' asked Stella.

'Not that I know of,' admitted Guy.

'Then whoever it was must have returned to the house drenched.'

'And with chattering teeth too,' said Guy feelingly. 'The water is as cold as ice.'

'Yes, I think we must look for someone who arrived back at the house with wet clothes,' said Angela.

'Not necessarily,' said Stella. 'It would make much more sense for him to strip before going out in the boat, and leave his clothes by the shore.'

'Ye-es,' said Angela. She looked as though she were about to say something else, but thought better of it.

Guy picked up a pebble and aimed it idly at the boat. It glanced off a rowlock and entered the water with a gentle splash.

'Supposing it was an accident,' said Angela. 'Let us assume that for some reason Edward acted so far out of character as to go out voluntarily in a rowing-boat on a cold night. Why did he do it?'

'Perhaps as a means of calming down and collecting his thoughts,' said Stella. 'Some people like to work off a bad temper with vigorous exercise.'

'Was he the type?'

'I shouldn't have said so, but people are odd. Sometimes they do totally unexpected things.'

'How did the accident happen, then?'

'That's easy enough,' said Guy. 'If he really was such a duffer on the water then he probably went out dragging the painter behind him or something, then when it got tangled up in weeds he fell overboard and drowned while trying to free it.'

'There's something in that,' agreed Angela. She looked absently down at the ground, turning over the various possibilities in her head.

'I've always thought this was such a pretty spot,' said Stella, 'but it's been spoilt now. I shall never look at it in the same way again.' She stood up and shivered. 'Let's go back to the house.'

'My shoe-buckle has come undone,' said Angela suddenly. She bent over to fasten it, then gave an impatient exclamation. 'I think it might be broken. Do go ahead. I shall catch you up.'

Angela busied herself with her shoe as Guy and Stella disappeared into the woods. As soon as they were out of sight she straightened up and went cautiously over to the fallen tree trunk. Something was sticking out a little way from a crack underneath it. With a little difficulty she succeeded in extracting the thing carefully and brushed the dirt off it. She stared at it, puzzled. Although it was damp and faded and part of it was torn away, it was unmistakably a photograph of a pretty young woman. The picture had evidently been trapped in the crevice of the tree trunk for some time, and was so damaged that it was impossible to judge how old it was, but Angela guessed it had been taken some years ago. Just for a moment she thought she recognized the face, but then almost instantly the impression was gone and she shook her head.

She heard the others calling her and, recollecting herself, thrust the picture in her pocket and hurried after them. Was the photograph connected to this business? If so, how? And who was the woman?

Chapter Seven

'THERE'S UNCLE JOHN,' said Stella as they reached the lawn.

John Haynes was a bluff, hearty-looking man with greying hair and moustache. He hailed them jovially.

'Ah, there you are, Angela,' he said. 'Louisa said I should find you out here somewhere. She's still clinging to this nonsense about Edward. I told her not to listen to Ursula—the woman is mad, quite frankly—got a ridiculous bee in her bonnet—but she went ahead and called you anyway. Have you been down to the lake? What do you think of Underwood?'

Angela duly expressed her admiration of the house and grounds and he nodded complacently.

'Yes, it's a pleasant spot, isn't it? I know it's not the fashion to be sentimental, but I must confess I love the old place. The others wanted to get rid of it, you know, said it was a millstone around all our necks, but I—well, I could never agree to sell it, however much it costs to keep it up. Ha! They can't make me sell now, can they? Not now they're dead. But you won't dig up anything, I can promise you that. Poor Philippa had been ill for years—heart trouble, you know, and Winifred always was a batty old trout—just the type to break her neck through her own carelessness.'

He broke off from this startling outburst to shout to a large retriever that was nosing around in some undergrowth.

'Does the house belong wholly to you now?' asked Angela.

John Haynes made a noise that sounded like 'harrumph'.

'Not wholly, no. I got Philippa to leave me her share in her will. Promised to think about selling if she did. Silly old fool—can't think why she believed me. Susan and Ursula inherited a quarter share each after Winifred and Edward died, but between you and me I'm pretty sure I shall come to an agreement with Susan—her mother gave all her money to spiritualist societies and educational institutions for deserving orphans, that kind of thing, so Susan was left flat broke. Ursula hasn't a leg to stand on. She can whistle for it if she likes, but unless she agrees to sell her share to me it's all so much gas.'

'I take it, then, that you don't believe the deaths were anything but natural.'

John snorted.

'Of course they were natural! Any half-wit can see that. Why my wife should take it into her head to believe anything that woman says is beyond me, but there you have it—she's allowed herself to be influenced and now she sees shadowy figures with raised daggers behind every gate-post.'

'But don't you think it odd that your brother should choose to go out on the lake on a freezing winter's night? Especially when, by all accounts, he loathed the water.'

'So Ursula says. I can't say I remember his having such a hatred of it. If you ask me, it's perfectly natural that a man in a huff should decide to work it off with a turn on the lake. It's what I should do myself.'

'I understand that nobody was present at either of your sisters' deaths.'

'Not that I know of. In Philippa's case, she simply went to bed and didn't get up again. I missed all the excitement with Winifred. I gather she came down with quite a thud.'

'Uncle!' said Stella reproachfully.

John Haynes looked sheepish.

'Well, I dare say that was in poor taste, but it's no use pretending there was any love lost between Winifred and Edward and me, although I was rather fond of Philippa.'

'Louisa said you were in your study when Winifred fell,' said Angela.

'Yes. I was in the middle of something and didn't take any notice of the row for a bit. Eventually I couldn't ignore it any longer and I came out to find out what in heaven's name was going on, only to find the old girl sprawled out on the hall floor with her neck snapped in two and everybody running in fifty directions at once.'

'I see,' said Angela.

'Perhaps Robin will be able to tell you something more about it,' said Guy. 'He was found bending over Winifred's body, so he must have been the first to arrive.'

'Yes, he or Donald,' said Angela.

'Ah, Stella, that reminds me,' said John. 'What's all this I hear about a disagreement between you and Don?'

Stella scowled.

'It's none of your business,' she snapped. 'But seeing as I shan't be speaking to him ever again you may tell him from me that he's a horrid pig.'

Guy raised his eyebrows.

'I say,' he said. 'Poor Don.'

'Never mind "poor Don,"' said Stella. 'I'm the one who's had to put up with him and his beastly moods. Well, that's all over now. He can find some other silly girl to follow him around. I shan't be taken in by him again.'

She turned on her heel and stalked off.

'Too bad,' said Guy, gazing after her. 'I wonder what it's all about this time. Her work again, I shouldn't wonder.'

'Her work?' said Angela. 'Louisa said she is a nurse.'

'Yes, and a very fine one too if what I hear is true,' replied the young man. 'She wanted to be a doctor, but her father wouldn't hear of any daughter of his doing that kind of thing, so she was forced to be content with nursing. Don would like her to give it up after they get married but she doesn't want to. It's caused plenty of rows between them, I can tell you. They're each as stubborn as the other.'

'Damn' silly quarrels,' said John. 'He ought to keep his mouth shut and give her her head. That's the way to get round a woman. Let her think she has the upper hand and she'll be as quiet as you like. But just try to forbid her from doing something and you'll know about it! Ten to one she'll decide to give it up anyway once the children come along. I shall have to have a word with him when he returns—make him see what he's about. Stella's a good girl, and he'd be a fool to let her slip through his fingers.'

'I'm sure he'll come round,' said Guy. 'I'll bet my life on it.'

There was a wistful expression on his face as he said it, which did not go unnoticed by Angela.

They left John and walked up to the house together.

'Did you find any clues?' asked Louisa eagerly as they entered the drawing-room.

'Not exactly,' said Angela. 'But then, I didn't expect to after all this time.'

'No, I suppose not,' said Louisa. 'It all happened weeks ago now, and it rained for the whole of April, so any evidence will have been destroyed long ago.'

'Yes, but I have a better picture of events in my head now, so it was useful in that regard at any rate.'

'Have—have you reached any conclusions?' asked Louisa hesitantly.

'No, but I haven't spoken to everyone. I have yet to meet Ursula.'

'You're going to speak to Ursula, are you?' said Guy. He grinned maliciously. 'I'm sure you'll find her a *very* interesting person. Robin, too.'

Louisa threw him a reproving look.

'Old Dick Trent was looking for you earlier,' she said. 'He said something about the bull getting into the lane and taking all the cows with it. Perhaps you ought to go and speak to him.'

Guy's features twisted into a grimace of comical horror.

'Oh Lord,' he said. 'Not again. That bull is the bane of my life. I swear I could work two mornings a week and spend the rest of the time fishing if it weren't for that dratted animal.'

He saluted Angela and left.

'He's a great help to us,' said Louisa, 'but sometimes he needs just a *little* reminder to get on with his work.'

Angela laughed.

'Like most young men, I imagine,' she said. 'He is rather young to have charge of the whole estate, isn't he?'

'Yes, he is, but he knows the place inside and out. Philip found him about ten years ago. He'd just come down from Oxford—he was a scholarship boy, you know, and terribly clever. He won prizes for his studies, as well as for boxing, cricket, swimming and all kinds of other sports.'

'Quite the all-rounder,' observed Angela. 'What did he mean about Ursula? I must say, I am growing more and more curious to meet her.'

Mrs. Haynes laughed.

'You shall, my dear. She and Robin live in Datchet.'

'Then to Datchet I must go,' said Angela. 'Oh, I almost forgot.' She brought out the photograph. 'Do you recognize this?'

Louisa took the picture and looked at it, mystified.

'No, I can't say I do. She's rather pretty, in an old-fashioned kind of way. Who is she?'

'I have no idea. I found it down by the lake just now.'

'Do you think it has something to do with all this? Is it a clue?'

'I don't know,' said Angela, 'but I should very much like to find out.'

She took leave of her friend and left the house. She was heading for the gate when a thought suddenly struck her and she walked out onto the lawn and gazed at the upstairs windows.

'Still here?' said John Haynes at her shoulder. 'Haven't you solved the mystery yet?' He chuckled at his own wit. 'No, and nor shall you. I should give it up if I were you—it's all a waste of time, although very kind of you to offer to help Louisa, of course.'

'Well, we shall see,' replied Angela pleasantly.

'What are you investigating now?' he asked.

'Nothing,' said Angela. 'I was just wondering how your gardener proposes to subdue that ivy. Look, it will soon be halfway across that upstairs window.'

'Yes, I must get one of the younger men to see to it, although I'm afraid old Briggs will be dreadfully offended. He is failing now, and isn't the man he was, but I let it slide as he's a faithful old thing—been here since my father's time, or even longer.'

'Whose room is that?'

'I'm not entirely sure. Donald's, I think. Or is it the guest bedroom next door? It's one or the other, anyhow.'

Angela was unable to pin him down to any more definite answer, so was forced to be content with that. She then took the photograph out of her pocket and showed it to him.

'Do you know who this is?' she asked.

John stood stock still for a moment.

'Why, that's—' he began. There was a long pause. 'Where did you say you found it?'

'At the little cove by the lake.'

'Oh? What odd things one finds in the strangest places these days.'

'Then you don't recognize it?'

He shook his head.

'Can't say I do. Perhaps it belongs to a servant or one of the tenants on the estate. Might have blown in from anywhere when you come to think about it. London, even!' He laughed. 'Well, goodbye.'

He strode away. Angela put the photograph in her bag, thinking hard. She was sure he had recognized the woman. Why, then, had he denied it?

CHAPTER EIGHT

THE HOUSE IN which Ursula Haynes lived was at the end of a quiet lane not far from the railway station. A gleaming white construction with a modern, featureless aspect, it perched uncomfortably among the lush shrubbery and well-tended lawns that sloped gently down to the river some hundred or so yards away.

Mrs. Marchmont was admitted by an unsmiling parlourmaid into a stark, pale entrance hall that gave little indication of its owner's personality, since it contained almost no furniture and no knick-knacks or ornaments of any kind. Angela was eyeing a spindly tubular chair doubtfully and pondering whether or not to risk sitting on it, when she heard footsteps approaching from above.

'Mrs. Marchmont,' said an imperious voice. 'I am Ursula Haynes.'

Angela squinted upwards, but the bright sunlight shining in through a window on the half-landing prevented her from seeing anything but a straight, slim shadow. There was a long silence, then the figure descended and its face came into view. Angela's first impression was one of absolute rigidity. Ursula Haynes was of only average height, yet she carried herself so upright that she seemed rather taller than she really was. Her figure was spare and her face cold and unsmiling. Her short hair, which was black with streaks of iron-grey, was in perfect order, and her dress, although elegant, was similarly severe in its tailoring. Altogether, it looked as though not one molecule had been wasted in her construction.

Mrs. Haynes scrutinized her visitor for a second, then held out her hand and unbent so far as to permit herself a small smile.

'So John and Louisa have finally admitted that this affair requires investigation,' she said. 'But of course it would have appeared most odd had they refused to cooperate. That must be why they have asked a friend to look into it, rather than engaging a detective with no connection to the family.'

In spite of her expressed dislike of being described as a detective, Angela was stung.

'I assure you that I have not been asked to take sides, if that is what you mean,' she said. 'I am approaching the inquiry as objectively as anyone can do in my position. I have no wish to protect the guilty party—if indeed there *is* a guilty party.'

Ursula clicked her tongue impatiently.

'Of course there is a guilty party,' she said. 'Only a fool could imagine that three deaths in similar circumstances in the space of a year were mere unfortunate accidents. But Louisa was always—well, never mind. Please come this way.' She turned and led the way into a large, square drawing-room that was as sparsely furnished as the hall. 'Do sit.'

Angela, feeling rather as though she were back at school and being examined on her French grammar by a particularly dour mistress, sat gingerly on the edge of the least delicate-looking chair she could find. It had a sloping seat and a slippery cover, and some effort was required to avoid sliding off it and onto the floor. The room had large windows that looked out onto the garden and the river, and again Angela was struck by the contrast between the house and its situation.

Ursula sat bolt upright with her hands folded neatly in her lap, and looked at her visitor expectantly. She was clearly waiting for Angela to begin, and offered no opening.

'Is she intending to make me feel at a disadvantage?' said Angela to herself. 'If so, she's making a jolly good job of it.' Determined not to admit defeat, she said out loud, 'Tell me why you believe your husband's death was not an accident.'

'Of course it wasn't an accident,' said Ursula. 'There's no "believe" about it. Mrs. Marchmont, my husband was a milksop. He hated the outdoors and would never have dreamed of getting into a boat, least of all on a winter's night while wearing his evening things.'

Angela raised her eyebrows at the description.

'I see,' she said. 'Then what do you think happened?'

'It's perfectly obvious what happened. Somebody knocked him out, then bundled him into the rowing-boat and tipped him overboard in the middle of the lake. He couldn't swim, and so he drowned. Whether or not he regained consciousness before he died I cannot say. I can only hope he was unaware of what was happening to him.'

She might have been placing an order with the butcher, so dispassionate was her manner as she spoke.

'You communicated your suspicions to the police, I believe,' said Angela.

Ursula bristled.

'I did, but I might as well have saved myself the time and trouble. Simpletons, every one of them—incapable of seeing the obvious even when it is dangled in front of their noses.'

'But I understood they looked into the matter. Surely they must have thought there was something in your theory, in that case?'

'Not at all. I have no doubt that they would much rather I had gone away and forgotten all about it. But I had no intention of doing so.' A thin smile played briefly about her lips. 'Let us say that the inquiry had to do less with conviction on their part than with the fact that I made myself somewhat objectionable until they did as I wished.'

It was the first glimpse of humour Angela had seen in her, and it disappeared as quickly as it had come. Ursula went on:

'I imagine you are aware that the inquest returned an open verdict. I should advise you to disregard that. A lack of evidence does not mean that there is nothing to find.'

Angela acknowledged the point.

'When did you first suspect that the deaths of Philippa and Winifred may not have been all they seemed?' she asked. 'Was it before your husband died?'

'Oh, I make no claims to cleverness in that regard. Like everyone else, I thought that Philippa's death was perfectly natural and that Winifred had met with an unfortunate accident—which was, moreover, quite in character. It was only when my husband was killed that I started to look with suspicion on the events of the previous two gatherings.'

'What is your theory, then?'

'I am not an expert, of course, but I do know that Philippa had been taking digitalin for her heart for many years, and that she was very careless in leaving bottles of the stuff lying about all over the house—she was always complaining that she could not find it. Now, everybody knows that it is necessary to be extremely careful with digitalin, since when taken to excess it is a deadly poison. What could be more simple, then, than for a person of malicious intent to procure some of her medicine and put it in her food or drink?'

'But I seem to remember hearing that digitalin has a very bitter flavour. Wouldn't she have tasted it?' Angela stopped as she dimly remembered something that Louisa had said. What was it? Something about Philippa's having complained about the dinner that night.

'I have no idea,' said Ursula. 'As I said, I am not an expert.'

'So presumably you are also of the view that Winifred did not fall over the balustrade accidentally, but was pushed.'

Ursula bowed her head.

'Winifred was a very silly creature,' she said, 'but having reflected, I have come to the conclusion that even she was not such a fool as to lean out far enough to topple over.'

'But I tried it myself, and was worried that I might fall.'

'You are a tall woman,' said Ursula. 'Winifred was not more than five feet one or two. She would have to have been balancing precariously on her stomach with her feet off the floor in order to fall accidentally.'

This was a point that Angela had not considered.

'Then you think that someone pushed her while she was reaching out?' she said.

'Or, more likely, that they grabbed her by the ankles and simply tipped her over. Nothing could be easier. She wouldn't necessarily even have seen who did it.'

'Who *did* do it, in your opinion?'

Ursula rose suddenly to her feet and thrust her face malevolently towards Angela.

'Look for the motive,' she hissed.

'I—,' began Angela, taken aback.

'Who had the most reason to kill them? Not I—Edward's death was to my disadvantage and my son's, as we lost five thousand pounds by it. The same goes for Susan, since her mother left her nothing. Who benefits? Who? Mrs. Marchmont, go back to Underwood House and find out: *what is John Haynes hiding*?'

A dumbfounded Angela was saved the necessity of replying by the entrance of a young man with a sulky expression, who stopped short when he saw her.

'I beg your pardon,' he said, and looked questioningly towards Ursula.

'Robin,' said Ursula, 'this is Mrs. Marchmont. She is a friend of Louisa's. You will remember I told you about her. Mrs.

Marchmont, this is my son, Robin.' She had regained her normal frigid poise, as though nothing had happened.

Robin Haynes held out his hand and narrowed his eyes warily. Angela had the uncomfortable feeling that she was being examined and classified like an unfamiliar species of moth or beetle. Apparently the result of the study was satisfactory, for his face lengthened into something akin to a smile.

'Ah, yes,' he said, 'the lady detective. We shall all have to be very careful not to incriminate ourselves.'

Despite his joking manner, there was something forced in his tone and Angela studied the young man, curious to see what kind of son Ursula had produced. Robin Haynes had a puny, under-nourished look about him and a mouth that turned down at the corners, as though a complaint hovered perpetually on the tip of his tongue. With a head of sleek, dark hair which as yet had no silver in it, he bore a striking physical resemblance to his mother, but unlike Ursula, who easily dominated the room with her presence, he seemed to cultivate a deliberate shrinking insignificance that would make him easy to overlook if he wished it.

'I shall leave you to question my son alone,' said Ursula, and departed. Robin cast a glance after her as she left and relaxed visibly.

'What has she been saying to you?' he asked abruptly.

'Your mother has been telling me about her suspicions,' replied Angela. 'She believes that your father's death was murder. What do you think?'

Robin bridled at the direct question.

'Well, really,' he said, 'I haven't the faintest idea. Mother is usually right in these things, though, so I dare say she has good reason for saying it.'

'Do you agree that it was out of character for him to go out on the lake?'

'How should I know? If everyone says so then it must be true. I haven't given the matter much thought.'

'I understand he was unable to swim.'

'That's what Mother said. I dare say she's right.'

'Does he have an opinion of his own?' said Angela to herself. Aloud, she went on: 'Did you see him go out that night?'

'Yes, of course. We all did.'

'Did you know he had left the house?'

'No, I hadn't the slightest idea of it.'

'Did you go outside yourself that evening?'

'Go outdoors in the middle of the night in February? Not I!'

'Very well,' said Angela, seeing that he could not or would not say anything about his father's death, 'I am also trying to find out what happened to Philippa and Winifred. According to Louisa, when Winifred fell over the balustrade and everybody rushed into the hall, you and Donald Haynes arrived on the scene first—indeed, you were found bending over the body.'

Robin inhaled sharply and glared at her.

'And if I was? What are you suggesting? She was my aunt. Why shouldn't I tend to her when she had just suffered a terrible accident? Anyone would have done the same.'

'Oh dear, I seem to have started off rather badly,' thought Angela. 'Forgive me,' she said to Robin. 'I expressed myself clumsily just then. I merely wanted to know whether you saw what happened.'

'No, I didn't see what happened. Nobody did, as far as I know.'

'Where were you when she fell?'

He waved a hand.

'Somewhere about. I can't remember.'

'Are you sure of that? Presumably you heard her fall, or you would not have run to her as quickly as you did. Try and think, Mr. Haynes.'

'Well then, I suppose I was in the library. Yes—yes, that's where I was.'

'And you heard a cry and the sound of something landing heavily?'

He winced and nodded.

'Yes. She was lying on the floor. When I knelt over her I saw that her head was at a funny angle. I could see immediately that there was nothing to be done. I have delicate nerves, and I'm afraid I was rather sick.'

'Who arrived first on the scene, you or Donald?'

Robin clicked his tongue impatiently.

'I really can't remember. Does it matter?'

'Perhaps. Or perhaps not. I can't say at the moment.'

'Well—' he paused. 'I think Don got there before me. Yes, I'm sure of it. I ran out of the library and he was already there.'

'What was he doing?'

'Just standing there, looking shocked and breathing hard. He was awfully white in the face—as was I, I should imagine.'

'Did you see anybody else? Upstairs, for example?'

'Don't you think I should have mentioned it if I had? There was nobody. Everyone was downstairs at the time.'

'Apart from your cousin Susan. Louisa said she came out of her room and fainted when she saw what had happened.'

'Ah yes, I'd forgotten about her. Yes, she was upstairs.'

'Do you remember where John Haynes was?'

'Uncle John? No, I can't say that I do. He was probably hiding away somewhere. He hates these family gatherings as much as the rest of us so he escapes to his study whenever he can.'

'Do you believe Winifred's death was deliberate? I know your mother believes it was,' went on Angela hurriedly, seeing him about to speak, 'but what do *you* think?'

Robin glanced round, as though making sure Ursula really had left the room.

'It looks odd in the light of what happened to my father,' he admitted finally, 'but really, I couldn't tell you. I saw nothing suspicious.'

'And what about your Aunt Philippa?'

'I know Mother thinks she was poisoned, but she had heart trouble, so it was hardly a surprise when she died.'

'Do you remember anything about the events of that evening? You don't remember what you had for dinner, for example?'

'Of course not. I can barely recall what I had for dinner a week ago. Surely you can't expect me to remember a meal that I ate last year.'

'There was soup,' said Ursula suddenly, making them jump. She had come back into the room so quietly that they had not heard her approach. 'It was a mulligatawny. I am not fond of mulligatawny. That is how I remember it. What else we had I couldn't say.'

'Lamb,' said Robin, as though the memory had just struck him. 'Of course, it was lamb. And a rather indifferent soufflé to follow.'

'How was the soup served?' asked Angela.

'I don't understand what you mean,' said Ursula.

'I mean, did it arrive in a tureen or already served into separate dishes?'

'I don't remember,' said Ursula. Robin shook his head in agreement.

'Was coffee served afterwards?'

'I imagine so,' replied Ursula.

Angela tried again.

'Louisa said Philippa complained about the dinner. Do you remember that?' she asked.

'Philippa was always complaining,' said Ursula. 'She was never happier than when finding fault with something. After a while, one tended to ignore it. To answer your question therefore—no, I do not remember her expressing discontent about that in particular, although that is not to say she did not.'

'And she went up to bed as normal? She did not mention feeling unwell?'

'No more than was usual,' said Ursula. 'She liked to make the most of her indisposition, you see. That was another thing it was easier to ignore. Otherwise one would have been dancing attendance on her from morning to night.'

The sun streamed cheerfully into the room, as though inviting all those hiding inside to throw open the doors and run into the garden. Angela was starting to feel wearied by the oppressive atmosphere in the house and the unfriendliness of its inhabitants.

'I have just one more question,' she said. 'Do you recognize this?'

She produced the photograph of the young woman. Robin glanced at it incuriously.

'No, not at all,' he said.

Ursula looked at it for a little longer, then handed it back to Angela with a shake of the head.

'I have never seen her before,' she said. 'Who is it?'

'That's what I want to find out,' said Angela. She rose. 'Thank you for your help,' she said.

'I am sorry you have so little evidence to go on,' said Ursula almost graciously, 'but perhaps you will succeed in unearthing something that the police have overlooked.'

'Perhaps. If you think of anything else that might help, do please let me know.'

'I shall. And remember what I said.'

As Angela walked down the front path of the house, she glanced back briefly and saw Ursula and Robin standing side by side at the window, staring darkly at her as they watched her leave. Once out of sight, she gave a little shiver and hurried away from the house as fast as she could.

CHAPTER NINE

THE SUN CONTINUED to shine as Mrs. Marchmont stepped off the train at Waterloo, and the day was such a warm and pleasant one that she decided to walk home rather than take a taxi. Besides, she wanted an opportunity to reflect on what she had learnt so far. Accordingly, she set off at a leisurely pace across the bridge, pausing once or twice to admire the expansive view of the city that can be gained only from its river.

On Northumberland Avenue, her way was impeded by a throng of people standing outside a theatre waiting to be admitted to the matinée performance of a comic play that had been receiving highly favourable reviews from the London critics. The crowd formed such a solid mass that there appeared to be no means of passing through it for a person of normal size, so after one or two unsuccessful forays Angela turned and prepared to cross to the other side of the road.

The next few minutes were ones of confusion. Afterwards, Angela had no clear recollection of what had happened, but she was quite certain that someone had shoved her hard in the small of the back, and all she knew next was that she was sprawled in the middle of the road, staring helplessly at the inexorable approach of a large motor-van as it bore down upon her. Several people screamed, and one shouted 'Look out, miss!', then there was a loud screech as the van (thank heaven for effective brakes!) came to a halt just inches away.

''Ere! What's all this then? What do you think you're doing?' cried the indignant driver, descending with all speed from his cab.

'I'm dreadfully sorry,' said a dazed Angela, sitting up. 'I don't know what happened.'

'Well there ain't no call for it—jumping in front of a person like that. You might have been killed, and then wouldn't there be trouble? I got rounds to do, see? And I'm already late.'

'You leave her be,' said a fat woman. 'Can't you see she's hurt?'

'No, no, I'm quite all right,' said Angela, almost sure she was telling the truth. She stood up carefully and dusted herself down. As far as she could judge, apart from grazed hands and knees and a severe blow to her pride she was unharmed.

'Miss, miss, he's got your bag!' exclaimed a small boy suddenly. The cry went up.

'He pushed her!'

'Catch him!'

'Quick! He's got her handbag!'

'Somebody stop him!'

There was a commotion and a certain amount of excited shrieking as several men and a quantity of boys broke away from the throng and bolted all in the same direction just as Angela realized that the article in question was indeed missing.

'There you go,' said the fat woman comfortably. 'Now he's for it. Are you feeling better now, miss?'

'Yes thank you. Did you see what happened?' said Angela, who had by now quite recovered her faculties.

'Someone pushed you into the road and then ran away with your bag,' replied the woman. 'That's a low trick, if you ask me. They'll catch him now, though, you mark my words.'

'Who was it?'

'Why, I couldn't rightly say—I didn't see him myself.'

'Please, miss, he was a big, tall man with a stoop,' said the small boy excitedly.

'Don't talk nonsense,' said a faded-looking woman. She turned to Angela. 'He's talking nonsense, he is. He was medium-sized and thin, with a grey suit and a beard.'

'He was tall, I tell you. And his suit wasn't grey, it was dark blue. And it was a moustache, not a beard,' said the boy stubbornly.

'And he had a scar on his cheek,' chimed in a middle-aged man, who appeared to be the faded woman's husband.

'What do you mean, he had a scar on 'is cheek?' demanded his wife. 'How do you know? You were looking in the other direction, like always. You never see what's right in front of your nose, do you? And look at all them other men chasing 'im. Why didn't you help? You could have been a hero for once, 'stead of standing there like a rabbit.'

'How am I supposed to chase him if I never saw him?' said the man, looking mutinous.

'You said he had a scar so you must've seen him.'

'According to you, I was looking the other way. You can't 'ave it both ways, can you?'

'He never had no scar that I saw, miss,' said the boy quietly, so as not to get drawn into the dispute.

'I wouldn't know, myself,' said the fat woman. 'Beard, moustache, blue suit, green suit—he could have had all or none of them for all I know. Like I said, I never saw nothing.'

The theatre doors had by now opened but many of those in the crowd were showing a marked reluctance to enter given the free entertainment on offer right before their eyes. Why, this was much better than a play! Meanwhile Angela, feeling increasingly foolish and embarrassed at the undisguised stares and frank curiosity of the assembled multitude, pretended to be examining the grazes on her hands as she tried to decide what to do next. 'Shall I go to the police straight away?' she said to herself. 'Really, I suppose I ought to stay here until some of these people return from the chase. I don't imagine for a second they'll catch him, though.'

Just then a great cheer went up and, to Angela's surprise, the crowd parted to reveal a small group of people, led by a flushed and panting young man, who approached her and shyly but proudly presented her with none other than her own bag, seemingly undamaged.

'Did you catch him, then?' demanded the fat woman.

The youth shook his head.

'Headed into Covent Garden, didn't he? Disappeared down an alley and we lost him. But we found this on the ground. I guess it must be yours—either that or we've pinched some other lady's bag by mistake.'

There was a ripple of laughter at this pleasantry. Angela smiled, glanced into the bag and saw that nothing seemed to be missing.

'Begging your pardon, miss, but it was left open so I had a quick look inside to see if anything might have been taken. I don't think he got your purse at any rate.'

Angela was suitably effusive and generous in her gratitude and the young man departed, beaming and blushing furiously as he was patted on the shoulder from all sides. The crowd gave a collective sigh of satisfaction at a good afternoon's fun happily resolved, and gradually melted into the theatre. The motor-van driver shook his head in admonishment and went on his way, leaving only the small boy, who hung about hopefully, unwilling to leave in case some other exciting misadventure should befall the smart lady.

'Are you going to the police, miss?' he asked.

'No,' replied Angela. 'I've got my bag back and there's no real harm done other than one or two bruises. No, I shan't be bothering them today, I think.'

The boy's face was the picture of disappointment.

'But what about the robber?' he said. 'He'll get clean away. Why, he might be murdering an old lady in her bed with an axe this minute!'

Angela could not help laughing at this bloodthirsty vision.

'I do hope not,' she said. 'Very well, I'll tell you what I will do. I have an acquaintance who is a very high-up policeman, and when I see him I shall report the matter to him and ask him to investigate. Will that do?'

'I'll say,' said the boy, nodding vigorously. 'A high-up policeman! Is he a Scotland Yard 'tec, your friend?'

'He is indeed, and a very important one too,' said Angela. She tapped her nose mysteriously.

'Coo!' said the boy, opening his eyes wide. 'Is he one of them what investigates murders and suchlike?'

'Yes, murders, thefts, blackmail, drug-running, espionage—all sorts of things. Why, he was one of the men who brought the McBride gang to justice, and he has a bullet-wound in his side to prove it!'

The boy clasped his hands together and almost danced in excitement.

'I wish *I* could meet him,' he said. 'I'm going to be a detective just like him when I grow up.'

'Oh? Then you will have to work very hard and start practising now. Tell me again what the man who stole my bag looked like. He was tall with a stoop and a moustache, I think you said.'

The boy looked down and shuffled his feet uncomfortably.

'I *thought* he was,' he admitted. 'But now I wonder whether I was looking at the right fellow. There was such a row going on that I might have got the wrong one.'

'Then you would not swear to your earlier description?'

He shook his head sheepishly.

Angela smiled. 'Don't worry,' she said. 'It is not easy to be an accurate observer, but I have no doubt that the next time you are a witness to a crime you will remember everything you saw.'

The boy looked relieved.

'I think I ought to be getting home now,' she went on.

'Get you a taxi, miss?' said the boy.

'Yes please,' said Angela. She was still feeling rather shaken after her experience and decided it was better not to risk the walk.

The taxi arrived and Angela got in. The boy stayed to salute her.

'Don't forget to tell your 'tec friend,' he said. 'He'll catch the fellow, you'll see!'

'Of course,' said Angela. She nodded and winked.

'Good gracious!' she said to herself as the taxi departed, 'A bullet-wound in his side, indeed! I must be quite light-headed after that fall to be talking such bunk.' Then she sat back in her seat and laughed until the tears rolled down her face.

Chapter Ten

AFTER A HOT bath and a light repast Angela felt much better, and submitted without too much protest to being fussed over by her maid, Marthe, who was horrified to hear of her adventure.

'But *madame*,' she said, 'You ought not to have been wandering around the city alone. It is full of *des méchants* and assassins—bad men who lie in wait around every corner to cut one's throat. I have always said it, have I not? And now I am proved right. Look at your poor hands! And your silk stockings, torn to rags!' She clicked her tongue and shook her head. 'Promise me you will not go out alone again without a man to protect you.'

Angela laughed.

'Don't be absurd, Marthe,' she said. 'To hear you, anyone would think that London was the seventh circle of Hell. I was merely unfortunate this afternoon. An opportunistic thief thought he should get good pickings from me, that's all. I shall of course be more careful in future.'

Marthe threw up her hands in despair.

'What will become of you, *madame*? Very well, I wash my hands of it, but I beg of you—do not take any risks.'

'Don't worry, I shan't,' replied Angela. 'Now, bring me some coffee and a paper and pencil. I should like to think for a while.'

She sat down at an elegant little table by the window, from where she was accustomed to amuse herself in observing the passers-by as they went about their daily business. Having spent much of her adult life in New York, Angela had grown to prefer big cities to small towns, and was pleased with the situation of her flat, which afforded an excellent view of the street below. On this occasion, however, she was not concerned with the goings-on outside, her thoughts being occupied by other matters. She sat staring at nothing much as her coffee cooled beside her and the sun began to sink. After a while she shook herself, nodded firmly and bent to her task, scribbling rapidly for several minutes. Occasionally she paused to collect her thoughts or cross something out. Finally she threw down her pencil, picked up the paper and read through what she had written. It was as follows:

> John Haynes
> Motive: did not want to sell house. Deaths of his sisters and brother made it easier for him to keep same.

Opportunity: ? not known in case of P and E (was he really in his study when W fell?).

Ursula Haynes

Motive: claims to have none, although she inherits E's money.

Opportunity: none in case of W, as was in drawing-room when she fell.

Robin Haynes

Motive: see above. Financial scandal? (see Inspector J).

Opportunity: claims to have arrived on scene of W's fall after DH.

Susan Dennison

Motive: none known (did she want her mother out of the way so she could come to an arrangement with John about selling Underwood House?).

Opportunity: only person known to have been in the right place to kill W.

Donald Haynes

Motive: ?

Opportunity: according to Robin, was first on the scene when W died.

Mr Faulkner

Motive: money, and lots of it! Inherits five thousand pounds outright from each of the three. Opportunity: none, apparently. Has an alibi for each occasion (see Inspector J to be sure).

1) Find out more about what everyone was doing when P and E died. Furthermore:

- How was the soup served on the night of P's death? Did they have coffee?
- Who can swim?

2) Speak to Donald and Susan.

3) Look at the will.

Angela regarded her work mournfully.

'Is this really the sum of all I have discovered in the past few days?' she said to herself. 'For shame, Angela! You must do better than that. Ah yes, I almost forgot.'

She picked up the pencil and appended a note in large letters: 'WHO IS THE WOMAN IN THE PHOTOGRAPH?'

'And perhaps I should also add, "Why did John say he didn't recognize it?"' she said.

She stood up and crossed the room to where she had left her handbag. The picture had seemed familiar to her the first time she looked at it. Perhaps it would come to her now. She opened the bag and felt inside, but could not find the photograph. She frowned and pulled everything out, then straightened up in puzzlement and summoned Marthe.

'Marthe, did you find a photograph of a woman in my coat pocket?' she asked.

'But no, *madame*,' replied Marthe. 'There were a number of things that—as I have told you before many times—one does not expect a lady *à la mode* to carry in her pockets, such as a pen-knife and some string and a quantity of liquorice. But no, there was no photograph.'

Suitably chastened, Angela dismissed the girl and rifled through her things again without success. The picture had gone.

'How very odd,' she said. 'But how—'

She stopped as she thought back to her adventure on Northumberland Avenue that afternoon. Had the picture fallen out of her handbag when it was stolen, or had it been taken intentionally? But why should anybody want to steal an old photograph when there was plenty of money in the bag for the taking, as well as a gold cigarette-case? Now for the first time it occurred to her that perhaps she had not, after all, been the victim of a casual thief, but had in fact been deliberately attacked.

'Who was it, then? And why did he do it?' she said to herself. 'Was it the owner of the picture? Did he merely wish to retrieve it by any means necessary, or did he also intend to do me harm? Why, had that motor-van stopped even one second later I could have been badly hurt or even killed.'

She shivered as she recalled the brief thrill of terror she had experienced as the vehicle bore down upon her. Until that moment she had had no intention of calling the police, but now she felt in need of advice. She suddenly noticed the soreness in her grazed hands and knees and winced. It was almost as though they were tingling in agreement.

'Very well then,' she said, and lifted the telephone-receiver, then paused and smiled wryly. 'But I shan't mention it to Marthe.'

Inspector Jameson was away on a case, Scotland Yard informed her, but was expected back the next day. Mrs. Marchmont left a message, then returned to her paper and added one or two notes.

'An early dinner and then bed, I think,' she said, and was as good as her word.

The next morning she summoned her chauffeur, William, and regarded him for a moment with her head on one side.

'I have a task for you, William, which I hope you will accept, even though it is out of the way of your normal duties,' she said.

William pricked up his ears with interest.

'You know I'm always happy to help, ma'am,' he said in his customary drawl. 'Just say the word and I'll do it.'

'Wait until you hear what it is before you give your promise. I have been engaged by a friend to discover whether or not three members of her husband's family were murdered, and I should like your assistance in the inquiry.'

William raised his eyebrows in surprise, then broke out in a wide smile that gave his freckled face the look of a rosy sun.

'Murder, eh? Why, I should be mighty pleased to do anything I can in the investigation.'

'Very good. I think it only fair to warn you beforehand, however, that there may be danger involved. You will, of course, have heard that I myself was attacked yesterday afternoon, although no harm came of it, thankfully. Now, the attack may or it may not be connected to this case, but I should like you to be on your guard at any rate.'

William's smile grew even wider.

'Danger, you say? Take me to it!' was all he said.

Angela could not help laughing at his carefree air.

'I see you would rather put yourself in peril than not,' she said. 'But I am afraid the first thing I want you to do is quite ordinary. I am going down to Underwood House this morning, and you shall come with me. While we are there, I should like you to insinuate yourself with the servants and find out one or two things. Can you do that, do you think?'

'Can I!' the young man exclaimed. 'You just watch me.'

Angela told him what she wanted, and he listened carefully and nodded.

'That ought to be easy enough,' he said.

'Yes, I am sure you will do an admirable job of exerting your charms on the maids, at the very least,' Angela smiled. 'I expect their heads will be quite turned by your American accent.'

'We-ell, that's a mighty fine compliment you just paid me, ma'am,' said William, his drawl even more pronounced than usual.

'Oh, and you need not admit to them that, as a matter of fact, you were born in Peckham,' said Angela slyly, as he prepared to leave the room.

William's smile grew so wide that his face looked as though it were about to split in two, and a touch of pink tinged his cheeks.

Chapter Eleven

THE WEATHER WAS holding nicely and Mrs. Marchmont, ensconced comfortably in the back seat of the Bentley, admired Beningfleet's high street as they passed through it, its higgledy-piggledy houses and shops seeming to doze gently in the sunshine as the villagers went about their daily business. William was in great high spirits, and she listened to his amusing anecdotes with half an ear as she turned various thoughts over idly in her mind.

She was brought up short when she caught sight of the Hayneses' solicitor, Mr. Faulkner, striding purposefully in the direction of his office, which was situated in one of the more attractive buildings not far from the square.

'Stop!' she said. 'I want to get out.'

William duly obliged.

'Wait for me here,' she said, and hurried after Mr. Faulkner.

'Good morning, Mrs. Marchmont,' said the solicitor genially, turning as she hailed him. 'A fine day today, I'm sure you'll agree. And how goes your little investigation?'

'Rather inconclusively, I'm afraid,' replied Angela. 'I was just on my way to call on Louisa when I saw you and was hoping you could spare me a few minutes. I wanted to take a look at Philip Haynes's will, as you did not have your keys with you last time I visited.'

'Ah, the will. I must confess I'd forgotten about it, but—oh! Yes, of course, that reminds me of something I meant to tell you the last time we spoke, which had completely slipped my mind. The inevitable consequence of age, I fear. It did not seem important at the time—and indeed I may have been guilty of not taking it very seriously when she told me about it, but it has since occurred to me that it may possibly have a bearing on this case.'

'Oh?' said Angela, her curiosity aroused.

'Yes. Shall we sit here? It is such a beautiful morning it seems a shame to cower in my stuffy old office as though we were afraid of a little sunshine.'

He indicated a bench placed in such a position as to afford weary walkers a restful view of the Downs beyond the edge of the little town. They sat. Angela regarded him expectantly but for a few moments he appeared to have forgotten his purpose as he stroked his chin and his features gradually gathered into a perplexed frown. At length he seemed to come to himself and turned to Angela with a wry smile.

'I beg your pardon,' he said. 'But I wonder whether I mayn't after all be making a mistake in telling you this, since her story was vague in the extreme and is, when all is said and done, quite unlikely to bear any relation at all to the business at hand. I should hate to set you off on a wild-goose chase.'

Angela laughed.

'If you were hoping to dampen my curiosity with that I'm afraid you have failed miserably,' she said. 'Now I am simply dying to hear it. Don't worry about sending me off on a false scent—I have no intention of taking any action precipitately.'

The lawyer's eyes twinkled in acknowledgment.

'Yes, I ought to have remembered that the surest way to arouse a lady's interest is to tell her that there is nothing to tell,' he said. 'Very well, then, but remember that there may be nothing in it. The person to whom I am referring is Winifred Dennison. Some time ago she came to me with a confused tale in which, in short, she accused a person or persons whom she was not willing to name of having cheated her out of a large sum of money.'

'Indeed?' said Angela.

'I believe I mentioned to you before, and probably you have heard it from others, that Winifred was an extremely unworldly woman. She was the type to be taken in by any hard-luck story one might care to tell her, and as a result she was frequently the object of charlatans, swindlers and other persons of questionable character claiming to represent good causes of various kinds. When she came to me with this tale, therefore, I confess I paid little attention to it, as I assumed that she had once again been "stung", as the vulgar phrase has it, by a petty confidence-man with a plausible story. It was not until after she died and it was discovered that all her money had gone that I began to think that perhaps there was something in it.'

'Do you remember what she said, exactly? When was it that she came to you?'

'It must have been about a year ago—not long before she died, as a matter of fact. It was late in the afternoon and I was about to go home which, I am ashamed to say, may have influenced my actions—or rather lack of them. She drifted into my office in the peculiar way she had, scattering scarves and hat-pins as she went, and said she wanted to consult me about a private matter. I had just begun to hint that perhaps a more suitable time could be found in which we could converse at our leisure, when she launched suddenly into a highly confused account of a fast-growing investment fund into which somebody—she would not say who—had persuaded her to put a large sum of money. The fund was meant to be as safe as houses, and she had been told that she could withdraw her money at any time. She had hoped to increase her capital significantly, as there were a number of charitable concerns which required her assistance, and she had initially agreed to leave the money with this person for a period of one year on the promise of a return of something in the region of thirty per cent.'

Angela pursed her lips as though to whistle but stopped herself just in time.

'Good gracious!' she said instead.

'Quite,' said Mr. Faulkner. 'At all events, it so happened that one of her projects found itself in need of funds rather sooner than she had expected, and so she asked to withdraw some of the money before the year was up. This, it seems, was not at all to the liking of her mysterious correspondent, who at first tried to dissuade her from doing so, then attempted to convince her that she was under a legal obligation to keep the money on deposit. According to her story, she stood firm—most unlike her, I should say—and pointed out that as she had not signed any agreement, she was perfectly entitled to have her money back whenever she chose.'

'She hadn't signed anything!' exclaimed Mrs. Marchmont.

'It appears not. And so, after some further prevarication, Winifred's unnamed adviser finally agreed to pay her the sum she had requested. She waited a month, but the funds were not forthcoming and, what was worse, her correspondent appeared to have begun to avoid her, since her letters went unanswered and he could not be contacted by telephone, although she tried on several occasions. It was at this point that she came to consult me but, as I said, I did not give the matter the attention that perhaps it deserved. On the contrary,' he went on, 'I am ashamed to say that I made excuses for this person, and encouraged her to wait another week or two. A fortnight later, she was dead.'

'And you have no idea who the person was?'

'None at all. It does strike me, however, that her reluctance to give his name is suggestive.'

'Yes, it does seem to indicate that whoever it was must have been a friend or member of the family. Why refuse to give his name, otherwise?'

Mr. Faulkner inclined his head.

'That would appear to be a rational deduction,' he said. 'But to go any further than that would be indulging in mere speculation.'

Angela was just about to ask again to see the will when the lawyer, who had been gazing past her down the street, suddenly started, glanced at his watch and gave an exclamation.

'Dear me! I have been so caught up with the fine morning and the charming company that I had quite forgotten I have an appointment. I am five minutes late already, and you must know I make it quite a rule never to keep a client waiting.'

He rose to his feet, as did Angela.

'I'm afraid I must rush,' he said. 'You will forgive me, won't you? But of course you will. Think of me trapped among my musty old papers while you enjoy the beauty of this delightful morning.' He waved an expansive hand and indicated the Downs in the distance. 'Indeed, if you have time, I highly recommend you take a trip to Beningsdown Hill. There is a very fine view from the top.'

'I should love to. But when can I see Philip's will?'

'Another time, another time,' he said. 'Believe me, I shall be only too delighted—' he bowed and was off.

Angela returned thoughtfully to the Bentley, where William was polishing the paint-work in a desultory fashion. He stood to attention when he saw her.

'William,' she said, 'you saw the gentleman I was just talking to, I believe?'

'Yes ma'am,' he replied.

'Did you see the woman who went into his office a few minutes before him?'

'I guess I did. Straight as a ramrod, looked like a fury. That the one you mean?'

Angela smiled at the apt description.

'That's the one,' she said. 'I want you to watch the building until she comes out, and if the solicitor comes out with her I'd like you to see if you can hear what they say. You don't object to eavesdropping?'

'Eavesdropping? Why, ma'am, how can it be eavesdropping if I chance to overhear a conversation between two people in a public street?'

'My thoughts precisely,' said Angela. 'It's a shot in the dark and I don't suppose it will come to anything, but you may as well try. In the meantime, I shall walk the rest of the way to Underwood House. You follow after.'

She set off at a brisk pace, smiling faintly. It was curious, she thought. There was no reason why Ursula Haynes should not visit Mr. Faulkner, but the lawyer had been so anxious to prevent her from seeing it, directing her attention towards the beauties of the countryside, that her suspicions had been immediately raised. There might be nothing in it, but she resolved to keep an eye on them in future.

Chapter Twelve

UNDERWOOD HOUSE LOOKED almost handsome in the sunshine, its grey frontage, which on cloudy days had a dark, unwelcoming aspect, seeming to shake off its customary gloom and smile kindly upon all comers. Two or three men bearing ladders and gardening tools were crossing the lawn towards the house as Mrs. Marchmont approached, and she watched as they stopped below the window that she had pointed out to John Haynes as being half-covered by ivy. One of the men was wrinkled and stooped, and he touched his hat politely as she drew near.

'Good morning,' said Angela. 'I see you are going to tackle that ivy.'

'Yes, ma'am,' replied the old fellow. 'Shot away when my back was turned, she did. Got to keep an eye on them creepers, you have, or they'll squirm their way into every crack and cranny and before you know it, the whole house'll come down. Dangerous things, they are.'

'You sound as though you weren't fond of them.'

The old man sensed a sympathetic soul.

'No I'm not, and never will be,' he said. 'Nasty, sneaking things they are, and ivy most of all. A rose, now, or a nice box 'edge—why, you know where you stand with them. Show 'em who's the master and they'll do your bidding. But ivy'll slither up behind you and strangle you dead before you know it. You can't beat her. You can only keep her down.'

'But there's such a lot of it. What will you do with the dead stuff once you've cut it back?'

'Why, we'll let her dry off awhile then build a nice big bonfire, of course,' he replied with some relish.

The ladder had now been placed and one of the other men was preparing to climb it.

'Do you know whose window that is, Briggs? It is Briggs, isn't it?' asked Angela.

The gardener beamed and drew himself up to his full height with difficulty.

'That's right, ma'am. Been with the Hayneses at Underwood House for nigh on sixty years, I have. I knew Mr. John when he was a lad this tall. Knew his father when he was a young man, too.' His face darkened. 'It's not my place to say it, but he's dead and gone now—you may guess where—so I shall. He was a bad man.'

'Philip Haynes?'

'The very one.'

'In what way was he a bad man?'

'I don't rightly know how to put it, ma'am, not being what you might call overly book-learned. But he *played* with people, if you catch my meaning.'

'Played with people?'

'That's right. Just as though they was dolls or toy soldiers or pieces on a board. He liked to set his family one against the other just for the fun of watching 'em fight. You could almost see him sitting back and clapping his hands every time he pulled it off. He was like a man I once knew, who used to come to Beningfleet every year when I was quite a young lad. He had a puppet-show and all the children used to come and watch. My, it was clever, the way he got the puppets to talk to each other, just as though they was real people, and not dolls being dangled about by someone behind a curtain. Just like that, old Mr. Haynes was.'

'Did you never wish to leave?'

'Not I. He always treated me kindly enough, I'll say that. It was his family what got all the unhappiness, not the servants. Besides, I was fond of Mrs. Haynes, God rest her soul. Who knows what trials she had to bear, all those years she was married to him. Still, she's gone to a better place now, and I won't say it's not a mercy. Take it all the way back there, Tom, that's right,' he called to the young man at the top of the ladder, who appeared to be having some difficulty.

'I do hope he won't fall off,' said Angela.

'Wasn't so long ago I should have gone up there myself, but Mr. John won't let me now,' said Mr. Briggs regretfully.

'He is quite correct,' said Angela. 'You are much better off directing things from down here.'

'P'raps you're right,' he said. 'I won't deny I've got a stiffness in my back. *Roomer*-tism, they call it. Call it what you like, says I, but it all boils down to one thing—old age, and there's no cure for that. Further to the left now,' he called out.

'Whose room did you say that was?'

'That one? That's Mr. Donald's bedroom. He's just come back from one of them foreign places. What was it they called it? The Ague. Seems a funny thing to me to call a place after a disease, but you never know what them foreigners will take it into their heads to do.'

'It's Donald's room, you say,' said Angela.

'It is now. Years ago it was Miss Christina's.'

'Who is Miss Christina?'

'She was the second child and the eldest girl, the one who ran off.'

'Do you mean Philip Haynes's second daughter? I seem to remember hearing about a girl who died.'

'That's her all right,' agreed Briggs. 'Terrible sad, it was. She was always a headstrong child, so it was no wonder that she came to blows with her family when she grew up.'

'When was that?'

He scratched his head.

'Ah, I don't rightly remember, but it must be thirty years or more. The old Queen was still on the throne, I do know that.' He lowered his voice. 'They do say—'

But what they did say Angela never knew, as they were just then interrupted by a cheery call from Stella Gillespie, who had spotted the visitor from a downstairs window and was coming out to greet her, accompanied by Guy Fisher. Mr. Briggs touched his hat once again and resumed his supervision of the ivy-cutting operations.

'There you are,' said Stella. 'We wondered where you had got to.'

'Am I late? I beg your pardon,' said Angela. 'I happened to bump into Mr. Faulkner in the village and have been talking to him.'

'Mr. Faulkner? He's the solicitor fellow, isn't he?' said Guy. 'He used to come here quite often before old Philip died, but I haven't seen him for some time now.'

'I don't like him,' said Stella. 'He's wily. There's something underhand about him.'

'Do you really think so?' said Guy, with interest. 'I say, now you mention it I suppose he does give rather that impression. Perhaps it's the way that he glances at one sideways rather than directly, as though he didn't want one to see what he was thinking.'

'Perhaps, but it's not just that. I always have the feeling that he knows something about me that I should rather he didn't, and that he is studying me in order to decide upon the best way to use that knowledge,' said Stella.

'I say!' said Guy. 'Are we to understand that you have a guilty secret? Tell all, my child, tell all. Neither of us shall breathe a word, you have my promise—although we may indulge in a little light blackmail.'

'Idiot,' said Stella. 'Mrs. Marchmont understands what I mean, don't you, Mrs. Marchmont?'

'I think I do,' replied Angela with a smile.

'And do you agree with me?'

'I should say that Mr. Faulkner knows very well what he is about,' said Angela cautiously.

'No doubt,' said Guy, 'but never mind him now. I am itching to know how our lady detective is getting on with her investigation.'

'Oh yes,' said Stella. 'Have you spoken to Ursula? What did she say? Did she accuse us all of being in it together?'

'Not exactly,' said Angela.

'Did you like her?' asked Guy maliciously.

'I found her very interesting,' replied Angela.

'You see, Stella? I told you she wouldn't tell us anything. She is far too discreet for that.'

'Naturally, I am as silent as the grave,' said Angela, who indeed had no intention of revealing anything at all about the progress of her inquiry if she could help it.

'Don is back, by the way,' said Guy. 'He returned last night. You can question him now.'

Stella glowered but said nothing, and Angela guessed that she and Donald had not yet made it up.

'I do have one or two questions I should like to ask him,' she said. 'Shall we go in?'

Guy turned to accompany her but Stella forestalled him.

'I think I shall go for a walk,' she said. There was a determined light in her eyes. 'Are you coming, Guy?' She set off towards the woods without looking back.

Guy hesitated, clearly torn between the two of them.

'Do go if you like,' said Angela. 'I can find my own way in.'

'Are you sure you don't mind?' said Guy. His tone was light but his eyes followed Stella's retreating figure.

'Of course not.'

He flashed her a grin and ran off after the girl.

'Oh dear,' said Angela to herself. 'I do hope she's not going to break his heart.' She turned and walked into the house.

Chapter Thirteen

ANGELA HAD CAUGHT only a brief glimpse of Donald Haynes the last time she saw him and so she was surprised to discover how extraordinarily good-looking he was. He was the sort of young man whom romantic novelists of the more fatuous kind would describe as 'saturnine', with intense dark eyes and a lowering brow. His habitual expression was sombre, but occasionally his face would light up and his mouth widen into an infectious grin, which transformed him completely. Angela judged him to be the sort of man who would be unlikely to wear his passions lightly, and was curious to know what had caused the disagreement between him and Stella.

He readily agreed to answer any questions Mrs. Marchmont might care to ask him.

'Ask away,' he said. 'Although you'll find I have nothing to tell you. Quite frankly, I don't know what Mother was thinking, listening to that silly woman's wild accusations. She's always had a screw loose somewhere, and this has given her just the excuse she was looking for to make a fuss about things.'

'Do you mean your Aunt Ursula?'

'Who else? I hear you've met her, so you must have seen for yourself how batty she is.'

'Do you really think so? I shouldn't have used that word myself. She appeared quite rational to me.'

'To you, perhaps, but of course you are an outsider. For my part it seems as though everywhere I turn these days there she is, dropping dark hints to me about I don't know what.'

'What kind of hints?'

He gestured impatiently.

'Why, I don't know. Something about having discovered something that I should rather nobody knew about. I haven't the faintest idea what she meant.'

'She said she had discovered something about you?'

'That's what she *said*.'

'And you have no idea at all what it was?'

'None at all. Perhaps you should ask Mother and Father. Apparently they are in on the secret too.'

'Oh?'

'What was it she said? Something like, "I know all about you and your mother. John has tried to keep it quiet all these years, but I have had my suspicions for some time now. Make no mistake—I could tell all if I wished to, but I won't for now. I must decide how to proceed." You see? Bats.'

'Do you or your mother have any dark secrets you should rather nobody knew about?' asked Angela as lightly as she could.

'*I* have none at all, unless she was referring to the fact that I am rather deeply in debt to my tailor. But Mother found out about that last week—that was an uncomfortable few minutes, I can tell you! As for Mother, you shall have to ask her yourself. Perhaps she has a murky past that none of us knows about, but of course you would know that better than anyone, as you have known her for longer.'

Angela smiled, then asked, 'Could she have been referring to her suspicions about the deaths of your aunts and uncle, do you think?'

'I expect it had something to do with that. I do wish she would say what she meant, though. We all know she suspects something or someone, but she won't say exactly what or whom, except that Father is meant to know all about it. She just hints darkly, and that's no use to anyone. We shall never find out what happened that way.'

'Well, that is why I am here, to try and find out the truth. Let us start with your Aunt Philippa. Ursula has suggested that she may have been poisoned by someone who put digitalin in her food, as the manner of her death was consistent with her having had a heart attack. Now, as I understand it, that evening you all had mulligatawny soup, followed by lamb and a soufflé and then coffee. I have never poisoned anybody myself, but I imagine the easiest way to do it would be to put it in either the soup or the coffee.'

'I should say you are right,' he agreed.

'But which was it? It all depends on opportunity. How is the soup served in this house, by the way? I mean, is it brought in in a tureen or in separate dishes?'

'We have a large tureen for that kind of thing.'

'Very good. So you see, if our hypothetical murderer wished to poison the soup, he must have found a way to introduce it into Philippa's dish after it had been served to her, otherwise you would all have been taken ill. Do you remember who was sitting next to her at the table that evening?'

'Probably me,' said Donald. 'I usually sat next to her. I don't know who was on her other side, though. And I didn't put anything in her soup.'

'No. I imagine it would be very difficult to introduce a drug into someone's food without their noticing, in fact. That leaves the coffee, which seems to be an altogether more likely prospect. How was that served?'

'It's always served from a coffee pot which is left on the side for everyone to help themselves or each other.'

'And you don't remember who helped whom to coffee that evening?'

'Hardly, after all this time.'

'I thought not—and I doubt anyone else does either. Your mother said something about Philippa's complaining about the food. Do you recall that?'

'No. Aunt Philippa fussed rather a lot, you know, so one would tend not to notice.'

'Yes. Very well, now we come to your Aunt Winifred. I understand you were the first to reach her when she fell.'

'Was I? I don't remember.'

'Your cousin Robin said so.'

'I suppose I must have been, then. Yes—now you mention it, I do seem to remember seeing everyone rushing out of the drawing-room into the hall, so I must have been there first, mustn't I?'

'What were you doing in the hall?'

'Why, I heard the cry, of course. I had been looking for Father in the study, but he wasn't there, and I was just coming out when she fell. I ran along and there she was, lying on the floor. Wait a minute, though—' he stopped. 'Of course, I remember it all now. I wasn't there first at all. Robin must have got there before me, because he was kneeling next to her when I arrived.'

'Are you sure of this?'

'Absolutely. I remember it distinctly.'

'What was he doing?'

'Looking for her pulse, I expect. He sat back in a hurry when he saw me, then said, "I don't know how it happened, Don." Then everyone else came running out and he bent back over her and said "She's dead!" Then he was sick and had to go and lie down for a while.'

'So everyone thought she had fallen accidentally. And why should you think any differently? It was only when Edward died that suspicions began to arise. One might almost say that to lose two relatives may be regarded as a misfortune, but to lose three looks like—what, Donald?'

'I don't know what happened to Uncle Edward,' said Donald. 'Nobody does. And I doubt we'll ever find out.'

'Then you don't subscribe to the theory that the three of them were murdered?'

Donald's face darkened and assumed a curious expression.

'I have my own views,' he said, 'but I don't suppose anyone will share them.'

'What do you mean?' Angela asked, taken aback at the sudden intensity of his manner.

'Has it ever occurred to you that a house may have a personality of its own?'

'Why, I—'

'Underwood House is more than one hundred and fifty years old,' said Donald eagerly. 'Think of all the things it has seen in that time! Births and deaths and marriages, and love and hatred—perhaps even violence. You may think me crazy, Mrs. Marchmont, but I believe that buildings can absorb the influence, or the energy, of those who live in them, and that they will grow to love those who love them best. Aunt Philippa and Aunt Winifred and Uncle Edward never liked the place. They plotted against it in order to get rid of it. And so it took its revenge.'

'Do you mean you believe the house itself killed them?'

He waved a hand.

'Nothing so simple. I am not so mad as to believe that a building is capable of putting poison in someone's coffee or pushing them over a balustrade. Of course not. That would be absurd. But I do believe in sympathies. I don't know exactly what happened, but I am certain that there was some mysterious influence at work, one which we are unable to understand—may never understand, in fact.'

An almost fanatical light had come into his eyes. Angela was quite startled at how suddenly his detached manner had transformed into something altogether more impassioned.

'I take it that you are fond of Underwood House, then?' she said.

'Why should it come as a surprise that a man should feel affection for his childhood home?' said Donald. 'Father is exactly the same.'

'I can understand it in your case,' said Angela, 'because you were brought up here by loving parents who were able to shield you from your grandfather's influence to some extent, but I have always understood that your father had an unhappy childhood at Underwood. His brother and sisters certainly had no fondness for the place if they wanted to get rid of it.'

'I don't believe Father suffered quite as much as the others. He is far more easy-going by nature, you know, and was usually sensible enough to remove himself when any scenes arose. The others were younger and took things much more to heart. Besides, he's terribly wedded to the idea of his responsibility as the eldest son to carry on the family name and pass on the estate. You know of course that I was adopted? Now, let me tell you that I have never been allowed to feel it—rest assured that no natural son could have been more kindly treated. But it must inevitably have been a source of private disappointment to Father that he and Mother were unable to have their own children, although of course he is much too honourable to say anything about it. And I know it was a blow to him when Grandfather left Underwood to all four of his children, instead of to Father alone. I think he may have felt it a reproach for his inability to pass on the house to a "true" Haynes. But I am as much a Haynes as any of them,' he went on, still with the same fiery glint in his eye, 'and when the house becomes mine one day everyone shall know it.'

'Do you expect to inherit the house, then? I thought Ursula and your cousin Susan had an interest?'

'Oh yes. I think Susan has already agreed to sell her share to Father, and he hopes that Aunt Ursula will do the same eventually, although I can't see her giving it up without a fight.'

Just then, Louisa Haynes entered with a distracted air.

'Has anybody seen Stella or Guy?' she asked. 'It's nearly lunch-time. Angela, darling, you will stay to lunch, won't you?'

'I believe they went for a walk in the grounds,' said Angela, 'and yes please.'

'Those children have the most dreadful habit of disappearing just before meals. I don't know *what* is to be done with them,' said Louisa. 'Well, it can't be helped. The bell will ring in a minute, and if they miss it then they shall just have to do without.'

Angela noticed that Donald's features had relapsed into their customary gloom, but he said nothing. Was he concerned about Stella and Guy? She observed him covertly, thinking about their conversation. He had directly contradicted Robin's story about who had arrived first on the scene after Winifred fell. Which of them was telling the truth? And another curious thing: John had claimed to be in his study at the time of the fall, but Donald had said that his father was not there when he looked. Where, then, had John been?

CHAPTER FOURTEEN

'THERE YOU ARE,' exclaimed Louisa as Stella and Guy entered the dining-room, laughing and flushed as though they had been running. 'What on earth possessed you to run off half an hour before lunch?'

'I'm sorry, Aunt Louisa,' said Stella, taking her place at the table. 'I forgot to put my watch on and I didn't realize how late it was.'

'She speaks only the truth,' said Guy. 'And I should take the blame upon myself like a gentleman were it not for the fact that in this instance it was entirely the lady's fault.'

'Beast,' said Stella. 'You could have kept an eye on the time yourself.'

'Alas, no,' said Guy mournfully. 'You forget that only yesterday the good people of Asprey's told me that my watch was no more, had gone to a better place—in short, could not be mended. I must now wait until some kindly rich widow takes pity on me and buys me another.'

'Or you could go somewhere other than Asprey's and pay six pounds for a new one instead of thirty,' said Stella.

'What a ridiculous notion,' said Guy. 'One must keep up appearances at all times, however difficult that may be on a straitened stipend such as my own.' He assumed an expression intended to convey a state of virtuous penury.

'I suppose I am to take that as a hint,' said John, laughing.

'Not at all, sir, not at all,' said Guy, as though the thought had never entered his head.

'By the way, Angela,' said Louisa, 'did you ever find out whose photograph that was?'

'No,' said Angela. 'I showed it to Ursula and Robin but they couldn't tell me.'

'Which photograph?' asked Stella curiously. 'May I see it?'

'I'm afraid not, as I rather unfortunately lost it yesterday.'

She told them what had happened, making light of the attack on herself, as she had no wish to worry Louisa. Even so, they all exclaimed in sympathy.

'But I don't understand,' said Stella. 'Why did he take the picture and nothing else? Are you sure that was the only thing missing, Mrs. Marchmont?'

'Quite sure,' said Angela.

'What is your theory?' asked Guy.

Angela smiled.

'I'm perfectly certain that the photograph was not stolen at all,' she said. 'Whoever took my bag was being hotly pursued by a group of enthusiastic bystanders, and so must have had only a moment or two to rifle through it before he was forced to abandon it and make his escape. The pursuers found it lying on the ground, open, and with nothing else missing from it. I therefore deduce that, since the thief can have had no possible reason for taking an old photograph, it must have fallen out of the bag and blown away.'

Was it her imagination, or was there a slight, almost imperceptible easing of tension in the room as she spoke? Had someone given a silent sigh of relief, perhaps? She did not believe for one second that the portrait had blown away, although she was much too sensible to reveal her true thoughts on the matter to the people most closely concerned with the case. But could one of the smiling, chattering people here really be the person who had pushed her with such violence into the path of a speeding motor-van?

After luncheon Louisa suggested that she and Angela go into the morning-room. John had gone out, while Guy had returned to work and Stella had disappeared to write a letter. Donald, who had toyed with his food in morose silence, muttered something about having some conference papers to look over and went off to the library. As he left, he grinned cheerfully at Angela, who was not yet accustomed to his lightning-quick changes of mood and was therefore a little startled.

Before they had even sat down Louisa said excitedly, 'Now, my dear, you must tell me exactly what you have discovered so far. I have been simply dying to know. Or are you going to be terribly discreet?'

Angela laughed, although in reality she had now begun to grasp the true implications of the task that had been entrusted to her and her heart sank within her as she looked at her friend's eager, expectant face.

'I don't know that there's much I can tell you,' she said. 'I've found out one or two things that are suggestive, although by no means conclusive, and I'd like to look into them further before I say or do anything irrevocable. I should hate to cause trouble unnecessarily, and the situation is of course rather delicate.'

Louisa looked disappointed but said, 'Naturally, I understand.'

'I did find out one rather mysterious thing, however,' went on Angela. 'Tell me, do you know anything about what happened to Winifred's money?'

'Why, no. I always understood that she had given it away to some of her causes before she died. Poor Susan was left with practically nothing.'

'Then she never mentioned to you anything about having been the victim of a fraud?'

'A fraud? What kind of fraud? No, I had heard nothing about this.'

'Apparently, someone she knew had persuaded her to put a large sum of money into an investment fund, on the promise that she could withdraw it whenever she chose. However, when she came to ask for the cash to be returned to her, this adviser—whoever he was—prevaricated. Two weeks later she died without ever having received her money.'

'Gracious me! No, I knew nothing at all about it. Where did you hear about this?'

'From Mr. Faulkner. He told me that she came to him to complain about it and ask what she ought to do. He advised her to wait a little longer before taking any further steps.'

'Oh dear! Then where is the money now?'

'I don't know,' said Angela, 'although I have no proof that the story is true. I heard it from Mr. Faulkner who in turn heard it from Winifred, and I gather she was not exactly reliable when it came to relating the facts of a matter with great accuracy.'

'No, she wasn't,' agreed Mrs. Haynes. 'But surely there must be some documentary evidence somewhere? I am sure that Susan would have said something had she found it when she was going through her mother's things.'

'According to Mr. Faulkner, Winifred said that she hadn't signed anything. It appears to have been quite an informal arrangement, which lends more weight to the theory that her adviser was somebody close to her. It would also explain why no written evidence had been found.'

'I see,' said Louisa. 'Well, it's quite obvious that it must have been—have you any idea who—' she stopped, but gazed at Angela with a hopeful expression. 'I don't want to influence you, of course,' she said.

'I guess you are thinking of Robin,' said Angela. Louisa looked relieved.

'Well, naturally, one doesn't want to accuse somebody unfairly without evidence,' she said, 'but Robin *is* the first person who springs to mind. He wanted me to give him some money too, you know.'

'Really? When was that?'

'Why, it must have been at around the same time he was asking Winifred, if what you say is true. It seems he was more successful with her than with me.'

'Then you decided not to invest?'

'Yes. It wasn't that I didn't trust him—he is in Peake's, you know, and does lots of clever and complicated things with bonds and shares and what-not. He wanted me to give him this money to put into some kind of fund that would pay out at a rate much higher than anything I could get in the bank. But he tried to explain what the fund did and I'm afraid I couldn't quite grasp what he was saying. To tell the truth, it all sounded a little *underhand* to me. But you know lots of people who do that kind of thing, don't you, so perhaps you understand it better than I.'

'Financial matters can be rather hard to comprehend,' conceded Angela.

'At any rate, I thanked him but said that I was unwilling to invest any money in something I didn't understand, and from what you say it looks as though I was right to say no.'

'Do you know whether he asked anybody else to invest their money? John, for example? Or Philippa?'

'Not John,' said Louisa. 'John would have sent him away with a flea in his ear. But I suppose he might have asked Philippa. Do you think it could be a possible motive?'

'It certainly sounds as though it might be,' said Angela. 'If we assume that Robin took the money and lost it—perhaps in some risky investment—and that Winifred was badgering him for it and possibly threatening to expose him, then that would be a motive for murder, yes. However, that doesn't explain the deaths of Philippa or Edward unless they, too, were victims of the same fraud. And would Edward have turned in his own son?'

'I see what you mean. I don't know. I doubt he would have done anything without Ursula's say-so, and I can't imagine that she would have wanted to see Robin go to prison. And as far as we know, Philippa's money was intact when she died.'

Angela nodded.

'So you see, it's not quite as simple as it seems,' she said.

'Shall you find out the truth, do you think, Angela?' Louisa asked suddenly.

'I don't know,' said Angela.

'*Is* there a truth to find out?'

'I am beginning to think there must be. There's nothing I can quite put my finger on, and yet—'

'And yet what?'

'I'm not sure. Everyone has been ready enough to answer my questions, but I get the impression that they have all held something back. I sense that there is something going on underneath the surface of which I am not aware—that there is an angle to the mystery that I have not yet considered. And you may think me superstitious, but I have the strangest feeling that someone resents my presence here.'

'Do you mean Robin? If he is guilty of fraud then he must be terrified of being found out, so naturally he wants you gone.'

Angela examined her fingers. How could she tell her friend that it was not from Ursula or Robin that the uncomfortable feeling of being resented came, but from someone in this very house? She could not identify the person or people behind it, but that the source of the sensation was Underwood House she was certain.

'Louisa, do you really wish me to continue with this investigation?' she asked at last.

'Why, of course I do,' her friend replied.

'But what if I should turn up something—something unpleasant?'

Mrs. Haynes went still for a second, then drew herself up.

'What could be more unpleasant than murder?' she said stoutly. 'Angela, you needn't suppose I haven't thought about it—what might come to light, I mean. I am perfectly aware that we are all under suspicion—even I. But murder is a terrible thing, and if anyone *is* guilty, then he must be made to face justice. Better that than for us all to mistrust each other for the rest of our lives. Please don't worry about me. I believe in the people I love best, and I rely on your intelligence and good sense to find out the truth.'

'If that is how you feel, then there is no more to be said,' said Angela. 'I only hope I can justify your faith in me.'

She called for her car and bade goodbye to her friend, promising to let her know as soon as she found any new evidence.

'Well, William,' she said, as the Bentley swept smoothly down the drive. 'What have you got for me?'

'Why, I'm not rightly sure, ma'am,' he replied. 'You must be the judge of that.'

'Go on.'

'All right. I did as you asked, and hung about outside for, I don't know, must've been a half hour or thereabouts. I guess the Bentley never had such a good polishing as it did this morning! Anyhow, after a while the stiff lady came out, together with the lawyer fellow, who looked for all the world as if he was making certain sure that she left. He gave her one of those old-fashioned bows, but evidently it cut no ice with her, because she speared him with a gimlet-eyed stare and said something I didn't hear. So I moved a little closer, and heard him say in a puzzled kind of way, "My dear Mrs. Haynes, as I have repeatedly said, I am at a loss to—". But what he was at a loss to do I never found out because she wouldn't let him finish. She interrupted him sharply, saying, "Do not think, Mr. Faulkner, that I shall allow you to dismiss me so easily. My son and I have been unfairly done out of our inheritance, and I intend to find a way of getting it back. You are hiding the truth from me, but believe me, you shall not prevail." Then she turned and stalked off.'

'And did you see how he looked?'

'I did happen to catch a glimpse of him. I should say he looked decidedly wary.'

'Wary,' repeated Angela thoughtfully as the car left the village and began to pick up speed on its journey back to London. What did it all mean? What did Mr. Faulkner know that was seemingly so vital to Ursula? Presumably it must have something to do with Philip Haynes's will—the will that Angela had not yet succeeded in seeing. Was Ursula angry that Mr. Faulkner was enjoying the benefits of Philip's fortune? A fortune that had once belonged to her and Robin before Edward died? She was not the kind of woman to accept defeat easily. Did she suspect that the solicitor had come by the money dishonestly—had influenced the writing of Philip's will in some way? Or did she even think that he had committed the murders himself? Angela remembered how keen Mr. Faulkner had been to present her with his alibis for the three evenings in question. Could they really be that unshakeable? She would have to ask Inspector Jameson.

Mrs. Marchmont sighed to herself. What was the solution to the mystery at Underwood House? Who was behind the mysterious deaths?—for she was now almost certain that the deaths of Winifred and Edward, at least, had not been accidental. It was tempting to plump for Robin as the most obvious suspect, especially if it were indeed he who had taken his aunt's money. Fear of exposure would certainly constitute a strong motive for murder, and—whether she liked to admit it or not—he was the most unprepossessing of all the people she had spoken to so far. There was also the fact that Louisa was clearly hoping against hope that he was the guilty party. Yes, Robin's guilt would certainly be the easiest way out. And yet—and yet Angela was not convinced. Somehow Robin did not fit into the picture as a murderer. Why should he kill his father, for example? There was no apparent motive there. Unfriendly and ill-favoured he might be, but violent? It was difficult to imagine him holding his father's head under water as he struggled, or pushing his aunt to her death thirty feet below. Perhaps he might have poisoned Philippa—that seemed more his type of method—but again, why?

Angela shook her head. She was uncomfortably aware that there was one person in particular who appeared to know more than he was prepared to reveal, and she wondered how on earth she was going to tackle him. John Haynes had left the house immediately after lunch, so she had been unable to question him, but truth to tell that was something of a relief as she had not yet decided upon the best way to approach him. How exactly did one go about asking the husband of a friend whether or not he was hiding a guilty secret without offending both the husband *and* the friend?

'I shall have to think about that later,' she said to herself.

'Very wise, ma'am,' said William, from the driver's seat.

Angela started. She had not realized she was speaking aloud.

'*Some* people have servants who don't presume to comment on their employers' decisions,' she remarked to nobody in particular.

William grinned.

'Is that so, ma'am?' he said. 'Begging your pardon, but would these happen to be the same people whose servants aren't required to eavesdrop on dangerous murder suspects?'

Angela opened her mouth to speak, then closed it with a snap and looked out of the window.

Chapter Fifteen

'I AM GOING to visit an artistic lady today, Marthe,' said Mrs. Marchmont, standing in front of the long glass in her bedroom and considering her reflection dispassionately. 'What do you suppose would be the most suitable thing for me to wear?'

Marthe thought for a moment.

'The peach *marocain* will be too formal, I think,' she said. 'I have seen these types of people before. They are not *chic*. They like to hide themselves under ugly garments that sweep and swoop, so everyone will believe they are dedicated to their art above all and have no time to attend to their *toilette*. Pah!' She wrinkled her nose in disgust. 'How stupid they are! To dress well, make no mistake, that is also an art. Very well, perhaps the dark-blue tunic in *mousseline de soie*, with the silver pendant and earrings in which *madame* looks so elegant.'

'That will be perfect,' said Angela. 'You are very right in what you say about dressing well, and I am glad I have you to guide me, Marthe.'

Marthe preened, then turned briskly to her task. Angela allowed herself to be primped and adorned to the girl's satisfaction, then sallied out in a rather daring new turban that she had been unable to resist buying on a recent trip to Paris, despite its fabulous price.

Susan Dennison—or Euphrosyne Dennison as she was known in her own milieu—lived and worked in a mews house in a run-down part of Chelsea that was considered quite the capital of English Bohemia. Angela was shown up three steep flights of stairs to an enormous attic space which was airy and bright, and which would no doubt be absolutely bathed in sunlight on a less overcast day than the present one. The room had the typical appearance of an artist's studio, with bare, dirty floor-boards, uncovered windows and detritus of all kinds piled up in the corners. Paintbrushes and jars of water lay on every surface, while canvases in various stages of completion stood around the walls. The smell of turpentine and oil-paint was all-pervasive. Angela approached an easel, on which stood what was presumably Miss Dennison's latest creation, and viewed the work with a critical eye. It was painted in the modern style and appeared to represent a plump and resplendent nude with greenish-tinged skin, surrounded by a writhing mass of snakes that were devouring a mound of rotting fruit. Angela was not an expert, but as far as she could tell the artist displayed some sign of talent.

'That is my *New Eve*,' said a deep voice behind her. 'I hope to have it ready for an exhibition I shall be putting on later this summer.'

Angela turned to look at the speaker. If she had thought of Euphrosyne Dennison at all, she had pictured a girl with a slight, coltish figure and an ethereal manner. She was therefore surprised to be confronted by a woman with strong brows and a heavy jaw who could only be described as short and stout. She was swathed in a diaphanous collection of silk robes and scarves in garish colours that gave her something of the appearance of a plump and exotic bird. Her unexpectedly delicate hands were stained with paint. Angela thought of Marthe and suppressed a smile.

'You are Mrs. Marchmont,' said Miss Dennison, but did not introduce herself. 'Please, sit down. You won't mind if I work as we talk.'

Angela looked about her, but the only thing she could see to sit on was an old packing-case. She sat on it gingerly, wondering whether an apparent disdain of the need for comfortable chairs was a family trait common to all the Hayneses. Euphrosyne Dennison showed no sign that she was aware of the deficiencies of her quarters, but took up a paintbrush and palette and began dabbing ferociously at the canvas.

'Is it nearly finished?' asked Angela.

Miss Dennison stood back and squinted at her handiwork.

'I cannot be sure yet,' she replied. 'There is something about it that does not please me. Technically, I can see no faults, you understand—yes, my powers are revealed undiminished in this work—and yet—and yet—I do not know. Perhaps the Muse has failed to cast its sweet spell over my endeavours on this occasion. I fear it lacks what one might call the Divine Spark.'

'Dear me, how provoking,' said Angela politely.

Miss Dennison gave a cluck of impatience, then removed the painting from its easel and stood it against the wall.

'I shall return to it later,' she said. She picked up another unfinished picture, placed it on the easel and set to work.

'Aunt Louisa tells me you are looking into the death of my mother,' she said.

'I am,' said Angela, 'and of your Aunt Philippa and Uncle Edward also.'

'And what have you discovered so far?'

'Very little in the way of concrete evidence,' said Angela. 'Although I have found out one or two things of interest. For instance, I have discovered that your mother believed she had been defrauded of all her money by a friend or relation.'

Euphrosyne Dennison looked up in surprise.

'Oh yes?' she said sharply. 'Who?'

'She would not say. I heard about it from Mr. Faulkner, the solicitor. He said your mother came to him with the story a week or two before her death. The unnamed person had persuaded her to invest all her money with him and was proving dilatory about paying it back. Did you know about this?'

Miss Dennison had by now recollected herself and turned back to her painting. She made a dismissive gesture with her shoulders.

'No, I knew nothing about it,' she said, 'and if I had, why should I have been interested? My mother was perfectly at liberty to do whatever she liked with her money.'

'But it would have been *yours* now, had this mysterious person not taken it,' Angela pointed out.

'I despise money,' declared Miss Dennison grandly. 'I am above such considerations. Of course, I do not expect others to understand the meaning of Art, but suffice it to say, Mrs. Marchmont, that its true adherents are transported to a higher plane on which material things are revealed in all their petty insignificance.'

'But even an artist such as yourself needs money on which to live. How can you pay for your materials without it? And this garret—you must have to pay rent, surely?'

Susan bridled.

'I have friends who assist me in these matters,' she said haughtily, 'and I understand that my paintings bring in a good deal, although I am not familiar with the details.'

'Then I guess there is no use in asking you about your grandfather's will and why you think he left his money as he did,' said Angela.

'Oh! Grandpapa!' exclaimed Miss Dennison. She drew out a handkerchief and put it to her eyes. 'Excuse me,' she said, 'but I am still prostrate with grief over his passing.'

This was a surprise. Angela had assumed that no-one in the Haynes family regretted Philip's death, but it looked as though she had been wrong.

'I beg your pardon,' she said. 'I had no idea that you were so fond of him.'

'Yes,' said Susan. 'I was his favourite, you know. We spent hours together when I was very young. I told him all my girlish secrets and he told me some of his. I was inconsolable when he died—quite inconsolable.'

'Did he tell you, then, why he left so much of his money only conditionally to his family? Why, in short, it was to revert to Mr. Faulkner should any of them die?'

'Grandpapa had a very mischievous sense of fun,' said Miss Dennison. 'He liked to play tricks on people. Perhaps it was something to do with that. And he was always making new wills. He showed me his final one, I remember, shortly after he wrote it—or at least the part about the money reverting to Mr. Faulkner. "That may not look like much to you, my girl," he said, "but mark my words, it will put the cat among the pigeons when I am gone."'

'Can you remember what it said, exactly? It all seems rather mysterious.'

'There was nothing mysterious about it. The wording was quite clear and straightforward, although I don't remember what it said—just something about Mr. Faulkner being to receive the money on the terms communicated to him in the event that any of Grandpapa's children should die.'

'*On the terms communicated to him*,' repeated Angela thoughtfully. 'Are you sure that's what it said?'

'I don't know if they were the exact words, but it was something very close to that, certainly.'

I wonder what he meant.'

'I have no idea,' said Miss Dennison. 'Perhaps they had agreed between themselves that the money should be used for a particular purpose. That is how I understood it.' She was mixing a colour as she spoke, and to Angela's astonishment suddenly spat onto the palette.

'I never feel that a painting is *truly* complete unless it contains the *essence* of the artist himself,' she explained, as she blended the gobbet of spittle into the colour. 'I put part of myself into every work I produce—and not just saliva, you understand, but also—'

She broke off to concentrate on a tricky section of the picture, much to the relief of Angela, who hastily brought the subject around to Winifred's death. But Susan had little or nothing to tell about the deaths of any of her relatives. She had observed nothing on the occasions of Philippa's and Edward's deaths, and very little when her mother had died.

'I heard it all but had no portent at the time of the tragedy that was about to befall me,' she said with a dramatic shudder. 'I heard the slamming of the door as she came out of her room, then a great thud and a scream broken off. Poor Mother.' She applied the handkerchief to her eye again.

Angela stood and prepared to take her leave.

'You will let me know if you find out anything more about your mother's money, won't you?' she asked.

Euphrosyne Dennison waved a paintbrush in a manner that might be taken as assent, then paid no more attention to her visitor, who decided that, all things considered, it would be easiest to show herself out.

Chapter Sixteen

MRS. MARCHMONT RETURNED to her flat late in the afternoon to discover a message from Inspector Jameson, who had called while she was out. She immediately picked up the telephone and asked to be put through to Scotland Yard. The inspector was there and saluted her cheerfully.

'And how is your little investigation going?' he asked.

'Slowly and uneventfully,' she replied. 'I've found out one or two interesting things, but nothing that you could make a case with. In fact, I shouldn't have called you at all had someone not tried to kill me the other day.'

The inspector was instantly alert.

'Someone tried to kill you? Are you sure?'

'I can't be certain, but I think so.'

'This is most alarming. I am very sorry. Believe me, Mrs. Marchmont, I had no intention of putting you in danger—indeed, I should never have dreamed of asking you to do it had I thought for even one second that this could happen.'

'Please don't worry, I'm quite all right,' said Angela, feeling as though she had perhaps made too much of it. 'As I said, I can't be sure that whoever it was actually wanted to kill me.'

'Tell me what happened.'

With some confusion, Angela began her story but he interrupted her almost immediately.

'No—no—not over the telephone, perhaps. Better to discuss this in person. Would you object to coming to Scotland Yard? What time is it? I say, is it that time already? I had no idea. No, don't come here. But—' he hesitated, then went on, 'I don't suppose you are free this evening? Should you be dreadfully offended if I asked you to dinner?'

'Not at all,' replied Angela. 'I should be delighted. I have no engagements that cannot be cancelled, and I should very much like to discuss the case with someone, as I fear I am getting into rather a muddle with it.'

'Then that's settled,' he said firmly. 'I shall call for you at seven o'clock, if that is not too early. We policemen keep respectable hours, you know.'

'That will be perfect.'

'Goodbye, then. Oh, and by the way,' he added, 'if a murder attempt is your definition of uneventful, I should be very much interested to know what sort of thing you consider to be exciting.'

Angela laughed and hung up.

Jameson arrived punctually and at Angela's suggestion they went to a quiet spot in Mayfair where they could talk undisturbed. The inspector listened intently as Angela recounted all that had happened in the past few days, and seemed particularly interested in Winifred's accusations of fraud.

'But you see,' said Angela, 'I have no proof that she was cheated out of her money. She refused to tell Mr. Faulkner the name of her correspondent, she apparently signed nothing, and even her daughter claims to be uninterested in the fate of her inheritance—although from what I have seen of Susan Dennison, that may be an affectation. This is where the amateur detective falls down. I cannot investigate her financial affairs myself. To find out anything more I am going to need your help.'

'Well, we can certainly make some inquiries of her bank,' said Jameson. 'I shall put a man onto it tomorrow. So you say Louisa Haynes suspects Robin?'

'Yes, and after what you told me on the train, I must say it was my first thought too.'

'What did you think of him?'

'Rather an unprepossessing type,' said Angela frankly. 'I don't mind admitting that he and his mother gave me the shivers when I met them. I should not like to be the one to cross Ursula, in particular.'

'Yes, she is a character, isn't she?' agreed the inspector. 'And I think from what you have said, it may be time to pay another visit to Master Robin.'

'What of the doings in the city? Have you heard anything more about that?'

'No, it all seems to have gone quiet on that front lately,' replied Jameson, 'but as I said, it could all blow up any day now.

I don't suppose you read such things, but veiled rumours have even reached the press about the troubles at Peake's, although the company was not mentioned by name.'

Angela had indeed read the article in question and, after putting two and two together following her earlier conversation with the inspector, had taken steps to ensure that she had no money deposited with Peake's.

'And you are quite certain, you say, that you did not see the person who pushed you into the road?' went on Inspector Jameson.

'I am afraid not,' said Angela. 'I was caught completely off guard. Perhaps I have led a sheltered life, but I don't generally expect to be shoved in front of speeding motor-vans by mysterious assailants whenever I leave the house, so I was not paying much attention to anything. And, of course, he waited until there was a large crowd to protect him, in order to make his escape unnoticed. It was unlucky for him that he happened to be spotted and pursued.'

'And since you lost the photograph, I presume you have not been able to find out who it belonged to.'

'No, but I have a little idea of my own about that which I shall tell you about later, since I have nothing to back it up at present and don't know where it fits in—or even if it does fit in, in fact.'

Inspector Jameson looked serious.

'Do be careful, Mrs. Marchmont,' he said. 'I am wondering now whether I ought to have asked you to do this. I had no wish to place you in the way of danger but you appear to have put the wind up somebody or other. Perhaps you should give it up.'

'I can't give it up now—I promised Louisa that I would continue. And in any case, I am not afraid. I've been thinking the matter over and have come to the conclusion that the chief purpose of the attack was probably to get the photograph back, although whoever did it was not above trying to get me out of the way at the same time. Don't worry, inspector—my friends will tell you that I am far too fond of myself to put my life knowingly in peril. I shall keep a sharp eye out for anything suspicious from now on.'

'I see your mind is quite made up,' said Jameson, 'and I am not in the slightest bit surprised. I have been hearing quite a lot of things about you lately, Mrs. Marchmont, and your name is quite a byword for tenacity in certain circles.'

'Oh?' asked Angela, intrigued. 'Which circles are those?'

'Tell me, do the words "Blue Iris" mean anything to you?'

Angela started, then eyed him suspiciously.

'How—?' she began, then stopped. 'Ah,' she said, suddenly understanding, 'I thought your name was familiar to me. I shall now put my powers of deduction to the test. Let me see: at a guess, I should say that you have a brother, or possibly a cousin in the Foreign Office. Am I correct?'

The inspector smiled.

'A brother, yes,' he said. 'Henry sends his warmest regards. He was quite enthusiastic in your praise, and believe me when I say that it takes a lot to rouse Henry from his habitual state of half-witted somnolence.'

'It is a long time since I saw him,' said Angela. 'He was very kind to me and had far more faith in my abilities than I did myself. Indeed, I still maintain that I did very little.'

'That is not the view of the powers that be. They credit your efforts with having been instrumental in drawing America into the War.'

'Nonsense,' said Angela briskly but with some embarrassment. 'Anyway, don't let's talk about that—it was all such a long time ago now that I have forgotten most of it. I am more concerned with the present. I wanted to ask you about Mr. Faulkner's alibis.'

'Do you mean for the nights on which Philippa, Winifred and Edward died?'

'Yes. I have no particular reason to doubt them, but he has such a strong motive and he seemed so keen to tell me about the important personages with whom he had been dining on the nights in question that I thought I had better ask you. Of course, it may just be that he was anxious to make sure I knew of his innocence before I started blundering around suspecting him, but it would be remiss of me not to check. On two of the nights in question he was actually dining with the same person. Can that really be a coincidence?'

'As far as I know it is. Both Sir Maurice Upton and Lord Willesden swear that Mr. Faulkner was with them on the first two occasions and the third occasion respectively. Whether he deliberately arranged things so, however, I cannot say.'

'I must speak to him again about showing me Philip's will,' said Angela. 'I have not managed to see it so far, and I should very much like to read it myself.'

'Do you think it may contain a clue?'

'I don't know, but the provisions of it are so very odd that I wonder whether it mayn't be the key to the matter. I have been thinking about it ever since I saw Susan Dennison earlier. Philip showed her the will before he died, you know, and made a rather mysterious remark about it.'

'What did he say?'

'According to Susan, he pointed to the clause that allows Mr. Faulkner to inherit, and told her that it would put the cat among the pigeons.'

'And so it did. No mystery about that.'

'Yes, but the clause was worded rather strangely. It mentioned something about Mr. Faulkner being to receive the money *on the terms communicated to him*. I wonder whether Philip and he had a private agreement about how the money was to be used. Have you ever heard of such a thing?'

'I can't say that I have. It does sound rather odd—but then, of course, Philip was an odd man. Do you think it may have some significance?'

'I don't know. Perhaps it's nothing, but I intend to have a look at that will all the same. On second thoughts I think the easiest thing will be for me to go to Somerset House.'

Jameson called for the bill and they emerged into the chill of the evening.

'I shall see you safely to your door,' he said. 'You may pooh-pooh my concerns, but I am not happy at the idea that someone wishes you harm, so I should like you to promise me that you will be very careful from now on.'

'Don't worry, I shall,' said Angela. 'I assure you, no woman could be more jealous of her own comfort and safety than myself.'

'You tell a convincing lie, Mrs. Marchmont, but you forget that I have heard all from Henry,' said Jameson.

'One does such reckless things in one's youth,' said Angela vaguely. 'Besides, I have William to take care of me.'

'Who is William?'

'My chauffeur and man-of-all-work. I found him in America a few years ago. He's dreadfully impertinent but quite devoted.'

'Well, do please be careful,' said Jameson, unconvinced, and Angela promised that she would.

Mount Street was only five minutes' walk away and as promised, Inspector Jameson saw her safely inside the building and bade her goodnight, reminding her as he did so to call him at any time if she needed help. Once he had gone, Angela hurried up to her flat. She passed through the dimly-lit drawing room and into the bedroom beyond, which was in darkness. Cautiously, she pulled aside a curtain and peered out. At first she saw nothing but then, after a few moments, a shadowy figure slid out from a doorway opposite and set off down the street. It was impossible to see who it was from that distance. Angela let the curtain fall and thought very hard.

Chapter Seventeen

THE OFFICES OF Addison, Addison and Gouch, solicitors, were located discreetly behind an unassuming black front door on Bedford Row. Mrs. Marchmont rang the bell and was shown immediately into the comfortable rooms occupied by Mr. Addison the Younger (Mr. Addison the Elder having long since retired from practice). Mr. Addison, a jolly, rubicund man who, to his great misfortune, looked more like a milkman than a solicitor, beamed as he shook his visitor's hand and indicated a seat.

'How delightful to see you again, Mrs. Marchmont,' he said. 'I'm terribly sorry I can't spare you more time this morning, but Mr. Gouch has rather unfortunately broken his arm and I have had to take over his cases for the next week or two.'

'Please don't mention it,' replied Angela. 'It was very kind of you to see me at such short notice. I shan't keep you long.'

'I understand you want to ask me about an inheritance.'

'Yes,' said Angela. 'I won't bore you with the whole story, but I have been poring over the will of one Philip Haynes, who died a couple of years ago leaving behind him some testamentary instructions of a rather curious nature.'

She explained the provisions of Philip's will and how his money was to be divided. Mr. Addison listened carefully, eyebrows raised.

'That is indeed somewhat unusual,' he said when she had finished. 'And, as you may have noticed, it puts the solicitor in rather a position of power—firstly of course because he is the ultimate beneficiary of twenty thousand pounds, and secondly because he is also the executor, and as such is in a position to dictate the course of events to a certain degree.'

'Yes,' agreed Angela. 'That had not escaped my notice. The contents of the will don't seem to have caused much surprise among Philip's family, who knew him as a mischievous eccentric, given to playing malicious tricks on them all, but as an outsider, I must confess I am curious. Why did he decide to stipulate that, after any of his children's deaths, the money revert to his solicitor, of all people? His family disliked each other, so if he had really wished to sow discord among them, surely it would have made more sense from his point of view to play them off against one another, for example by having the money that would normally pass to one particular family member revert to a hated relative.'

'I see what you mean,' said Mr. Addison.

'I have a very active imagination so it's entirely possible that I am making something out of nothing,' said Angela, 'but when Philip Haynes's granddaughter happened to mention to me that a particular phrase had been used in the will, my curiosity was aroused. Yesterday, therefore, I went to Somerset House to see the document for myself. I spent quite some time reading it, but no matter how hard I looked, I could see no trace of the phrase or anything like it. The granddaughter had been quite certain it was there, but she also said that her grandfather had been fond of changing his will, so I can only assume that a later will was signed which superseded the earlier one. All the same, I should like to know what it meant. Tell me, Mr. Addison, if you were to read a will in which someone left a bequest to someone *on the terms communicated to him*, what should you think?'

Mr Addison pricked up his ears.

'That was the phrase in question, was it?' he said. '*On the terms communicated to him*. That is very interesting and suggestive. My word,' he went on enthusiastically, 'I know of such things but have never actually come across one myself. I believe they are quite rare these days.'

'What do you mean?' asked Angela.

'Why, it sounds very much as though Philip Haynes intended to set up a secret trust.'

He rose and went to a bookshelf, then selected a weighty reference work and brought it back to his desk. Angela waited as he found the page he wanted.

'Hmm—hmm. Ah, yes,' he said. 'Very interesting indeed. Are you familiar with the concept of the secret trust?' he asked.

'Not at all,' said Angela.

'Secret trusts have been used for centuries as a means by which a testator may bequeath assets to a particular person without mentioning him or her by name in the will. They have traditionally provided a convenient means for mistresses and illegitimate children to receive an inheritance without causing embarrassment to the legitimate family. I shall not waste your time by expounding on the finer points of *McCormick v Grogan* or *Rochefoucauld v Boustead*, but the way it works is this: let us say that A wishes to leave a certain sum to B without A's family knowing he has done so. He writes a will ostensibly leaving that sum to C, having first obtained C's private consent to act as trustee. In law a trust is then deemed to have been created. Following the testator's death, C receives the bequest in accordance with the deceased's apparent last wishes, but is then bound by law to hold it in trust for B.'

'And this is expressed in the will using the phrase I mentioned?'

'Yes, or a similar expression—one which in any event makes it clear to anybody reading it that C has been given separate instructions regarding the ultimate destination of the assets.'

'In that case, then, it is known that a secret trust has been created but not whom it is intended to benefit?'

'That is so, yes.'

'It certainly sounds as though Philip may at one time have intended to leave some money to a person or persons unknown,' said Angela. 'Presumably he changed his mind later on, though.'

The solicitor beamed even more widely.

'Ah, but here we come to the most interesting point—we cannot be sure that he *did* change his mind. Incredible though it may seem, the law allows a secret trust to be created without its being mentioned in the will *at all*. Let us suppose that A wanted to leave some money to his mistress, B, but did not wish his wife to get wind of the fact. In this case he could simply say "I leave a thousand pounds to C," and nobody would be any the wiser that he and C had in fact reached a private agreement for C to pass the money on to B.'

'Nobody except C and possibly B, I assume,' said Angela. 'It seems a terribly risky thing to do—create a secret trust without mentioning it in the will, I mean. What if C decides to keep the money?'

'Ah!' said the solicitor, nodding vigorously. 'I see you have spotted the biggest flaw in the thing. Yes, it would be very easy for the trustee to keep the money if he wished. Since secret trusts may be agreed verbally—in fact, are likely to be agreed verbally by their very nature—they can lead to all sorts of disputes. Without witnesses, it may be very difficult to prove that a secret trust ever existed. I imagine that many an intended beneficiary has been cheated out of his rightful inheritance over the years.'

'To return to the case in question,' said Angela, 'is it possible that, after changing his will, Philip Haynes maintained the agreement with his solicitor to form a secret trust but did not mention it expressly in the later version?'

'It's certainly possible, but we have no way of knowing without speaking to the solicitor himself—and if he is bound by secrecy then he is hardly likely to tell you.'

Just then a clerk entered discreetly and gave Mr. Addison a meaningful look. The solicitor glanced at his watch and nodded.

'Is there anything else you should like to ask me about?' he said politely.

'No, I think that's everything,' said Angela. She rose and held out her hand. 'You have been enormously helpful, thank you.'

Mr. Addison shook her hand and gave her another beaming smile.

'Do call me if you think of anything else you would like to know,' he said.

Angela stepped out into the street and walked towards Holborn, intending to return home. The day was a fine one, however, so she decided to make a little detour to Lincoln's Inn Fields to enjoy the sunshine. Sitting on a bench, she reviewed the information she had received from Mr. Addison. There was scant evidence for it, to be sure, but it looked as though there might be more to Philip's will than met the eye. It had always seemed odd to her that Philip should leave his children only a life interest in what should have been their birthright. And then to stipulate that the money revert to his solicitor after their deaths? It was unaccountable, wholly unaccountable. But if Philip's true intention had been to provide in some way for some other person—perhaps a relative unknown to or unadmitted by the family—why, then, that was much more comprehensible. But why had he done it in such a roundabout way? Surely the easiest thing would have been to leave some money directly to Mr. Faulkner, to be held on trust for the person in question. Why give his children a life interest in the money only to snatch it back from their families after their deaths? It seemed almost as though Philip wanted to deny his grandchildren part of their rightful inheritance. Susan, in particular, had ended up with nothing after Winifred's unfortunate speculation and yet she had claimed to be his favourite grandchild. And what of the wording of the will? Mr. Addison had seemed convinced that the earlier version revealed an intention to create a secret trust. Had Philip changed his mind about the trust, or had he deliberately rewritten the will to make sure that it would remain wholly secret?

Angela sighed. Only one thing in the whole business was clear to her: that Philip Haynes had been a most ill-natured character.

'Lucky for me I never had to make his acquaintance,' she said to herself. 'What a difficult man he must have been! It's little wonder his family turned out as they did. A miracle, in fact, that John has managed to remain relatively unaffected by it all. I imagine much of that is Louisa's doing.'

And what of John, in fact? For the first time, it occurred to Angela that he was the only one left; that he, the eldest child, had outlived his younger sisters and brother. Had he been fonder of them she should have felt sorry for him, but he did not seem to require her sympathy. Could he be in danger himself, though? If Philippa, Winifred and Edward had indeed been murdered—whether for their money or for some other motive—then as Philip's last remaining child surely he was the next target. Whoever was behind the deaths was ruthless, and would clearly stop at nothing in order to gain his ends. Perhaps she should warn John of the potential danger.

But—but—was there something more to it than that? She had long felt that he was concealing something—and Ursula too seemed to think that he knew something about the matter which he refused to reveal. Could it be the unthinkable? Angela now forced herself to face a question that up to now she had pushed from her mind: *was John the murderer*? His love for Underwood House and desire to keep it for himself gave him ample motive. He had persuaded Philippa to leave her share of the house to him—and shortly afterwards, Philippa had died. Winifred had wanted to get rid of Underwood, and she had died too, leaving her share to Susan, who had been more amenable and had agreed to sell it to John. That left only Edward—and after his death, Ursula. And, judging by the conversation William had overheard between Ursula and Mr. Faulkner, she was smarting from the loss of Edward's five thousand pounds. Perhaps she would be more willing to sell her share of the house to John now. Had John been relying upon that supposition? Certainly, there was no shortage of motive. But what about opportunity? If Donald was to be believed, John had *not* been in his study, as he claimed, when Winifred fell from the upstairs gallery. And as for Philippa and Edward—why, it would be almost impossible to provide alibis for their deaths.

Angela felt a sinking sense of dismay. Her clear, logical mind told her that there was no use in denying what should have been obvious long ago: that, assuming all three deaths were caused by the same agency, then John was the most likely suspect. Ursula certainly seemed to think so, although she had not said so expressly for reasons best known to herself.

'How can I ever face Louisa if he is the guilty one?' she said to herself. 'It will break her heart. Why couldn't she have taken my hint and asked me to stop the investigation when I gave her the chance?'

But there was no use in thinking about that any more. What was past was past, and Angela knew that she must carry on to the end now, come what may.

Chapter Eighteen

THE FIRST THING Mrs. Marchmont did when she returned to her flat was to put through a telephone-call to Mr. Faulkner. She had little hope of achieving anything by it, but it had to be done.

'Faulkner speaking,' said the solicitor as he came on the line.

'Hallo, Mr. Faulkner, it's Angela Marchmont here,' said Angela. 'I'm sorry to trouble you, but I have a question about Philip Haynes's will.'

'Hallo, Mrs. Marchmont. What is it you wish to know?'

There was no sense in beating about the bush. Angela took a deep breath.

'Did Philip ever create a secret trust with you as the trustee?' she asked.

There was the briefest of pauses at the other end of the line, then came a laugh.

'A secret trust? Whatever gave you that idea? No, there was no agreement of the sort. What made you think there might be?'

'Something Susan Dennison said to me the other day. She told me that she had seen her grandfather's will, and that the clause referring to the money which was to revert to you contained a phrase which seemed to imply that you had been told what to do with it.'

'Indeed? How very odd. But I think she must be mistaken, since there is no such phrase in the will as far as I know.'

'No,' agreed Angela. 'I went to Somerset House yesterday to have a look at it myself, and I couldn't find anything of the kind. But I understand that Philip Haynes was forever changing his will, and wondered whether Susan was talking about an earlier version of the document.'

'I wrote every one of Philip's wills, and can assure you that none of them contained a phrase of the type you mention. No doubt Miss Dennison was telling you what she truly believed, but I am afraid she is very like her mother, who was somewhat vague in many respects. I mean no impoliteness when I say that I should not like to rely on her as a witness in court.'

'Then you never agreed with Philip to hold money on trust for someone, under a secret provision contained in either an earlier will or the final version?'

'That is the case,' he said firmly.

There seemed nothing else to be said, so Angela thanked him and hung up. She had not expected him to admit it—indeed she would have been surprised if he had, but his denial meant she was unable to proceed with what had looked like a promising line of inquiry.

'Still,' she said to herself, 'perhaps some new evidence will come to light later. I shan't give up hope.'

The next morning she drove down to Underwood House with William.

'Let us see if you have any more success with the servants today,' she said.

William nodded feelingly.

'I hope so, ma'am,' he said. 'There was one young lady in particular who seemed kindly disposed towards me. It was a pity that the housekeeper insisted on sticking so close by the whole time. She's a fierce one, right enough! I guess she suspected that I was there to fool around with her girls.'

'Whereas nothing could have been further from the truth,' said Angela blandly.

William grinned.

'At any rate, I couldn't get any of them to talk to me and give me the low-down. I just hope it's the housekeeper's day out today, or that she's come down with a cold. Nothing too serious, you understand—just enough to keep her sniffling in her room and out of the way.'

Louisa was out but Stella was at home. She seemed a little depressed.

'Hallo, Mrs. Marchmont,' she said. 'Are you still investigating?'

'I'm afraid so,' said Angela. 'As a matter of fact, I wondered if you wouldn't mind showing me upstairs. In particular, I'd like to know which bedrooms were occupied and by whom on the day of Winifred's death.'

'Oh? Do you have a clue, then?'

'Not exactly—I just want to get things straight in my mind,' replied Angela.

'Well, then, come with me. I shall show you who slept where.'

They went up the stairs and came onto the galleried landing. Angela looked around her and leaned over the balustrade at the point where Winifred had fallen.

'I believe Ursula was right,' she said.

'Right about what?'

'She said that it would have been very difficult for Winifred to fall accidentally since she was not tall enough. Look here.' She stretched her arm out towards the chandelier. 'You see I can only just reach the light from here myself and I am rather tall, but I understand Winifred was a very short woman, so it would have been much harder for her.'

'Do you think she wasn't leaning over at all, then?'

'She may have been—obviously we will never know. But the balustrade is a high one so she would have been unlikely to fall accidentally, that is all I meant. Ursula thinks that somebody grabbed her by the ankles and tipped her over, and I must say it looks as though the theory may be a sound one.'

Stella shuddered.

'How horrid!' she exclaimed.

'Now,' went on Angela, 'I believe I am correct in saying that this room here was occupied by Susan.'

'That's right. She was nearest the stairs.'

'And whose is this one?'

'That's Don's.'

'Ah!' said Angela keenly, but made no further comment.

They carried on along the passage, with Stella pointing out the various family and guest bedrooms.

'Which was Winifred's room?' asked Angela as they turned into a new passage.

'That one,' said Stella, pointing. 'The second one along.'

'That's rather odd,' said Angela. 'May I?'

She opened and closed the door. It shut with a click.

'Why did you do that?' asked Stella.

'Would you mind awfully doing something for me?' asked Angela without replying.

'Of course not.'

'Go into this room and wait there for two minutes, then come out and slam the door behind you.'

Stella raised her eyebrows but nodded and entered the room without comment. Angela returned to the gallery, slipped quietly into the guest room which had been occupied by Susan and shut the door behind her. After a few minutes she heard Stella calling her and came out onto the landing.

'There you are,' said Stella. 'Whatever were you doing?'

'Did you slam the door?' asked Angela.

'As loudly as I could. Didn't you hear it?'

'No,' said Angela thoughtfully. 'I didn't.'

'You're being jolly mysterious.'

'Am I? I don't mean to be,' said Angela. 'I have just been trying to reconstruct the events of that afternoon in my head.'

'And where did that little pantomime fit into the picture?'

'I'm not sure yet,' replied Angela and would say no more.

They returned to the drawing-room where they found Guy Fisher frowning over a letter written in a large, ornate scrawl.

'Hallo, Mrs. Marchmont,' he said. 'Still pursuing your inquiries, I see. There have been no more attacks, I trust?'

'Happily not,' replied Angela.

'Still, I suppose that is one of the hazards of being a private investigator. It must be very tiresome having to be constantly on one's guard against sudden assaults by assassins brandishing knives and bludgeons.'

'What a dreadful idea!' said Angela, laughing. 'Nothing could be further from the truth. In fact, the most difficult task so far appears to be that of pinning down my witnesses to speak to them. Everyone always seems to be out and about or engaged with someone else when I want to speak to them. Indeed, I had so much trouble in catching Mr. Faulkner at a free moment that I had to go to Somerset House in order to get a look at Philip's will.'

'Faulkner? Typical of a solicitor. Yes, I hate it myself when people won't do what is required of them,' said Guy. 'I have a case in point right here in my hand.' He flapped the letter at them with a grimace. 'And now I suppose I shall have to go and do something about it.'

He got up and left the room without ceremony.

'He seems rather cross,' observed Angela.

'Yes,' said Stella. 'I think he finds his job a little difficult sometimes. He is forever having to sort out disputes between tenants, and it makes him grumpy. I think he would prefer to live a life of idleness really.'

She spoke fondly, and Angela looked up.

'You like him very much, don't you?' she said.

'Yes, I do. We have lots in common. We are both orphans, for one thing, so we know what it is like to feel an outsider.

And he always cheers me up when I am feeling blue, which seems to be quite often lately.' She stopped and closed her lips.

'And I rather think he likes you, too,' said Angela gently.

Stella looked up, then back down.

'Perhaps he does,' she said.

'I hate to see a young man with a broken heart,' Angela went on, only half-jokingly.

'I have no intention of breaking anybody's heart,' said Stella.

'No, but you could do it without meaning to.'

'And what if I—share his feelings?'

'Do you?'

Stella got up and paced restlessly up and down the room.

'I'm very fond of Guy and we should rub along well together, I have no doubt of that,' she said. 'I don't believe in all that romantic, happy-ever-after drivel any more. The most important thing is to find somebody I can trust—somebody who makes me feel safe.'

'Don't you feel safe now?' asked Angela in concern.

Stella turned to her with a white face.

'Oh, Mrs. Marchmont, if only you knew how frightened I've been!' she cried.

Chapter Nineteen

AT THAT MOMENT, Louisa and Donald came in, talking animatedly. Stella took one look at them and hurried out of the room.

'Whatever is the matter with Stella?' said Louisa. She did not wait for an answer and went on breathlessly, 'Angela, have you heard the news?'

'What news?' asked Angela.

'Why, that the police have visited Robin to question him about Winifred's money!'

'Oh,' said Angela. 'Is it certain, then, that her money was stolen?'

'It seems so,' replied her friend. 'Apparently, they went to her bank and discovered that a few months before she died she had withdrawn a large sum which constituted most of her money, but nobody could tell them what she did with it. I don't know how the police got wind of it or fastened onto Robin,' (here Angela stared hard at the floor) 'but at any rate they went to Datchet and asked him straight out whether he had had anything to do with it. Of course, he denied it all so they had to go away again.'

'Who told you all this?'

'Ursula. She called me in a great fury. She was convinced that one of us here at Underwood had been sneaking to the police. I did my best to persuade her otherwise, although I'm not sure I was successful. But of *course* none of us reported it,' she went on. 'Why should we dream of doing such a thing?'

Angela debated for a second but decided not to confess. She wanted to speak to Ursula again, but there would be no chance of that if Ursula knew that she had been the one to tell the police about Robin's supposed dishonest dealings.

'Perhaps it was the house,' said Donald darkly. 'Have you noticed how all those who have a dislike of the place seem to suffer?'

'That's hardly helpful, Donald,' said his mother impatiently. 'Really, I don't know where you get these fey fits from.'

Donald glowered but said nothing, then shortly afterwards excused himself and went out.

'I do wish he and Stella would make it up,' said Louisa. 'They have had rows before but this one has gone on for ages now.'

'Perhaps they won't make it up at all,' said Angela.

'Oh, but they must. Why, it's perfectly obvious to anyone who has seen them together that they're made for each other. I think I shall have to have a word with Stella.'

'I shouldn't if I were you,' said Angela. 'I think it would be better to leave them alone. These things have a habit of resolving themselves, and your interference might be more likely to cause harm.'

'Do you think so? I suppose you're right. You always are right, Angela.'

'Hardly,' said Angela. 'But listen, Louisa. I have a question to ask you while we are alone.'

'I am all ears,' said Louisa with interest.

'How shall I put this? Do you know of any person or persons to whom Philip might have wanted to leave a legacy without his family knowing about it?'

'A secret bequest, do you mean? Is that possible?'

'Yes—I have discovered that it is quite legal for a testator to bequeath some money to one beneficiary, intending all the while that it should be passed on to another person entirely.'

Louisa was surprised.

'I have never heard of such a thing,' she said. 'Why should anyone want to do that?'

'Lots of reasons,' said Angela, 'but the most obvious one is a desire to provide for illegitimate children.'

She paused delicately to allow Louisa to digest the significance of the remark.

'Are you suggesting that Philip might have had a secret family somewhere?'

Angela said nothing as Louisa considered the possibility, her head on one side.

'Obviously I can't say for sure, but I'd be very surprised if he did,' she said finally.

'But it might explain why he named Mr. Faulkner as the ultimate beneficiary of twenty thousand pounds. That is a very large sum to leave to one's solicitor at the expense of one's family. Perhaps Philip intended Mr. Faulkner to pass it on to someone unknown.'

'Well, if Philip was leading a secret life it must have begun long before I met John,' said Louisa, 'because I know nothing about it.'

'I didn't want to ask John as I wasn't sure how touchy he might be on the subject,' said Angela.

'Oh, go ahead and ask him. He has long since given up being embarrassed about his family,' said Louisa with a laugh. 'But I'm sure he would have told me if he knew of anything of the kind.'

Angela was privately unconvinced of this, but said nothing and shortly afterwards got up to go.

'I forgot to ask,' said Louisa, as she accompanied her friend to the door. 'Will you come to our family gathering on the 27th?'

'Do you mean the famous one of the will?'

'The very same. Do come, Angela. Just imagine what fun you will have watching us all scowl at each other and descend into idiotic bickering.'

Angela could not help laughing at her friend's rueful expression.

'Don't you think my presence will be unwelcome?' she asked.

'On the contrary, you might just be the calming influence we need. There are not many of the Hayneses left to fight each other,' she went on a little sadly, 'but I foresee trouble between Ursula and John and you could perhaps act as a useful buffer.'

'And here was I thinking that you had invited me for my sparkling wit and devastating repartee,' said Angela.

'Oh, that too, of course,' Louisa assured her. She clasped Angela's hand in hers. 'You *will* come, won't you, darling? I hate to admit it, but I shall be terribly frightened without you, given what has happened at all the other family meetings.'

Angela relented.

'Of course I will,' she said. 'I wouldn't miss it for the world.'

She left the house and got into her car. William was in high spirits, having been successful in his attempt to ingratiate himself with the servants. Mrs. Jones the housekeeper had not been present, and he had spent the morning being plied with tea and biscuits by a bevy of admiring maids. Over the course of the morning he had discovered that of the family, Mrs. Haynes was considered pleasant but forgetful; Mr. Haynes was irascible but well-liked, although he had been rather gloomy lately; Mr. Donald was a decent chap and very handsome too (if a little odd); Miss Stella had a secret, and Mr. Fisher was *such* a charming man and was still hoping that his watch could somehow be repaired. As for the guests, everyone was scared of Mrs. Ursula Haynes, Mr. Robin took liberties and Miss Euphonium—or whatever she was calling herself nowadays—gave herself airs.

All this was no more than Angela had already known or guessed.

'Did you find out anything about the dates in question?' she asked.

'Not as much as I should have liked,' said William, 'but I did find out from Annie that John Haynes usually poured Philippa's coffee for her after dinner. Of course, nobody can say whether he did it on the night she died as it was such a long time ago.'

'Naturally. And what about the 16th of February of this year? Did you ask about the laundry?'

'I sure did, ma'am. They were all quite certain that nobody had given them any dirty or wet evening clothes to clean. Might I take the liberty of asking why you wanted to know?'

'It's simple enough. Edward Haynes was drowned in the lake, so whoever did it must surely have got wet in the struggle. At the very least his jacket and shirt cuffs would be drenched—unless he was unclothed at the moment of the killing, which is of course a possibility.'

'Do you really think so? I don't see it myself. What was the victim doing while the killer was stripping off? Did he just stand there and exclaim, "Say, it sure is a fine evening for a swim. Mind if I join you?"'

Angela laughed.

'Hardly. But the murderer may have knocked him unconscious first, to make it easier to drown him.'

'I get it. He gives the guy the old one-two, then while he's out cold, strips off, bundles him into the rowing-boat and out onto the lake, throws him out then swims back to shore, leaving the boat behind.'

'Or holds his head under in the shallows. That might be easier,' said Angela. 'Then he would merely be throwing a dead body overboard rather than struggling to hold a live one under the water.'

'Well, it's a rotten trick whichever way you look at it,' said William indignantly.

'The whole business is rotten, William,' said Angela, 'and we have to find out who did it—and soon, or he might just do it again.'

Her thoughts returned to the events of the day, and particularly Stella's unexpected outburst. Who or what was Stella afraid of? Was it somebody at Underwood House, and did she know something about the mystery that she was concealing? Angela resolved to speak to Stella in private as soon as she could, and find out what had frightened her. She sighed. Nothing seemed simple. The further she delved into the case the more perplexing it seemed to become. One thing was clear, though: she was going to have to bite on the bullet and speak to John as soon as possible.

Chapter Twenty

TRUE TO HER resolution, a day or two later Mrs. Marchmont went down to Underwood House to speak to John. She went to his study and knocked quietly.

'Who is it?' said John.

'May I?' asked Angela, putting her head round the door.

'Ah, Angela. Come in. Are you snooping round here again?'

'I'm afraid so,' said Angela apologetically. John gestured to a chair and she sat. To her relief, it was soft and comfortable and showed no inclination to eject her onto the floor.

'So tell me, are you getting anywhere with all this investigating?' asked John in his abrupt manner.

'I very much hope so,' said Angela. 'I'm sure you must be dying to get rid of me by now.'

'Not a bit of it,' he said politely. He waved a letter at her. 'I was just looking at our—invitation, I suppose I must call it, although how one can be invited to dine in one's own home by a fellow who won't be there is anybody's guess. Anyway, we are all to present ourselves here like good little boys and girls and smile nicely, although of course the company is much reduced these days. Is there any way of getting out of it, I wonder? Can Father really have intended us to go on meeting and scowling at each other over dinner, especially now three of us are dead?'

'I don't suppose he intended anybody to die.'

John snorted.

'Don't you believe it! The old devil would be hugging himself with glee at the mischief he had caused, if he knew. In fact, I shouldn't be a bit surprised if he wrote the will as he did deliberately to set us all at each other's throats and see who would be the first to resort to murder.'

'Tell me, why *do* you think he made such a strange will?' asked Angela. 'You are the only one of his children left, and must have known him better than anyone living today. Why was part of your inheritance only a life interest? Why did he favour his solicitor over everybody?'

'I tell you, I have no idea. Perhaps old Faulkner had some kind of hold over Father—if anyone can match my father for cunning and trickery, it's that wily bird.'

Angela looked at her hands.

'What would you say to the suggestion that before his death, your father had asked Mr. Faulkner to hold the money on trust for someone else?'

'Someone else? Who do you mean?'

'Why, I don't know. I was hoping you might have an idea.'

'There is no-one else. Father didn't exactly encourage friendships, and the few friends he had are all dead now, as far as I know.'

'You don't think he might have had—a secret family somewhere?'

John went silent for a second, then burst out into a roar of laughter.

'Oh my, that's a good one,' he said finally, wiping his eyes. 'A secret family? Why, he was far too busy making his real family's lives a misery to have time for another one.'

'Can you be certain of that?' asked Angela.

'As certain as I am of anything,' said John. 'So that's your little idea, is it? Well, you may as well forget it at once. I don't say he was the best of men—quite the opposite—but I do know that my father rarely left Beningfleet, and it's such a small place that we should have found out years ago had there been any funny business going on, I'm quite sure of it.'

'I see.' Angela was disappointed. She hated to abandon her pet theory, but everywhere she turned she seemed to come to a dead-end. Still, there was no sense in flogging a dead horse.

'I also wanted to ask you something about the day Winifred died,' she said. 'I believe you said you were here in the study when she fell, but Donald says he was looking for you at the time and he came in here but couldn't find you. Are you quite sure that's where you were?'

John's face went purple.

'I—ah—' he began, then recovered himself. 'Of course I'm sure, although now you mention it I may have run outside for a moment or two to get some fresh air. This room gets very stuffy, you know. So Donald says he came in here, does he? I must have just missed him, then. Any other questions?' He appeared keen to change the subject.

'Ursula seems to believe that you, Louisa and Donald are hiding a secret from her. Do you have any idea what it might be?'

'Pfft!' said John dismissively. 'Who knows what the woman's got running through her head. One can never get a word of sense out of her. I shouldn't be a bit surprised if she drinks.'

'I think she suspects you of knowing who killed Edward and the others.'

'Bah! Nobody killed them, I keep telling you. Why does everyone keep insisting that there's some kind of mystery about their deaths? Listen, Angela, the only reason I agreed to Louisa's mad idea about getting you in was that I thought you might be able to prove once and for all that the whole thing was a mare's nest. And yet it seems you have fallen for all this nonsense too.'

'But I'm not at all sure it is nonsense,' said Angela, wondering at his obstinate refusal to admit that anything untoward might have happened.

'Of course it is. And even if it isn't you'll never prove anything, so why go stirring up the past and causing trouble when we're all perfectly happy as we are?'

'Because murder is wrong,' said Angela simply, 'and if it *was* murder then we need to catch the person who did it before he does it again.'

'Humph,' was all he said in reply.

'Has it occurred to you that you might be in danger yourself?'

'I?' said John incredulously.

'Yes, of course. Assuming that someone deliberately killed your sisters and brother, then as the only one left you could be the next target.' She did not add, 'Unless *you* did it.'

To judge by his surprised expression, this was a new idea to John.

'But why should anybody want to kill me?' he said.

'I leave you to work that out,' said Angela dryly. 'Have you offended anyone lately?'

He gave a sudden guffaw.

'Dozens of people, probably. I shouldn't be surprised if Louisa and half the servants wish me ill, given my general untidiness and the state I leave my clothes in. But that's hardly a motive for murder.'

'You have money and property,' Angela pointed out. 'A stronger motive you couldn't find.'

'I think Louisa and Donald might have something to say about that,' he said with another bark of laughter.

'But it isn't just them, is it? Other people have an interest in your death, too. Mr. Faulkner, for instance.'

'Are you saying he killed Philippa and the others?'

'No—he has alibis for the nights of their deaths, but perhaps he got someone else to do it. I don't say that's what happened,' she went on hurriedly. 'I'm just musing over possibilities. Please, John, I should like you to think about it carefully. If you know of anyone who might have a reason to kill you—however far-fetched that sounds—tell me so at once.'

Seeing she was serious, he bit back his impatient reply.

'I swear to you I don't know of anyone who wants me dead,' he said more gently, 'and I promise that if anything occurs to me I shall let you know.'

'Thank you,' said Angela. 'Louisa would never forgive me if I let you come to harm.'

'So the lady has to protect the gentleman in this case, yes?' he said, eyes twinkling. 'I must say, I never heard of such a thing.'

'I doubt it will come to that,' said Angela, 'but you never know. And now I have just one more question, then I shall leave you in peace.'

'Fire away,' said John.

'Do you remember the photograph I showed you a few days ago? The one that was lost when I was attacked in London?'

'Yes,' said John warily.

'When I asked you if you knew who the subject was you said you had no idea.'

'Well?'

'Was it a photograph of your sister Christina?'

Chapter Twenty-One

IF ANGELA HAD hoped to catch John by surprise she was not disappointed. He started and flushed, then finally gave a brief nod.

'How on earth did you find that out?' he asked.

'It was a lucky guess,' Angela admitted. 'When I saw the picture I immediately had the feeling that it looked like someone I knew, but I couldn't think who. When I looked at it later I realized that it was you she reminded me of—especially around the eyes. Ursula didn't recognize her so I knew it couldn't be Philippa or Winifred. In fact, my first thought was that it was a picture of your mother, but the age of the woman and the style of the clothes she was wearing led me to conclude that it was more likely to be Christina.'

'Well, it was. And what of it?'

'Was it you who dropped the photograph down by the lake?'

John shook his head.

'No, that wasn't me. I'd never seen the picture in my life before you showed it to me.'

'Then who dropped it?'

'I haven't the faintest idea.'

'But why did you say you didn't recognize it?'

He looked away and did not reply for a few seconds.

'It would have been her birthday soon,' he said eventually in a gruff voice. 'Every year I used to bring her forget-me-nots from the woods. They were always her favourite, even as a child. I brought her armfuls of them and she would clap her hands together and jump up in delight. She loved wild things—loved to run around in the open air and feel the fresh breeze on her face. She hated being stuck indoors. She wanted to be as free as the wild flowers, she always said.'

'She died many years ago, I understand,' said Angela gently.

'Yes, and it was all Father's fault,' he burst out. 'He goaded her continually until she couldn't stand it any more and was driven to desperate means in order to escape. At last she ran away, and I never saw her again. I wanted to go and find her, but Father lied and told us she had died. A few years later she *did* die, and it was only then that I found out she'd been alive all along, believing to the last that nobody cared enough about her to seek her out. I regret that very much.'

'I'm sorry,' said Angela. 'I didn't mean to reopen old wounds.'

John waved his hand.

'Don't mention it. I didn't think it *was* an old wound but you caught me off guard. I was very fond of her but it all happened a long time ago now, and what's done is done.'

'Then you have no idea what her photograph was doing down by the lake?'

'None at all.'

Angela was about to ask another question when they were interrupted by Louisa, who hurried into the room, full of suppressed excitement.

'My dears, I've just been speaking to the police on the 'phone. They wanted to know if we'd seen Robin. It seems he's disappeared, and they've discovered that quite a lot of money is missing from Peake's. They're all in an uproar there, and it could turn into a tremendous scandal if they don't find him soon.'

'Good Lord!' exclaimed John. He looked almost pleased. 'Can it really be true? Well, there's a turn-up and no mistake. You see, Louisa? I always said there was something shady about him. Ursula will be smiling on the other side of her face now, won't she? Perhaps this will stop her from bandying all these silly accusations about.'

'Do they want to arrest him, then?' asked Angela.

'It looks like it,' said Louisa. 'I wonder where he's hiding. I don't suppose he'll come anywhere near us.'

'What happened, exactly?'

The tip-off had come from within Peake's, it seemed. Two of Robin's fellow employees had for some time suspected him of engaging in illicit dealings, and had reported their concerns to their superiors, who in turn had quietly requested the assistance of the police. Robin, apparently unaware that he had raised suspicions, had been under discreet observation for some weeks now without anything coming of it, but events had suddenly been precipitated by the police's decision to question him about Winifred's money. This appeared to have thrown him into a panic and the next day it was discovered that he had fled with some jewellery and cash belonging to his mother, and that the firm was missing many thousands of pounds. Nobody knew where he had gone.

'I do hope it's all a mistake,' said the kindly Louisa after they had all exclaimed over the news. 'I know poor Robin isn't the most agreeable boy but I should hate to think he was a criminal. We all know Ursula can be a little difficult at times but after all, she has just lost her husband and Robin is her only son—the only person she has left to comfort her. What will she do if he goes to prison? John, perhaps we should invite her here for dinner. She must be feeling terribly alone at the moment.'

'I say, steady on, old girl,' said John, alarmed. 'I mean to say, I'm all for showing sympathy when a family member is in trouble, but this is Ursula you are talking about. We can't have her to dinner. Why, I shan't be able to eat a thing with her sitting there like a skeleton at the feast, glaring disapprovingly at us all.'

'John!' exclaimed his wife reproachfully.

'And besides,' he went on, 'she will be coming here on the 27th anyway for our little family party.'

'Oh!' said Louisa. 'I'd forgotten all about that. Perhaps you're right, then. We shall have her here on that evening. I may just telephone her, though, to make sure she's all right.'

'Do as you please,' said John, 'but I warn you now, she will take it amiss. She will be looking for someone to blame.'

The house was abuzz with talk of the latest events and since it was clear that nobody had attention to spare for anything other than Robin's disappearance, Angela excused herself and went back to London. There she put a telephone-call through to Inspector Jameson.

'Hallo, Mrs. Marchmont,' said Jameson when he came on the line. 'I imagine you've heard the news about Robin Haynes.'

'Indeed I have,' said Angela, 'and I must say it looks rather bad for him.'

'It does,' agreed the inspector. 'The silly fool has got himself into the devil of a mess.'

'What is he supposed to have done with the money from his firm?'

'Well, I'm not an expert myself, but it appears that he got himself into a dreadful hole by what is known as selling shares on the short side. I don't suppose you have ever heard of such a thing, but I shall try to explain what it means in simple terms.'

Angela knew all about selling short, but listened patiently.

'Let's suppose that you have it on good authority that the share price of a particular firm—let's call it Smith and Co.—is about to fall. Perhaps you have heard a rumour that the company made lower than expected profits last year, or that a new invention of theirs is not selling as well as they had hoped. If you are bold enough, you can borrow some shares of the company from a Smith's shareholder, sell them at today's price, then, when the market learns that Smith's is not doing as well as expected and the price falls, buy the shares back at the lower amount and return them to their owner, pocketing the profit for yourself. For example, let's suppose that you borrow a thousand shares and sell them at a price of twenty shillings for a total of one thousand pounds. After a few days, the market price falls to fifteen shillings. You then buy the shares back at the lower price and return them to their rightful owner, making yourself a handsome profit of two hundred and fifty pounds at the same time. Have I explained that clearly?'

'Quite clearly,' said Angela.

'Well, that is what Robin Haynes was doing—borrowing shares owned by clients of Peake's and taking short positions on them then keeping the profit for himself. Somehow, though, he forgot to ask permission before borrowing the shares. For a while he did rather well out of it, but then he made a couple of bad bets, which is when his problems began. I don't suppose you remember, but early last year the markets were full of excitement about Anglo-Pretoria, the mining company that struck an enormous seam of gold after doing very badly for some years.'

'I seem to remember reading something about it,' said Angela, who had made rather a lot of money from Anglo-Pretoria's stroke of good fortune.

'Unfortunately for Robin, he had taken a short position on Anglo's shares just before the news emerged of the discovery. The share price went up, instead of down as he had expected, and that meant he was forced to stump up a large sum of money to get the stock back to return to the client—money he didn't have and couldn't borrow. A similar thing happened on a couple of other occasions, and each time he tried to make up the money through wilder and wilder speculation. You can imagine the result.'

'That must be around the time he persuaded Winifred to let him invest her money,' said Angela.

'Yes. There was no investment fund paying fantastic returns, of course. That was a lie. Robin had merely convinced himself that he would be able to repay her the money by making up his losses and more on the stock markets.'

'Are Peake's in serious trouble, then?'

'I don't think they will sink, if that's what you mean. Robin has lost them many thousands of pounds but they have been trading for more than a hundred years so they know what they are about and will most likely weather the storm. I can't say what this will do to their reputation, though, when the news gets out.'

'Poor Winifred, to have been duped by her own nephew. No wonder he kept avoiding her. He must have been desperately trying to find a way of getting the money back quickly. I imagine her death shortly afterwards must have been quite a relief to him.'

'Ah,' said the inspector, 'but there is more to the story than you know. Once we heard that he had done a disappearing trick, naturally we went to his house.'

'I don't suppose Ursula took too kindly to that.'

'You could say that,' said Jameson, feelingly. 'In fact, I don't mind telling you that I should far rather tackle an armed gang any day than have to face Mrs. Ursula Haynes with a search-warrant.'

Angela laughed.

'At any rate, she had to let us in eventually,' he went on, 'and we searched through his things. Not that he'd left much that was of any use—as a matter of fact, it looked as though he'd had a very pretty bonfire before he went off.'

'Dear me,' said Angela. 'Presumably that was to get rid of any incriminating evidence of his illicit dealings.'

'That's what it looks like, although he may as well have saved himself the effort since we have plenty of proof at the Peake's end. He won't get away with it that easily. However, he must have been in a hurry because we did find one rather interesting thing that had somehow slipped down underneath the grate and escaped the flames mostly undamaged.'

'Oh?'

'Yes. It was a letter from Robin himself to his Aunt Winifred, pleading for more time to repay the money and begging her not to report him to the police or—worse—his mother. I assume Winifred must have been threatening to expose his unscrupulous dealings to the proper authorities.'

'That letter could be very useful to his cousin Susan should she ever wish to make a claim against him to try and get her inheritance back. It may be the only evidence that exists in writing, since I gather Winifred signed no agreement.'

'Yes, that's true,' said the inspector, 'but we at Scotland Yard are taking an even more serious view of the matter than that, given his presence on the scene immediately after Mrs. Denison fell to her death at Underwood House.'

'You think it proves he was the murderer?'

'It certainly points very strongly in that direction. Think about it—why should Robin Haynes have a letter in his possession that he wrote himself? Surely he must have sent it straight after he wrote it—or, if he had decided against sending it, why did he not destroy it at the time?'

'What is your theory?'

'Why, I think there is a very good chance that, faced with the threat of exposure, he was driven to extreme measures to avoid being found out. And what better way to stop his aunt from reporting him to the police or Peake's than by closing her mouth permanently?'

'And so he pushed her over the balustrade. It's certainly a possibility. But what of the letter?'

'Don't you think it's possible that when he was discovered bending over her body, he was searching her pockets for it? If it was found on her, then all his efforts would have been in vain, but if he could only get it back then there was a good chance he would not be found out.'

Angela considered it.

'Or perhaps he had nothing to do with her death and got the letter back by some other means,' she suggested.

'Who knows? All the same, I should very much like to catch Master Robin. I've already had a carpeting from the superintendent for letting him escape from under our noses when we were supposed to have him under observation. The super's a pal of Mr. Peake's and has been getting it in the neck himself, so I can hardly blame him. Still, I'm not exactly covered in glory at the moment, so I should like to find him as soon as possible. There's going to be a terrific scandal once this gets into the newspapers.'

'Might he have gone abroad?'

'He might. We're watching the ports, but he got a head start on us and could have been long gone by the time we discovered he was missing.'

The inspector then excused himself, anxious not to lose a minute in the hunt for his quarry, and hung up. Angela sat for a few minutes, thinking over what he had said. He had certainly made a convincing case for Robin's guilt in the matter of Winifred's death, she could not deny it, but what of Philippa and Edward? Nothing had been discovered up to now to suggest that he had had a hand in their deaths. Nor was there any suggestion that he had taken their money, so why on earth should he want to kill them? Was it possible that not all the deaths had been murder? Philippa in particular could certainly have died from natural causes—it was only the deaths of her sister and brother, in fact, that had raised the question of whether or not someone had had a hand in her demise. Nobody had had the slightest suspicion before that.

Very well, then, take Philippa's death out of the picture and what was left? Edward. Angela shook her head. She was as certain as she could be that Edward Haynes had not drowned accidentally but had been murdered. But what was the motive? There seemed to be none—or if there was, it was not, as far as Angela could see, the same as the one which had presumably led Winifred to her doom. No, on the face of it there seemed to be no connection between Edward's death and Winifred's other than the fact that they had both died at the gatherings ordained by Philip's will. Perhaps it was a coincidence. Could they have been killed by two different people? But no—that was no good as a theory either, since there was also the inescapable fact that Philippa, too, had died at one of the gatherings. That was stretching coincidence too far.

And then there was the feeling she had, one which she could not put into words, something that told her that, unknown to them all, there was a single, unseen hand at work behind the scenes, conducting events and impelling people to act. She had nothing to back it up, but her instinct told her it was true: that somehow, *someone* was influencing the Hayneses, Mr. Faulkner, the police—everybody concerned with the case, to act as he wanted.

'It's almost as though we are all dolls, being danced around idiotically on the stage by an invisible puppet-master,' she murmured to herself. 'But who can it be?'

She had missed something, she was sure of it. A clue or a vital piece of evidence. What was it, now? Something that would provide the key to the whole mystery. She cast her mind back. Was it something John had said to her that morning? Something to do with forget-me-nots, perhaps? Angela gave a wry smile at that. And she was sure there was something that she had been going to ask Stella the other day. What could it be?

'I must be getting old,' she said. 'My memory is obviously not what it was. I shall have to sleep on it.'

Then, in a spirited act of defiance against the hateful god Geras, she went out dancing and did not return home until past three.

Chapter Twenty-Two

MRS. MARCHMONT WAS just removing her hat and coat after returning from lunch with a friend when she heard the bell ring. Marthe answered it.

'Please, *madame*,' she said, 'there is a woman downstairs who wishes to speak to you.'

Her tone was not lost on Angela.

'A woman?'

Marthe clicked her tongue.

'A lady, then. Although she was not very polite. Her name is Ursula Haynes.'

Angela was surprised. What on earth was Ursula doing here? She suddenly felt a little nervous.

'Let her in, Marthe,' she said. She straightened up and smoothed her hair, then chided herself for her timidity.

Ursula arrived and looked about her, unsmiling. She was dressed smartly but severely in dark blue. There was no decoration about her, no trimming.

'Mrs. Marchmont,' she said. 'I have come to speak to you about my son, Robin.'

'Please, do sit down,' said Angela. 'Marthe, bring us some coffee.'

'I should prefer tea,' said Ursula.

'Tea, then.'

Marthe acquiesced without a word and went out. Ursula sat down on the edge of a chair but did not speak. Perhaps she was collecting her thoughts. Angela waited, determined not to be the first to break the silence.

'As I am sure you know, the police want to arrest my son,' said Mrs. Haynes finally.

Angela bowed her head.

'Yes, Louisa told me,' she said.

Ursula looked up sharply.

'That is odd, because I rather thought *you* had told Louisa,' she said.

'I?'

'You deny, then, that it was you who reported Robin to the police for fraudulent share-dealing?'

'I had nothing to do with it,' said Angela truthfully.

'A wholly trumped-up charge, I might add. I know he has enemies within the firm who have been looking for an opportunity to discredit him, although I never dreamed they would stoop to this.'

Her voice was filled with suppressed fury and her eyes gleamed.

'I understand he went missing before the police could arrest him,' said Angela.

'Yes. My son has a delicate disposition, and naturally the prospect of arrest filled him with horror in spite of his innocence, so he has gone into hiding.'

'Surely it would be better for him to face the music now, rather than dragging it out,' said Angela. 'After all, they are bound to catch him sooner or later and if he really is innocent then he ought to be here to defend himself. You can't deny that his running off like that looks very suspicious. If he came out into the open then he could fight the accusations. The police are only concerned with catching the right man, you know, and if they have made a mistake then sooner or later it will be found out.'

Ursula gave her a withering look.

'How very credulous you are, Mrs. Marchmont, if you believe that. At Peake's Robin is surrounded by people who plot against him and seek his downfall. They will have made certain that there was plenty of evidence against him before they made their move.'

This seemed so unlikely that Angela wondered at the blindness of a mother's love.

'Are you quite sure of that?' she asked. 'Why should he take Winifred's money, in that case?'

'Stupid woman!' spat Ursula, quite startling Angela, who wondered for a second whom she was referring to. 'She gave him the money quite of her own free will and badgered him to invest it for her. I know all about it—he told me what happened after the police first came to question him. She was dissatisfied with the return her inheritance was bringing in and was casting about for a way in which to increase her income.

He was unwilling to take her money, as he felt that she did not truly understand the nature of the risks she was running even though he had explained them carefully to her, but she was quite insistent. In the end he relented since she was family, but shortly afterwards disaster struck on the markets and all the money was lost.'

'The police seem to think that he used the money to shore up the losses he had already made through his own speculation,' hazarded Angela.

'Then they are dolts. It's all stuff and nonsense, I tell you.'

Marthe arrived with the tea and there was a short pause in the conversation as she served them. Ursula took a delicate sip, pursed her lips and put her cup down.

'And to add to everything else, it now appears that the police suspect Robin of murdering Winifred,' she said.

'Is that what they told you?'

'They did not say it in so many words, but I could see in which direction their questions were tending.'

'What did Robin say to that?'

'Of course he denied it, as it is not true.'

'I believe the police found a letter to his aunt among his belongings, begging her not to report him. Perhaps that is what made them start considering a possible connection to her death.'

'The letter was a forgery, no doubt,' said Ursula flatly.

There was no arguing with such wilful self-delusion, so Angela made no reply. Ursula sat stiffly for a minute or two longer then rose from her seat and began to pace up and down restlessly.

'You are no doubt wondering what is the purpose of my visit,' she said. 'Obviously I did not come here merely for the pleasure of chatting idly about my son.' She looked hard at Angela. 'The events of the past few days have come as a complete shock to me. It is not often that I am caught at a disadvantage, but on this occasion I find myself quite at a loss to know where to turn for assistance. I want to find my son and demonstrate his innocence, but the police are determined to do quite the opposite: find him and prove him guilty, so there is no help to be had from them. I have no family of my own and the Hayneses will do nothing, I know. That is why I thought of you.'

'Me?'

'Yes. I should like to engage the services of a detective, and you are the only one I know.'

Angela shook her head.

'I am afraid you are mistaken,' she said. 'I am not a private investigator. I was unfortunate enough to become embroiled in a rather notorious murder case a few months ago, and the newspapers somehow got the fanciful notion that I had solved the mystery. Louisa believed it all too, and I only agreed to help her because she is an old friend.'

'Then what am I to do?' cried Ursula suddenly in despair. To Angela's horror, she sank back into her chair, covered her face with her hands and wept. Angela looked about her desperately, wondering what on earth to do next, then searched fruitlessly in her pockets for a clean handkerchief. Fortunately, Marthe came to the rescue, presenting Ursula with the necessary article and pressing a cup of strong tea upon her. By this time, Angela had recovered her presence of mind and changed seats to sit next to her guest, who had unexpectedly proved herself to be human after all.

'I do beg your pardon,' said Ursula, regaining her composure and lowering the handkerchief to reveal reddened eyes.

'Not at all,' said Angela. 'I quite understand. And I am very sorry that I am unable to help you.'

She placed her hand on Ursula's arm in a gesture of sympathy. Ursula stiffened and drew back.

'Well,' she said, turning her face away. 'I did not have much hope of success. But I am quite alone and cannot help Robin by myself.'

'If you will permit me to say so,' ventured Angela hesitantly, 'you can most usefully help your son by hiring the best defence counsel you can afford.'

Ursula looked at her bleakly.

'You, too, believe him to be guilty, then,' she said. Angela said nothing, and she sighed, as though finally forced to accept the inevitable. 'I am quite alone,' she repeated.

'Then call Louisa,' said Angela decidedly. 'She is kind and will give you all the help she can if you will only let her.'

'But John hates me.'

'I don't believe John hates anybody,' said Angela, smiling. 'He is impatient, certainly, and does not suffer fools gladly, but he, too, is kind at heart.'

'That is what you say, but I am not so easily deceived.'

'What do you mean?'

'Why, can't you see how he has benefited from the deaths of his sisters and my husband? And now he has somehow convinced the police that Robin killed Winifred. I dare say it is only a matter of time before they decide he must have killed Edward and Philippa too. My son is not a murderer.'

'For what it may be worth, Mrs. Haynes, I agree with you,' said Angela. 'But unless we can find out who *did* kill them then he will be forever under suspicion.'

'You are right,' said Ursula.

'I believe you can help me,' Angela went on. 'I believe you know, or think you know something about what happened. You tried to get information from Mr. Faulkner but he could not or would not help you. Will you tell me what you suspect?'

Ursula looked up, surprised.

'What do you know about Mr. Faulkner?' she demanded, then gazed at Angela through narrowed eyes for a moment or two, as though weighing the decision.

'You are a friend of John and Louisa's,' she said finally. 'You are investigating on their behalf, and so naturally that will colour your conclusions. Perhaps you may even be persuaded to alter the facts a little in order to help them, to the disadvantage of my son.'

'I assure you I shall do no such thing,' said Angela with dignity. 'I have told Louisa repeatedly that I shall not flinch from the truth, however unpalatable it may be, and she has agreed with me that I ought not to.'

Ursula stared at her for another long moment, but it was impossible to tell what she was thinking. Finally she looked away and said, 'You are mistaken, Mrs. Marchmont. I have nothing to tell you.' She stood up. 'I am sorry to have taken up so much of your time. I shall do as you suggest and engage a legal adviser.'

Angela saw there was no use in pressing her.

'Goodbye,' she said. 'Do think about what I said. I promise you that I am concerned only with finding out the truth.'

Again Ursula gave her that assessing look, then left without another word.

Chapter Twenty-Three

IN SPITE OF all the best efforts of Scotland Yard, Robin Haynes could not be found. No-one of his description had been apprehended trying to leave the country, or escaping to the North on the train, or hiding in a barn. His mother still claimed to have no idea where he was—not that anyone dared question her too closely. In fact, it was not until Inspector Jameson took over the business of talking to Ursula himself that even that slight admission could be drawn from her. For the most part the police contented themselves with keeping a discreet eye on her from a distance, since even the stoutest of English bobbies has been known to quail before a certain type of elderly lady.

Angela, meanwhile, went down to Underwood on the train, this time in the hope of speaking to Stella in private. As she approached the house, she encountered Mr. Briggs as he pushed a heavy wheelbarrow with difficulty across the lawn. He beamed as he recognized her.

'Good morning, ma'am,' he said cheerfully. 'Another fine day we're having for the time of year.'

Resisting the temptation to offer to help him with his load, Angela returned his salute.

'I see you have managed to get the ivy looking beautifully neat,' she said, gazing up at Donald's bedroom window.

'Yes, and a devil of a time we had of it too—begging your pardon, ma'am,' he said. 'Young Thomas nearly came off his ladder more 'n once. He always was a foolhardy one, mind you. He'll break bones before he's much older, you mark my words.'

'Well, I'm sure Mr. Donald must be pleased to have a view out of his window again,' she said. She was about to pass on when a thought struck her. 'Wasn't that Miss Christina's room at one time?' she said. 'I believe you told me something of the kind.'

'That's right, ma'am,' replied the old gardener.

'Yes, Mr. Haynes was telling me her story the other day,' said Angela. 'It was all terribly sad, of course.'

'It was, ma'am. Mrs. Haynes, God rest her soul, was dreadful cut up about it. Some might say she never recovered, although it wasn't until a few years later that she died.'

'I understand that Christina and her father did not get along at all well.'

'No, they didn't. He was all for the de-*mewer* young ladies, was Mr. Haynes. By his way of thinking, they should all sit nicely in the parlour with their hands folded, looking pretty. But Miss Christina, she always was a wild one. She liked to run about in the woods and climb trees like a boy. I heard she used to swim in the lake, too—and I never saw a finer horsewoman.'

'Indeed? That must often have brought her into conflict with her father.'

'Yes, ma'am. My, how they quarrelled! And then he would shut her in her room to teach her a lesson, but there was no holding a girl like that.' He snickered admiringly. 'He never knew it, but she used to climb out of the window and shin down that very ivy what we've been talking about. Just like the ivy herself, she was—you could never keep her down.'

'She must have been a most enterprising young lady.'

'Yes, ma'am. She was that.'

'And then of course there was the final quarrel that led to her running away,' said Angela carelessly, as though she knew all about it. 'There was a young man involved, wasn't there?'

Mr. Briggs looked surprised.

'Oh, so Mr. John told you that, did he? I thought they preferred to keep the scandal well hidden. Mind, there's plenty of water flowed under the bridge since then, so I suppose he thought there was no harm in it, seeing as she's long dead and there's no-one can hurt her any more.'

Angela was gratified at her lucky guess.

'Who was he?' she asked.

'A local lad from the farm yonder. Not one of her kind. Just like her wilfulness, it was, to pick someone she could never marry. She stood her ground, too—wouldn't hear of breaking it off when her family found out about it. But it was all a mistake, and in the end he proved unworthy of her.'

'In what way?'

'Why, he put an end to it himself and near broke her heart at the same time. I did hear as Mr. Haynes bought him off, but I don't know if there's any truth to that. At any rate, shortly afterwards he died in an accident on the farm and by then it had all come out and it was too late for him to marry her even supposing they could have persuaded him to it.'

'You don't mean she was in trouble?'

Briggs pursed his lips and lowered his voice confidentially.

'That was the rumour in the servants' hall, ma'am,' he said. 'I can't say whether it's true or not. And of course, we never did find out because two days after her young man was killed, she climbed down the ivy for the last time and was never seen again around these parts. A few years later we heard she'd died.'

'And what about her child?'

'Nobody knows. Some said it had died at birth, some said it had been taken in by a wealthy family and some said there had never been any child at all. Choose whichever story you like, ma'am—I don't know which is the right one.'

'Mr. John Haynes was dreadfully upset by the whole affair, I imagine.'

'Yes,' said Briggs, nodding sagely. 'They were mighty fond of each other, those two. He wasn't so keen on his younger sisters and brother, Mr. John wasn't—they were too much under the influence of their father, so there wasn't much of what you might call sympathy between 'em. But he always looked after Miss Christina, his favourite, and I'm sure he would have taken her and the child in if he could have found them.'

'Gossiping again, Mrs. Marchmont?' said Guy Fisher, appearing suddenly at Angela's shoulder and making her jump.

'Briggs, I ought to warn you now, this lady is dangerous. If once you let her get into conversation with you, you will find yourself giving away all your guiltiest and innermost secrets before you know it. Why, within five minutes of meeting her, I involuntarily confessed to her that, as a child, I had been caught red-handed stealing apples from our neighbour's orchard and soundly beaten by my mother. She now knows my history as a common thief and won't believe a word I say ever again.'

'You will have your little joke, Mr. Fisher, sir,' said Briggs pleasantly. Taking the hint, he touched his hat and went on his way, pushing the wheelbarrow before him unsteadily.

'I take it from the smell of smoke in the air that they are having a bonfire today,' said Angela.

'Either that, or cook has burnt the pudding again,' said Guy. He spoke in his usual jocular manner but seemed distracted, as though he had something else on his mind.

'Has there been any news of Robin?' asked Angela.

He roused himself with an effort and shook his head.

'No, none at all. Wherever he is, he's gone to ground pretty thoroughly, I'll say that for him. If you ask me, I think he got out of the country before the hue and cry was raised. At this moment he is probably strolling along the Promenade des Anglais in a regrettable suit, or sunning himself on a hilltop overlooking Rome, counting his ill-gotten gains with glee and congratulating himself on how clever he has been.'

'You sound as though you envied him.'

'Indeed I do. Not his ill-gotten gains, naturally, but all the rest. I have always wanted to travel to far-off places, but have never had the opportunity.'

'Shall you go abroad one day, do you think?'

'I hope so. I have glorious dreams of taking my pretty young wife on a grand wedding tour to Florence or Venice or Stamboul. That's always supposing Ste—any woman should take leave of her senses for long enough to agree to marry me.'

'I'm sure there are many women of perfectly good sense who would be happy to accept you,' said Angela, smiling.

'I used to think that myself,' he said sadly, 'but at the last tally I have been turned down by twenty-three women—or was it twenty-four? I'm not sure I should count Mrs. Harrison, who runs the tea-shop, but really, her scones were so delicious that I was moved by an overwhelming urge to propose. And now I really must go, or I shall find myself proposing to you too and then we shall fall out.'

He went off and Angela turned, laughing, to go into the house, but was brought up short by the sight of Donald Haynes striding towards her with a purposeful look on his face.

'I say, Mrs. Marchmont,' he said. 'Might I have a word with you about Stella?'

CHAPTER TWENTY-FOUR

'WHY, OF COURSE,' said Angela in surprise.

Donald smiled briefly.

'Let's walk away from the house where we shan't be overheard,' he said.

'Shouldn't you be better off talking to Stella?' suggested Angela. 'I don't know what I can tell you that she can't tell you better herself.'

'But that's just it—she won't speak to me at all,' he replied crossly, 'and I don't know what it is I'm meant to have done.'

'Don't you? I thought you'd had a quarrel—something about her giving up work after you marry.'

He waved a hand.

'Oh, we quarrel about that all the time, but she knows very well that I should never stop her from doing it if she really wanted to. Besides, I don't believe she *does* want to keep working, since she only threatens to do it when she's in a miff with me. Listen, Mrs. Marchmont, you must be aware that Stella and I—well, we have known each other all our lives. We grew up together. We know each other as well as anybody can know another person. We are soul-mates. When we row, it's nothing but a brother-and-sister kind of scrap. It clears the air and we laugh about it afterwards. But this is different. We had a fight about something or other a week or two ago and she won't make it up, although goodness knows I've tried often enough to find out what it is that's bothering her. Whenever she sees me she runs off. How am I supposed to win her over if she won't even talk to me?'

'What was the last row about?'

'I'm not even sure I can remember. It was one of those "nothing" things, if you see what I mean. I said something in passing and she flared up and started accusing me of all kinds of mysterious transgressions that she wouldn't name. But it wasn't my sins themselves that offended her, so far as I could tell—no, believe it or not, it was the fact that I would not confide in her about them that exercised her. How could we get married, she said, when I was keeping secrets from her? She would stand by me through thick and thin, and she would see to it that I got all the help I needed, but she was damned if she was going to be shut out.'

'That's what she said, is it?' said Angela thoughtfully.

'I only wish I knew what I was supposed to have done. But she won't tell me. That's why I wanted to speak to you. I was hoping that you would talk to her on my behalf, at least to find out why she's so angry with me.'

'But wouldn't your mother be a more suitable person in this case?'

'Mother's tried, but Stella won't talk to her about it.'

'Then why should I have any more success?'

'She likes you—admires you very much. And besides, since you are an outsider she will find it easier to talk to you, as you ought to be free from any prejudice in the matter.'

Angela relented.

'Very well, I shall try,' she said, 'but I can't promise anything. She may prove stubborn.'

'She's that, all right,' said Donald fervently. 'But you are my last hope. After you I have—nothing.' He raised his hands and let them fall.

'Don't say that. I'm sure something will turn up. In fact, I shouldn't be a bit surprised if she comes round after I have gone. I believe this whole affair—and especially my investigation of it—is making everybody in the house somewhat agitated and nervous.'

'Do you really think so?' he asked eagerly, as though willing to snatch at any theory that might give him hope. 'I say, now you put it that way—it's not much fun for us all to have the police and detectives and what-not tramping around the place all the time, asking silly questions.'

'Thank you,' said Angela dryly, but he paid no heed, caught up with this new idea. He turned to her.

'When—do you have any idea—I mean to say—'

'When shall I be gone? That is what you want to ask, I believe?' she said, smiling.

'No—no, of course that's not—'

'I quite understand. I should feel the same in your position, and between you and me, I shall also be very glad when this business is finished. I only agreed to do it because your mother was so very persuasive that I could not say no. I am not a detective, you know, and perhaps that is why nothing has yet been resolved. *Cave* the meddling amateur,' she said with mock seriousness. 'Far from helping, he may make things even worse.'

'Not at all,' said Donald. 'I know Mother is terribly grateful to you for all that you've done up to now—and it's so much better than having the police here, and our names in the papers, and all that kind of unpleasantness.'

'Do you still wish me to speak to Stella, then, or should you rather try again with her once this is all over?'

'Yes, please do speak to her, Mrs. Marchmont. Who knows when this whole thing will be finished? It may take months, and by then—why, I don't know—she may have found someone else who can give her what she wants.'

He did not mention Guy, but he did not need to.

'I shall talk to Stella now, if I may, then,' said Angela. 'In fact, she is the reason I came here today. I wanted to speak to her about something else.'

'She has gone into the village, but she will be back soon. Will you come into the house?'

'If you don't mind, I think I shall walk down to the lake. I should like to reflect. I shall be back soon.'

She turned and headed towards the path that led through the woods. As she did so she saw Briggs again, hobbling across the lawn carrying something that looked like a bundle of old rags. He stopped as he saw her and held it up in exaggerated puzzlement.

Angela, since she was clearly expected to do so, obligingly asked, 'What's that?'

She moved to get a closer look. It was filthy and stained and burnt around the edges, but was nonetheless easily recognizable.

'Why, it looks like a dinner jacket,' she said.

'And trousis too,' nodded Briggs. 'Somebody had shoved them under the heap of rubbish to be burned. I nearly died of fright, I did—I thought it was a tramp who'd gone to sleep under it all to keep warm, and there we'd gone and set 'im ablaze. So I started to drag it out and saw it weren't nothing but a set of clothes.'

'But whose are they?' asked Angela. 'May I?'

She took what was left of the jacket gingerly and laid it out on the grass. A brief examination showed no laundry marks or other means of identification. A similar search of the trousers was just as unsuccessful.

'There's nothing in the pockets,' she said, and turned her attention to the sleeves of the jacket as Briggs looked on in polite mystification. 'Hmm. Inconclusive,' she said at last, then picked up the trousers and peered at the ankles. 'They have obviously been wet and muddy at some time, but they could easily have got that way by being shoved into a heap of garden rubbish. I don't suppose you know how long these clothes were there, Briggs?'

'No, ma'am,' he said.

Angela reached a decision.

'These things must be kept,' she said. 'I shall take them myself. Briggs, take these to the house and have someone wrap them up in a parcel for me, but be sure and keep quiet about it.'

'Right you are, ma'am. And don't worry, I shan't breathe a word to the family,' said the kindly Mr. Briggs, taking pity on poor Mrs. Marchmont, who was evidently in such reduced circumstances that she was forced to take whatever nasty old clothing she could scavenge from great folks' houses.

Angela thanked him and departed, happily unaware that below stairs she was now marked out as a destitute, although it would in future occur to her to wonder occasionally why the servants all seemed to single her out for especially kind treatment and extra cake.

Chapter Twenty-Five

THE SUN HAD gone in and a chill had descended when Angela entered the wood. She picked her way carefully along the rough path. The trees were already more thickly clothed with leaves than they had been a week or two ago when she had last come along here, so she did not see the lake until she came upon it unexpectedly as she rounded a bend and saw the little cove ahead.

She walked down to the edge of the water and dipped her hand into it, letting it trickle through her fingers. It was cold and clear, and she could see that the sand and pebbles sloped gently away without any steep drop. It would certainly have made more sense from the murderer's point of view to kill Edward here, rather than out on the lake where he would be likely to struggle and perhaps tip them both overboard. She half-closed her eyes, trying to visualize the events of that night. In her mind's eye she saw Edward standing by the dark shore, gazing out at the water. Suddenly, he heard something and turned round to see a shadowy figure approaching. Perhaps he nodded curtly and greeted the newcomer. Was he surprised to see him? Or was the meeting prearranged?

What happened after that? Angela pictured the stiff conversation, which gradually intensified into an altercation and then a struggle that Edward Haynes could never win. She imagined him, his arms and legs thrashing in a desperate fight for life as his assailant threw him to the ground and held his head mercilessly under the water until he grew still. Angela saw the murderer rise, panting, and glance contemptuously at the body of his fallen foe before setting to work, stripping off his own things, hefting Edward over his shoulders and lowering him into the rowing-boat. She saw him pull strongly out towards the middle of the lake and then stop to grapple with his load. She could almost hear the grunt and the splash as he consigned Edward to his watery grave. Perhaps he stopped to contemplate his handiwork for a moment or two—or to make sure his victim was truly dead. Then he dived neatly from the boat, causing barely a ripple, and struck back to shore with long, powerful strokes. He must have crept back into the house as quietly as possible, so as not to draw attention to the state of his clothes. Perhaps he had run upstairs and changed into another suit, then come downstairs to rejoin the company. Had he sat in the drawing-room, chatting idly and inwardly congratulating himself on his success? Or perhaps it had all happened after everyone else had gone to bed. There was no way of knowing.

One thing was clear, however: a man had murdered Edward, not a woman. A woman might have poisoned Philippa, or might have pushed Winifred from a height, but it would certainly have taken a man's strength to kill Edward with such violence, such brute force. But who was it?

Deep in her own reflections, Angela forgot the time and was only recalled to herself by the realization that she was getting very chilly. A stiff breeze had got up and she could smell the smoke from the bonfire as it burned elsewhere in the grounds. Her thoughts returned to the suit. As far as she could judge, it might fit any one of the men in the house—except perhaps Robin, who was more slightly built than the others. She would look at it more closely once she got home, and would keep it to give to Inspector Jameson as evidence, should it ever be needed.

She turned and made her way back towards the edge of the woods. Stella would surely be back by now, and Angela was keen to get to the bottom of the girl's mysterious outburst of a few days ago—as well as to fulfil her promise and intercede with her on Donald's behalf. The sky was even darker than before, and it looked as though a cloudburst threatened: there was that eerie silence that often precedes a storm. Angela tramped up the path, hearing nothing except the crunch of her own footsteps as she went. Even the birds were silent, waiting breathlessly for something, it seemed.

She suddenly felt an insect at her ear and brushed at it impatiently, then started in surprise as the air was rent by a sharp *pop!* followed by a cracking noise close by. Angela stared for a second at the pale groove which had suddenly appeared at head height along the edge of a nearby tree trunk, and knew immediately what it was. Quick as lightning, she threw herself to the ground and scrambled round to the other side of the trunk, ripping the knees of her stockings as she did so. She made it by the skin of her teeth—even one second later and she might have been dead, in fact, for immediately another two bangs sounded, followed by a *thunk* as one of the bullets hit the tree behind which she was now crouching.

Once the rushing in her ears and the beating of her heart had subsided, she froze and listened, thanking her stars that she was dressed in dun. For a few minutes the silence was complete, then came a low rumble of thunder. Angela pricked up her ears as she caught the faintest of sounds to her left, as though someone were using the peal as cover to move slowly through the trees. All was quiet again. He would have to make his move some time. Or was he waiting for her to come out? Well, he was a fool if he thought she was mad enough to stand up and reveal herself, or make a run for it. During her intrepid younger days, Angela had learned all sorts of tricks that had proved extremely convenient at the time—although she had never dreamed that she should have to put them to use again more than ten years later, when approaching staid middle-age. Nonetheless, she knew many useful things about how to hide, how to move as quietly as a mouse, and how to escape from sticky situations.

The first thing to do was to get him to show himself, or at least find out where he was. She flattened herself against the tree, keeping as low as possible, and peered round the trunk slowly, but could see nothing. She sat back and chewed her thumb. Did he intend to wait for her to emerge? Surely there was no need for him to do that—after all, he was the one with the gun. Sure enough, after a moment or two she heard someone take a cautious step or two. Then the steps became more certain. Angela grabbed a handful of pebbles and shied them as far as she could. They hit a tree some distance away with a loud rattle. The footsteps stopped and she heard whoever it was moving hurriedly in the direction of the noise. As quickly as she could, Angela wriggled over to a larger clump of trees that afforded better shelter and hid among them. She wanted to see who had attacked her and so peeped carefully through the leaves, trying to get a glimpse. But her shadowy assailant was evidently of the cautious type and there was no-one to be seen.

Angela looked about her. She did not know how good a shot he was, but had no wish to test his skills by providing an easy target for him to practise on. She had the advantage at present, since he did not know where she was hiding, so she judged the best thing to do was to try and creep as far away as possible without being spotted, and then to make a run for it.

Slowly, carefully, she lowered herself onto her stomach and inched her way forward, pausing frequently to listen and being careful to make no sound herself. Her goal was a thick shrub about five yards away, and she reached it without incident. The next move would be more difficult: she wanted to cut through the trees and reach the path further up, but there was a large area of open ground between her and the next patch of undergrowth which would give no cover at all.

There was nothing for it: she would just have to get on with it. Making no sound, she wriggled forward inch by inch. When she had gone a few yards she stopped to listen again. The silence was complete. Had he given it up and gone away? Angela waited another minute or two but heard nothing. She raised her head cautiously, then jumped as something flashed past her left ear this time and thudded into the ground just ahead of her. Throwing caution to the winds, she scrambled at all speed in the direction of the next clump of trees, but had gone barely two yards when the ground gave way beneath her and she plunged into a little gully that had been hidden from view, and where perhaps a stream had once flowed.

Angela gasped as she landed in a mess of dead leaves and cold mud, and lay there for a moment, winded. As she looked about her, she saw that the little channel wound for quite a way in both directions. Above her, the undergrowth grew across it and concealed her from view. This was a stroke of good fortune. With any luck, she could follow the watercourse along its length until she was out of sight of her attacker. As quickly as she could, she crawled in the direction in which she judged the path to lie, but her way shortly curved round and began to meander, and soon Angela had lost her bearings. She set her jaw and pressed on, as there seemed to be no other way out. Soon she was covered from head to toe in mud and filth. 'I shall catch a terrible chill—always assuming I don't catch a bullet in the head first, of course,' she said to herself with grim humour.

She scrambled along the channel for some way, moving as quickly as she could, then finally heard something that filled her with hope. It was the sound of voices talking and laughing nearby. She raised her head and peered out of the ditch, and saw to her relief Briggs and his men standing a little way away, enjoying the bonfire.

Just then, one of them—young Thomas, perhaps—caught sight of her and his mouth dropped open in astonishment. The other men saw him and turned to see what he was looking at, and their eyes grew wide as they beheld the sight of Mrs. Haynes's elegant friend kneeling in a ditch, her clothes and hair caked in mud and leaves.

'Hallo,' said Angela, rather feebly under the circumstances. They continued to stare at the mad lady. 'I'm afraid I fell into this ditch. Could someone help me out, please?'

Briggs recovered himself first and came towards her.

'Right you are, ma'am,' he said. 'Give us a hand, Tom.'

Thomas came forward and they helped her climb out.

'Thank you,' said Angela with as much dignity as she could muster. She took out a handkerchief and wiped her face and hands, then removed her hat and examined it. It was quite ruined. Smoothing her hair and straightening her clothes as best she could, she bade them good day and headed towards the house, leaving them all gazing after her in silence.

Chapter Twenty-six

IT STARTED TO rain. Angela debated her next move. She needed to wash and change her clothes, but had no desire to show herself in the house looking as she did. The best thing to do would be to find Louisa and enlist her help before anybody else saw her. But where was she likely to be at this time of day?

Praying that nobody was about, Angela started towards where she knew the morning-room to be, hoping that Louisa would be there and that she could attract her attention by knocking at the window. But her efforts to remain discreet were doomed to failure, because just then she came up against Inspector Jameson as he left the house through a side door.

'Good God!' he exclaimed involuntarily as he caught sight of her. He recovered himself quickly and put his hand up to his mouth as though to stifle a laugh. 'Isn't it a little chilly to be taking a mud bath?' he asked.

'Yes, it most certainly is,' she replied with some asperity. 'Where is Louisa? I should like to wash.'

'Goodness me!' exclaimed Mrs. Haynes, who had spied Angela through the window and now hurried out to join them. 'What on earth have you been doing, Angela?'

'I shall explain shortly,' said Angela, 'but for now I'd like to get out of these wet things before anybody else sees me. I have already scandalized the groundsmen and expect to be the talk of the village by tomorrow. Inspector, are you going back to town?'

'Yes, I was just leaving,' he said, seeing that something serious had happened. 'May I give you a lift? I have a car.'

'Thank you. That would be most welcome,' she said. 'I shan't be long.' Her teeth had begun to chatter, whether from cold or from shock she could not tell.

Louisa accompanied her upstairs, where she cleaned herself up as best she could and changed into some borrowed clothes, telling her friend merely that she had lost her footing in the woods and fallen into a ditch. Mrs. Haynes pressed her to stay longer and take some time to recover from her ordeal, but Angela was anxious to get away as soon as possible and excused herself.

'But I can't let you leave without even a cup of warm milk,' exclaimed Louisa.

'Really, I shall be quite all right,' said Angela. 'A hot bath at home is all I need. Why,' she went on to herself. 'I do believe I'm in a blue funk. Thank goodness I have a tame policeman to take me home before I make any more of an exhibition of myself than I already have.'

'By the way, this is for you, from Briggs,' said Louisa, taking a parcel from a table as they passed through the hall and handing it to Angela. 'He said to tell you that they're delicious served with just a dab of butter. Spring greens,' she explained on seeing Angela's mystified expression.

'Ah,' said Angela, enlightened. 'Tell him thank you very much.'

She took the parcel and went out to where the inspector was waiting for her by the car.

'Please, I'd like to go,' she said. She was feeling a little light-headed.

Jameson looked at her and realized that something was very amiss.

'Why certainly,' he said. 'Start the car, Willis,' he commanded the sergeant who was acting as driver.

Once they were safely on their way, Angela sagged back in her seat and closed her eyes for a moment. Then she straightened up, took a deep breath, looked the inspector directly in the eye and said, 'Inspector Jameson, I must apologize for not heeding your advice of the other day. I'm afraid you're going to think I've made the most awful fool of myself.'

'Why? What do you mean?' he asked, startled by her serious tone.

'Somebody tried to kill me in the woods not an hour ago,' she said.

Jameson sat up.

'Tell me what happened,' he said.

'Someone shot at me. Not just once, but several times. I was quite fortunate to escape.'

'Who was it?'

'I couldn't see him. He was hiding, or I was hiding, and we were never in view at one and the same time.' She grimaced in frustration. 'I'm very cross that I didn't manage to catch a glimpse of him. Or her,' she added. 'It could have been a woman, I suppose.'

She recounted the whole story to him and he listened in great consternation.

'I know you're going to tell me I should have been more careful,' she said, forestalling him as he opened his mouth to speak, 'and you're right. It was silly of me, but stupidly, I didn't believe the first attempt on my life was a serious one. Evidently I was wrong.'

Jameson shook his head in remonstrance but said nothing.

'But are you quite sure you are not hurt in any way?' he asked.

'Apart from a blow to my pride and a few grazes to my hands and knees, I am perfectly all right,' she replied.

'That is a great relief to me,' he said. His eyes were full of genuine concern but he attempted to make a joke of it. 'I am already in trouble with the super over the Robin Haynes fiasco, and I should hate to have to stand before him and explain the death of an amateur detective who was working on this case with my full knowledge.'

Angela smiled wanly, but inside she was furious with herself. How could she have been stupid enough to allow herself to fall into such a trap? She had known that somebody wished her harm and yet she had ignored the warnings of the police and walked into the woods in the most self-satisfied manner possible. And why had she very nearly lost her head? She would not have panicked like that in the forests of Belgium—although other lives besides her own were at stake then. Still, she could have kicked herself in vexation at her own incompetence.

Inspector Jameson was still talking.

'Now, Mrs. Marchmont,' he said, 'I really think it is time for you to withdraw from the case and let the police take over. An attempted murder gives us all the grounds we require to reopen the investigation officially, especially now that Robin has disappeared and there is some question about his financial dealings with his aunt.'

Angela narrowed her eyes and set her jaw. Oddly enough, the inspector's words were just the tonic she needed.

'I shall be more than happy to relinquish the chief of the responsibility to you,' she replied. 'You have resources that I lack. I cannot legally search Robin's house, for example, or arrest and question him. But you mustn't think for a moment that I have any intention of retiring altogether. I have put myself to some inconvenience over the past week or two for my friend Louisa's sake, and I think it is fair to say that I have made some progress in my inquiries. But there are still many things I want to find out. There are still many questions that remain unanswered and I intend to answer them. Inspector, I don't know who it was who came after me today, but let me tell you I absolutely *refuse* to be frightened off by whoever it was.'

'I do believe that your mysterious antagonist has rather put your back up,' said the inspector admiringly.

'Indeed he has,' said Angela firmly. 'I may have had a moment of weakness earlier, but I shall choose to attribute that to my dismay at the unnecessary destruction of a very expensive pair of silk stockings. However, you should be aware that, in general, I do not allow myself to be overcome by adversity.'

'I know it well,' smiled Jameson. 'I have heard it all from my brother.'

'Then please let me continue investigating alongside you, inspector,' she said. 'I should hate to have to stop just as I am starting to get somewhere.'

'To be perfectly truthful, Mrs. Marchmont, there's nothing I can do within the law to stop you from continuing your inquiries if you wish it,' replied the inspector, 'so from that point of view you are safe from me. In addition, I have seen and heard something of your capabilities and I assure you I have as much faith in you as I should in a fellow Scotland Yard man.'

Angela was flattered, especially in view of her earlier carelessness. She blushed slightly.

'However,' he went on, 'If we are to work together I think it only fair that you tell me what you have discovered so far, otherwise I shall be working in the dark.'

'Yes, of course,' said Angela. 'Well, then, I have something for you here.'

She unwrapped the parcel on her lap and showed its contents to the inspector.

'What is that?' asked Jameson.

'I can't prove it, but I believe it is the dinner suit worn by the killer of Edward Haynes on the night of his murder.'

The inspector whistled.

'I say,' he said, and took the jacket from her to look more closely at it. 'Where did you find it?'

'It was shoved under a heap of garden waste to be burned,' replied Mrs. Marchmont. 'Briggs the gardener rescued it and showed it to me quite by chance.'

'It's a pity he didn't find it before the fire was lit,' observed Jameson. 'But why did the murderer get rid of it?'

'Why, if he was wearing it when he drowned Edward, then the sleeves of the jacket and the lower legs of the trousers must have got soaking wet at the very least—if not completely ruined, and the servants might have talked if anyone decided to investigate. By getting rid of the suit he avoided awkward questions about what happened to it. Difficult to explain why one's dinner things are drenched, I imagine. I wonder why he decided to get rid of it today, of all days. I assume he has kept it hidden up to now.'

'Probably because you came along,' said Jameson. 'You have evidently put the wind up him—that's why he tried to kill you. But what have you found out that scared him so much? Granted, the first attempt on you may well have been an afterthought as he tried to get the photograph back, but what about today? Today was deliberate.'

'I don't know,' said Angela.

'Who knew that you had taken the path down to the lake?'

'Donald saw me go,' said Angela, 'and so did Briggs. Perhaps one of them mentioned it to somebody—or perhaps somebody even saw me from one of the windows.'

'Hmm,' said Jameson. 'What about Donald Haynes? He seems something of a hothead from what I have seen of him. Could he be behind all this? You said he had a bee in his bonnet about Underwood House, just like his father. Didn't you say he was spouting some kind of nonsense about the house trying to get rid of its enemies? That sounds a little unbalanced to me. Perhaps he has a monomania on the subject.'

'He is certainly an intense young man, but I don't believe that his rather unusual attitude to the house is a good enough motive for murder,' said Angela carefully.

The inspector eyed her suspiciously.

'You have something up your sleeve,' he said. 'That's not fair play. Come on, out with it.'

Angela paused.

'Yes, I confess I do have the germ of an idea, but I should like to look into it first before I tell you about it. I am in something of a delicate position, as you know, and I have no wish to unleash a scandal at this stage by getting the police involved. I promise I shall tell you all as soon as I have looked into it myself,' she went on quickly as she saw him about to protest, 'but you must remember that Louisa is one of my oldest friends and I shouldn't like to hurt her.'

'This is not a question of friendship, Mrs. Marchmont,' said Jameson. 'It is a question of murder, and all else must give way before it.'

'Naturally,' said Angela. 'I hope you don't believe for one second that I should put considerations of friendship above those of justice.'

'No,' he replied. 'I saw for myself in the Norfolk case that you are a woman who acts with integrity when the occasion calls for it.'

She lowered her eyes, then looked up again.

'Then please trust me on this occasion too. I promise I shall not withhold any secrets unnecessarily.'

'Very well,' he said reluctantly. 'But could you perhaps give me just a hint of what is on your mind?'

Angela smiled.

'I don't see why not. I am still not satisfied about Philip Haynes's will. I am almost certain that there is more to it than meets the eye, and that he intended to provide for someone who is not mentioned by name in the document, by means of a secret trust administered by Mr. Faulkner, the solicitor who drew up the will and the person who supposedly benefits from the deaths of Philip's children. Mr. Faulkner denies all knowledge of any such trust—as of course is only to be expected given his presumed position in the matter, but if I am correct, then he must know about it. I believe, too—although I have no evidence—that Ursula Haynes also knows or suspects something about the will, but has chosen to keep that knowledge to herself at present.'

'You think, then, that the secret beneficiary of the will is also the murderer?'

'That is what I intend to find out,' said Angela.

'And how do you propose to do that, if Mr. Faulkner denies the existence of the trust altogether?'

'I plan to do a little research on my own account,' she replied.

'And when will you tell me the results?'

'As soon as I have found out what I want to know,' she assured him. 'Tomorrow, I hope. Time is running short: it is the 27th of May in two days. The family will be gathering at Underwood House and I am concerned that there may be trouble.'

'Shall you be there?'

'Yes, Louisa has invited me to observe the proceedings. I'm not quite sure what I expect to happen, but I should like to be on the spot just in case.'

'Be careful, I beg of you, Mrs. Marchmont,' said Jameson.

'Don't worry, I shall,' said Angela grimly. 'Someone has made a fool of me twice recently, but rest assured I shan't let it happen a third time.'

Chapter Twenty-seven

'I SHOULD LIKE to ask a great favour of you, William,' said Mrs. Marchmont, as the young chauffeur stood before her in an attitude of polite attention. 'I believe somebody is trying to kill me.'

William's eyebrows rose.

'Naturally, this is a matter of no little concern,' said his mistress. 'To me, at any rate. I wanted to ask you, therefore, if you would be willing to act as a sort of bodyguard for me, at least for the next few days.' She held up a hand. 'Before you reply, please believe that I know you already to be a plucky young man, so don't think you have to accept in order to prove your worth. Please don't suppose I shall think any the worse of you if you say no. The task might be a dangerous one and I absolutely forbid you to put your life in danger purely because you fear for your situation.'

William's face had been growing increasingly pink and indignant during this speech.

'Why, I ought to be mighty offended that you should doubt me for even a second,' was all he said.

Angela gave him her broadest smile.

'Of course, I knew I should be able to rely on you,' she said. 'But it would have been very rude of me not to allow you the chance to say no.'

'I never say no to a lady in distress,' he said with dignity.

'Then I shall say no more,' said Angela, 'and after this case is all over we shall see about giving you a holiday in return for the extra duties now. I believe it is your birthday next month?'

He nodded.

'Good. You shall take two days then if you like.'

William grinned.

'I won't say no to that either,' he said.

'Very well,' replied Angela. 'Now, today I want to—' she broke off suddenly. William waited politely for a minute or two but she appeared to have forgotten his presence entirely as she sat, frozen, staring at the wall just over his left shoulder.

'Ma'am?' he prompted after a little while. She seemed not to hear, but continued to gaze, unseeing, at nothing. Finally she exhaled sharply and looked at him as though noticing him for the first time.

'Did I say two days?' she said in a tone of suppressed excitement. 'I meant a week. Take a week, William. Now, you may go.'

The young man looked at her oddly but had the good sense to leave the room without question before she changed her mind. Ten minutes later he was summoned back into the living-room by the violent ringing of the bell.

'Ah, William, there you are,' said Angela briskly, as though their earlier conversation had never happened. 'Bring round the Bentley, please. We are going out.'

'Right away, ma'am,' he said. 'Where are we going?'

'Somerset House,' replied Angela. 'I seem to be turning into quite a regular visitor there lately.'

Twenty minutes later they were motoring down Berkeley Street towards Piccadilly.

'I don't suppose you saw anyone suspicious outside the flat, did you?' she asked William.

'No-one, ma'am,' he replied, 'and I was keeping a sharp eye out. I think we're safe for now.'

'Good,' said Angela. She had great faith in William's sharp eye.

'You had better come in with me,' she said as they arrived at the Register Office. 'You can help me in my search.'

By noon she had returned to the Mount Street flat and was on the telephone to Scotland Yard. Inspector Jameson was away, following an urgent lead, she was informed. Someone bearing a close resemblance to Robin Haynes had been spotted in Aberdeen and the inspector had gone after him. He was not expected back until tomorrow at the earliest. Would Mrs. Marchmont like to leave a message? Yes, Mrs. Marchmont would be delighted to leave a message. She briefly communicated what she had learned to the voice at the other end of the line, and asked that the inspector be given the information as soon as possible. The voice promised to do so, and Angela hung up, hoping that the news would reach him soon.

She rang for William.

'Tomorrow we go down to Underwood House again,' she told him, 'and this is your chance to have a little adventure.'

The young man beamed.

'I'm game,' he said.

'Good,' said Angela. She coughed. 'I ought to warn you, however, that what I am about to propose may not be entirely legal.'

William's expression gave her to understand that, legal or illegal, it was all the same to him, but all he said was, 'Yes, ma'am.'

'Very well,' said Angela, and began to speak. He listened carefully and nodded.

'As I said, I only caught a glimpse of it, but I am almost certain that it forms at least part of what we are looking for,' she finished.

'If it's there, I'll find it,' promised William.

'There may be other things, but we don't want to arouse suspicion so I advise you to leave them where they are.'

'I get it,' he said.

'Mind, this person is very dangerous, and has already attempted to kill me twice. Be very sure, therefore, to avoid being caught. And don't run any unnecessary risks.'

'No fear of that,' he replied. 'You promised me a week's holiday and I'd hate to miss it.'

'Did I? So I did. What on earth was I thinking?'

William made his escape again.

The next afternoon they ran down to Underwood House. It was unseasonably warm for May and there was a closeness in the air that promised thunder. Angela wondered whether she was doing the right thing, or whether she should have left the entire matter in the hands of Inspector Jameson. But it was the 27th and the inspector was away, and she was dreadfully worried about what might happen today. Was the killer planning to strike again? If so, it was up to her to stop him if at all possible. She checked her handbag for the fourth or fifth time to make quite certain she had brought what she needed. She should not be caught unawares this time.

They drew up before the front door and Angela alighted.

'Remember, be careful,' she said to William.

'I will,' he promised.

'I am relying on you. You may send a message to me when you have done it and I shall come out immediately.'

She was shown into the drawing-room, where she found Louisa and Stella listening politely to Susan Dennison, who was holding court, swathed in layers of gold and orange and reclining superbly on a chaise longue. Susan nodded distantly to Angela and went on talking.

'Naturally, I take my inspiration from the latest European artists,' she was saying. 'One finds that English painters have no real sense of the *self*. It is so important to have that vital connection to one's inner essence; to shake off the constraints of the super-ego and embrace what the Germans call the *Es*, that is, our deepest, basest instinct. Only then can true Art emerge. I myself bring forth my *Es* every morning by circling the room three times on all fours, howling like a wolf.'

'Hallo, Angela,' said Louisa as soon as Susan paused for breath. 'As you can see, Ursula has not arrived yet but she will be here soon.'

'Has there been any news of Robin?' asked Angela, although she already knew the answer.

'Not yet. He has disappeared into thin air, it seems,' said Louisa.

'Taking Mother's money with him, I understand,' said Susan. 'I always thought there was something untrustworthy about him.'

'It might be better not to say anything to Ursula about that, my dear,' said Louisa. 'She will be dreadfully upset. The police are doing their best to find him and bring him back, so there's no use in making a fuss when we can't do anything about it.'

'I do believe she is upset,' said Angela. 'She came to see me the other day as she wanted me to find him. You will be kind to her, won't you, Louisa? She may look tough on the outside but I know she does feel it dreadfully.'

'Of course I will,' said Louisa, 'although she does make it rather difficult for one.'

Donald Haynes entered the room and looked immediately at Stella, who turned her head away. Angela was reminded that she had not yet had the opportunity to keep her promise and intercede on his behalf. He greeted Angela with a smile, then threw himself carelessly into a window-seat.

'Where is everybody?' he asked.

'Ursula hasn't arrived yet,' said Louisa. 'I don't know where your father is, but Guy is out today and won't be back until later.'

'Our gatherings are getting smaller and smaller,' he observed. 'There used to be quite a crowd of us but our numbers are dwindling. Who will die today, I wonder?'

Chapter Twenty-Eight

A BRIEF SILENCE followed his words.

'Donald!' said his mother after a second. 'Don't say foolish things like that, please. You forget we have company.'

Stella pressed her lips together and glared at him angrily. He looked a little ashamed.

'I'm sorry,' he said. 'It was meant to be a joke.'

'Well that kind of joke isn't funny,' said Louisa. 'Stella, ring the bell for tea, please.'

Donald jumped up and left the room.

'Oh dear, we seem to have started already,' sighed Louisa.

Angela made a valiant attempt to turn the conversation to the more neutral topic of her recent trip to France, and had some success, although she was amused to find that, within a very short time, Miss Dennison had led the talk away from that subject and back towards herself and her Art. This fascinating theme carried them all the way through tea, and Susan was just beginning to expound at length upon the technical incompetence and spiritual inferiority of the Italian Renaissance painters in comparison with herself, when Ursula arrived.

She entered the room with her usual erect bearing and economy of movement, and greeted them all frostily, nodding at Angela. There was no sign of the woman who had begged for help the other day; she was as poised and composed as ever. For a few moments, Angela was convinced that she would carry off the meeting with no mention of Robin at all, and was therefore astonished when Ursula went over to Miss Dennison and stood before her.

'The police have informed me that my son has been engaging in various illicit activities,' she said stiffly to Susan. 'They also believe that he may have persuaded your mother to give him all her money to invest, but instead used it to make up his losses from speculation. Unpleasant as it is to hear such accusations levelled against my only son, I am not a woman who shies away from the truth. When I was first told of the matter, I refused to believe that Robin was capable of such crimes. However, I have now had a few days in which to reflect, and have been forced to face the distasteful possibility that he may in fact be guilty.

'Nevertheless, while he may have failed in his duties as a son and an honest man, I am his mother and shall stand by him to the end. He will need my support—especially to fight the other absurd allegation against him, which is that he killed Winifred in cold blood.'

Susan stared at her in astonishment, speechless for once. Evidently no-one had told her of this.

'Dishonest he may be,' went on Ursula, turning to Louisa, 'but a murderer he is not, and I shall not stand to one side as his name is dragged through the mud for a crime he did not commit. I will fight the accusations to the last.'

'Naturally, my dear,' said Louisa. 'I shouldn't expect anything less of you.'

Ursula looked slightly disconcerted, as though she had expected a different reaction.

'I must warn you, Louisa,' she said. 'I shall not remain silent and see my son hanged for murder.'

'Well, we shall have to see what we can do to help,' said Louisa. 'Now, do sit down and have some tea and a scone. You are looking far too thin. Why, I'll bet you haven't eaten in days.'

Just then, Annie the maid came in and informed Mrs. Marchmont that her driver had an important message for her. She excused herself and went out to find William waiting for her in the hall. His broad smile told her that she was not about to be disappointed.

'Well? What have you got for me?' she asked in a low voice, so as not to be overheard.

'I reckon I got the goods all right, but they weren't where you said they'd be,' he replied. His jacket and the knees of his trousers were dusty.

'Tell me,' Angela commanded.

'Well,' he began, 'the first opportunity I got I slipped away quietly and went to the room you directed me to. The door was unlocked so I got in with no difficulty at all and wasted not a minute in setting to work and scouting around. I searched carefully through the things in the drawers of the little writing-table that was in there, but nothing turned up—not even so much as a tailor's bill. Then I went into the wardrobe and rifled through the pockets of all the clothes in there, but still no luck. I looked everywhere I could think of—darn near took the room apart, as a matter of fact, but there was nothing, so I came out again, wondering whether maybe it was all in a safe somewhere, and whether I was wasting my time.

'Then, as luck would have it, I was walking back along the landing when a little door opened just as I was passing, and a housemaid came out carrying what looked like an old vase. I wouldn't have even noticed the door if it hadn't been for her, as it was set back in a kind of recess. Anyhow, I stopped to pass the time of day with her and she told me, among other things, that the door led to the attic stairs. Oh, said I, so that must be where the family keep all their odds and ends that they've got no use for, am I right? And she said yes, the attic was full of things—old things, new things, things that had no place anywhere else and a lot more besides. Then she told me off for keeping her from her work, but with a kind of smile on her face so I knew she wasn't all that serious, and went away.

'Naturally, I went straight through that door and up the stairs to the attic, and I'm blowed if she wasn't right. It was like a regular Aladdin's cave up there. My first thought was that it would take weeks to search through it all, but then I started examining some of the things and saw that quite a few of them were marked with names. There was one thing in particular that caught my eye as being likely to hold what I was looking for. It was sitting on top of an old writing-desk and was one of those little document cases with an inlaid wooden lid—you've probably seen the kind of thing I mean. And what was most interesting about it was that it was monogrammed with a particular set of initials that might be familiar to you.

'I picked the box up and tried to open it, but it was locked. I hadn't seen a key anywhere in the bedroom so I assumed the owner of the box must carry it around at all times. For a minute or two I was stumped, but then I remembered what you said about the person being dangerous and maybe planning another murder, and I figured that if it was a question of saving somebody's life, then in this case the end justified the means.'

He paused and looked a little sheepish.

'What did you do?' asked Angela in some concern.

'I broke the lock,' he said. 'It was the only way,' he went on hurriedly at the sight of Angela's alarmed expression. 'I couldn't have gotten into it otherwise.'

'Well, it can't be helped now,' said Angela, 'although the owner of the box will now find out that all has been discovered. Perhaps you ought to go back up and hide it somewhere.'

'Too late,' said William. 'That's what I was getting to. I was looking through the papers in the box, my heart in my mouth, when I swear I heard a creak, followed by the sound of someone stifling a gasp, for all the world as though somebody was up there, watching me. I don't mind telling you I almost jumped out of my skin. I leapt up and shouted, "Who's there?"—mostly to prove to myself I wasn't a coward, to tell the truth—but nobody replied. I wanted to run away as fast as I could, but I forced myself to stay and find out who it was.

I grabbed one of the most likely-looking papers and put the box back, then went on a little hunt.

'There was a big old armoire standing in one corner, which looked like a possible hiding-place, so I crept over on tiptoe and peered round it. I didn't find anyone, but you'll never guess what I did find.'

'What?' said Angela.

'Why, there was a little makeshift bed, with a candle next to it, half burnt down, and the remains of some food and drink. It looked for all the world as though someone was living up there. Is it customary to put guests in the attic around these parts? I've heard these great families can be a little eccentric.'

'Not as far as I know,' said Angela. 'What happened next?'

'Well, by that time my nerves were getting the better of me, so I thought I would just take one more quick look around and then go. At that moment, I heard a sneeze quite close by, and—well I hate to say it, but I completely lost my head. I ran out of the door as fast as I could and shot down the stairs, and kept on running until I reached the kitchen.'

He looked so horrified at himself that Angela could not help laughing.

'Never mind,' she said. 'I should have done the same myself. You have done well—although it is a little unfortunate that you had to break the box open. We have now well and truly revealed our hand.'

'Only if the owner of the box happens to go up to the attic in the next day or two,' said William. 'You never know—the person in question might have better things to do for a while.'

'Let us hope so,' said Angela. 'Now, let me see the paper you took from the box.'

William reached into his inside pocket and handed over a folded sheet of letter paper. 'Is this what you were looking for?' he asked.

Angela glanced at it.

'Let us see,' she said. She perused it carefully, the furrows on her brow deepening with every passing second. Finally, she looked up at William with troubled eyes.

'Well?' he asked. 'Is it any good?'

'You have done well, William,' she said. 'This is extremely useful. And now we must find Mr. Faulkner as soon as possible. I believe he may be in grave danger.'

Chapter Twenty-Nine

WILLIAM WAS JUST about to ask a question when the front door opened and Guy Fisher came in. Angela folded up the letter and pocketed it smoothly, then nodded to William, who retired respectfully to hover in the background.

'Hallo, Mrs. Marchmont,' said Guy. 'Is everyone here? Have I missed anything thrilling? If I go into the drawing-room, shall I see Ursula and Susan grappling at each other's throats in unseemly fashion?'

'I do hope not,' said Angela. 'They were conversing quite politely when I came out.'

'A pity,' he said. 'It would add a certain piquancy to the proceedings, don't you agree?'

He went off, and Angela beckoned to William again.

'Quick,' she said. 'I am going to telephone Mr. Faulkner, and I shall need you to keep a look-out in case anybody comes. Or one person in particular, at any rate.'

'Got it,' he said.

Angela picked up the receiver and asked to be put through to Mr. Faulkner's office. After a short wait, an unfamiliar voice came on the line.

'Hawley speaking,' it said.

'Hallo, Mr. Hawley,' said Angela, 'this is Mrs. Marchmont. I wonder if I might speak to Mr. Faulkner. It's rather urgent.'

'I am sorry, Mrs. Marchmont, but I'm afraid he is not here at present,' said the clerk.

'Do you know where I might find him?'

'Well—' said Mr. Hawley hesitantly. There was a note of worry in his voice. 'To be frank with you, I don't know where he is. He did not come to the office today and has left no word of his whereabouts.'

Angela's heart sank.

'Is it usual for him to tell you where he is going?'

'Yes,' said Hawley.

'Have you tried calling him at home?'

'Yes, I telephoned this afternoon but no-one answered. Do you think he might be ill?'

Angela made a decision.

'Wait in the office, if you please,' she said. 'I shall be there in a few minutes. We must find him, and quickly. I only hope we are not too late.' She hung up, leaving Mr. Hawley feeling anything but reassured.

'No go?' asked William.

'He did not come into the office today,' she replied. 'Go and get the car quickly, William. There is not a moment to be lost.'

He ran off and Angela scribbled a note to Louisa. She had no intention of announcing her departure to the entire family.

'Give that to Mrs. Haynes, please,' she said, handing it to a passing servant. 'And be sure to put it in her hands yourself. I shall be back soon to explain further.'

She ran out to the Bentley and they set off to drive the half-mile into the village. When the car drew up on the edge of the square she spied the face of Mr. Hawley peering expectantly out of the window of Mr. Faulkner's office. He came out to greet her.

'Do you believe something untoward has happened to him?' he asked.

'I hope not,' Angela replied, 'but I suggest we go to his house and see if he is there. Perhaps he has been taken ill and could not answer the telephone. Does he live alone, by the way?'

'Yes.'

'No servants?'

'He has a woman who comes in from the village, but she does not live with him.'

'Then let us go. You shall show us the way.'

Mr. Hawley got into the Bentley and they set off. Mr. Faulkner's house was at the end of a lane quite on the edge of Beningfleet. It was square and comfortable, with a well-tended garden. The three of them alighted from the car and approached the front door. Hawley rang the bell and they waited. There was no answer.

'I wonder if his housekeeper came today,' said Angela. 'Does she have a key?'

'That I do not know,' said the clerk.

William was peering in through the window.

'I can't see anything,' he said. He moved to another window and peered again.

'Ma'am,' he said suddenly. There was a note of urgency in his voice. Angela joined him and he pointed wordlessly at something. Angela drew a sharp breath.

'We must get into the house somehow,' she said.

'What is it?' asked Hawley, sounding frightened.

'Blood, if I'm not much mistaken,' said William. He picked up a small rock from the garden. 'Stand back,' he said.

'Not that window,' said Angela. 'We must preserve all the evidence as much as possible. Try this one here. It's the dining-room and it doesn't look as though anybody has been in it.'

William wrapped his hand carefully in his handkerchief and gave a smart blow to the window with the rock. The glass gave way with a loud tinkle. He reached carefully inside and loosened the catch.

'Can you give me a leg up?' he asked Mr. Hawley.

White in the face, the clerk did as he was asked. William levered himself cautiously up and across the window-sill.

'Watch out for the broken glass,' said Angela. 'Now, go to the front door and let us in.'

William nodded and disappeared. A few seconds later there was a rattle at the door and it opened. Angela entered, with Mr. Hawley following unwillingly behind. William held up a slip of paper.

'I found this just here inside the door,' he said. 'It's a note from the housekeeper saying that she came this morning but couldn't get in.'

Angela glanced at it then looked round. They were in a gloomy entrance-hall panelled all in wood. Around the walls were hunting scenes and prints of horses. The place was almost silent: no noise could be heard other than the ominous ticking of a grandfather clock which stood in one corner. Angela noticed that a chair next to it looked quite new. She raised her head and sniffed the air. There was a smell of fresh paint.

'I believe he has been decorating,' she said.

She looked into the dining-room.

'New furniture, too,' said William, at her shoulder. 'I guess he's been spending some of his hard-earned cash lately.'

'Yes,' she said, but made no other comment. They reached the door of the living-room and William pushed it open.

'Must I—must I come in?' asked Mr. Hawley faintly. 'I am not altogether fond of the sight of blood.'

'Sit here, then,' said Angela. She left the clerk in the hall and followed William into the living-room. There was no mistaking what had happened. They stared for a few moments at the thing on the floor. Mr. Faulkner was lying on his back, his gaze fixed unseeing on the ceiling. The handle of what looked like a large kitchen knife protruded starkly from his chest, and a pool of dark liquid congealed around him.

'Stabbed through the heart,' said William. He moved forward.

'Don't touch him,' said Angela. 'The police will want to examine him.'

'I guess his luck ran out,' said William.

'He was playing a very dangerous game,' said Angela. 'His luck was bound to run out eventually. I suppose he thought he had played his cards very cleverly, but he reckoned without the fact that murder comes easily to someone who has already killed three times.'

'Oh Lord!' cried Mr. Hawley, who had plucked up the courage to join them and who was now staring, aghast, at the sight before him. 'Mr Faulkner! Who could have done such a terrible thing?'

'We must call the police at once,' said Angela. 'William, take Mr. Hawley out to the car. I shall telephone from here.'

William escorted the poor clerk outside, while Angela telephoned the local police and Scotland Yard and then came out to wait with them. After a short time a police sergeant on a bicycle came puffing up to the house.

'Now then, Mr. Hawley, what's all this nonsense I hear about Mr. Faulkner getting himself murdered?' he said, removing his hat and wiping the perspiration from his forehead.

'Oh, Sergeant Peters, here you are at last. No, no, it's not nonsense at all,' cried Hawley. 'Why, I saw it with my own eyes: his dead body lying in a pool of blood in his own living-room.'

'Good Lord!' exclaimed the sergeant. 'I thought it was just a silly prank by one of the boys in the village. You can't mean to say it's true?'

'I'm very much afraid it is, sergeant,' said Mrs. Marchmont. 'Allow me to show you. Unfortunately, we were forced to break into the house, but otherwise we have tried to touch as little as possible.'

She led Sergeant Peters inside and showed him where the body lay. As soon as he saw it, he stiffened and his manner became brisk and business-like. He was an officer of the law doing his duty, and he was now in charge. He ushered her from the house and eyed her suspiciously.

'Might I ask your name, madam? And what exactly brought you to this house?'

'My name is Mrs. Angela Marchmont,' said Angela, 'and I came to Mr. Faulkner's house because I suspected that his life was in danger. Unfortunately, it seems I was right.'

The policeman looked disbelieving.

'It is rather a long story,' said Angela, 'but perhaps it will make more sense to you when I tell you that this murder is connected to the recent deaths at Underwood House.' She fumbled in her bag and brought out something which she handed to him. 'In case you don't believe me, here is the card of Inspector Jameson of Scotland Yard. He has been investigating this case and I have been assisting him in his inquiries.'

The sergeant examined the card carefully. He still seemed a little doubtful.

'I have called Scotland Yard,' she went on. 'Inspector Jameson is on his way back from the North and they will send him down as soon as they can, but in the meantime we are to leave things in the hands of the Beningfleet police.'

Whether Peters would ever have believed her is a matter of some doubt, but fortunately for Angela a car then drew up carrying the local inspector, who had been rudely summoned from a quiet afternoon's fishing with news of violent happenings. It was he who had originally called in Scotland Yard to look into the mysterious deaths at the big house, and he knew Inspector Jameson well. He agreed to Angela's being allowed to leave on condition that she remain at Underwood House until the next day. She promised to do so and departed with William and Mr. Hawley, who was now looking rather faint.

They took the clerk home to his wife and then headed back to Underwood.

'Well, ma'am, I'll admit that I wasn't sure whether or not to believe you when you said there was a murderer about,' said William, 'but now I have to say you've got me convinced.'

'That is a great reassurance to me,' said Angela dryly.

'So, what's the plan now?' asked William.

'I'm not entirely sure there is one,' said Angela, 'but I should like to go into the attic myself and have a closer look at that box of papers before our quarry discovers that they have been disturbed.'

'But it's too late,' he replied. 'Don't you remember? Whoever was watching me in the attic saw me do it.'

'Ah, yes,' said Angela. 'The mysterious spy in the attic.'

'You don't seem too bothered about him.'

Angela smiled to herself.

'I think he has other things to worry about besides a box of letters,' she said. William glanced back at her curiously but she said no more.

'So, it's back to Underwood for more fun. These Hayneses are more trouble than a nest of vipers.'

'They are certainly a very *unusual* family,' she agreed.

'Do you need me to stand by again this evening, ma'am?'

'Yes. I have the feeling that something is going to happen very soon.'

'Like what?'

Angela wrinkled her brow and stared out of the window. The sky was black and it looked as though a storm were brewing.

'I don't exactly know,' she said, 'but whatever it is, I hope it will put an end to this business once and for all, without anybody else getting hurt. By killing Mr. Faulkner, the murderer has now killed the goose that lays the golden eggs. He must have been very desperate to do such a thing, and now he has cornered himself. He could do almost anything.' She leaned forward to emphasize her words. 'We must tread carefully, William. Somebody very dangerous is in our midst.'

CHAPTER THIRTY

IT WAS ALMOST seven o'clock when they drew up at the house.

'Everyone will be dressing for dinner,' said Angela. 'I had better do so too or I shall be late. William, be ready for my call. I don't know quite what is going to happen, but I should like you to be there when it does.'

She hurried upstairs and made a hasty toilet, throwing on her evening gown and adding, as an afterthought, a crimson velvet evening jacket with wide, draped sleeves. She smoothed her hair in front of the looking-glass, smiling as she thought how horrified Marthe would be at the perfunctory nature of her preparations, then returned downstairs to the drawing-room.

She was not quite the last to arrive. John and Susan were absent, but Louisa, Stella, Ursula, Guy and Donald were all dressed and making desultory conversation. Louisa gave her a significant look. She was obviously dying to ask where Angela had been but could not without throwing discretion to the winds. Guy had no such qualms, however.

'Why, it's our Angela, returned from her mysterious outing. Where on earth have you been, Mrs. Marchmont? We quite missed you. We have all spent the last two hours listening to Miss Euphrosyne and her theories on the nature of Art. I stifled my yawns as best I could but I believe at least one escaped through my left ear while I was holding my mouth shut.'

'Hush!' scolded Louisa. 'She may come in at any moment and hear you.'

'I'm afraid I was called away on urgent business,' said Angela. She took a deep breath and went on boldly, 'It appears that Mr. Faulkner, the solicitor, has been murdered.'

There were gasps of dismay and everyone began to ask questions at once. As soon as she was given the opportunity, Angela recounted briefly the events of the past two hours. Rather than reveal her part in the discovery of the body, she gave them to understand that she had been summoned to Mr. Faulkner's house by the police.

'But why should anyone want to murder Mr. Faulkner?' said Louisa.

'I can think of lots of reasons,' said Donald. 'As a solicitor he must have been privy to many secrets. Perhaps somebody wanted to close his mouth forever.'

'Of course somebody wanted to close his mouth,' said Ursula in a high, clear voice.

Everybody fell silent. Angela was instantly on the alert.

'What do you mean?' asked Louisa.

Ursula turned to her.

'You know exactly what I mean, Louisa,' she said. 'He knew far too much about this family and its dark history, and so he had to be silenced.'

'There you go again,' broke in Donald impatiently, 'dropping hints about who knows what. Why can't you just say what you mean?'

Ursula rose and walked over to the young man with deliberate steps. She stood before him and looked into his eyes.

'You of all people ask me why I do not speak up?' she said.

'Yes,' exclaimed Donald. 'I am sick of all this mystery. People keep dying and I should like to know why. You say you know something, Aunt Ursula, so why don't you just tell us what it is and stop all this beating about the bush?'

Something that might have been a short bark of laughter escaped Ursula's lips.

'Very well, then,' she said. 'I accept your challenge. Let it be said out loud for once. Absurd and dramatic as it may sound, we have a murderer among us. Tell me, Donald, why did you do it? Was he threatening to tell everybody your secret?'

Donald took a moment or two to realize that she was addressing him directly.

'What are you talking about?' he said, after a pause.

'Did he want money? He was a venal old fool. Perhaps that was his undoing.'

Angela remembered the smell of fresh paint in Mr. Faulkner's house, and the new furniture.

'Are you accusing me of murder?' said Donald, as Ursula's meaning dawned upon him. 'Have you gone quite mad?'

'I am not mad, no,' she replied. 'But perhaps you are. I have heard it said that most people who kill are mentally unhinged.'

'Mentally unhinged?' repeated Donald, going quite red in the face. 'Why, I am as sane as anybody here. If anybody is unhinged it is you.'

'Where were you this afternoon, Don?' asked Stella suddenly. 'I was looking for you because I wanted to talk to you, but I couldn't find you anywhere in the house.'

Ursula looked triumphantly towards Donald as though to say, 'You see? I am not the only person to have noticed.'

'Why—why—' Donald stuttered. 'I was—I don't know. I can't remember. Probably out in the grounds somewhere. Does it matter?' This attack from two fronts seemed to have quite overwhelmed him.

'It matters to me,' said Stella, so quietly that her words were almost inaudible.

'Of course Donald didn't kill anybody,' said Louisa. 'Ursula, what on earth makes you think he did? What could he possibly have to gain from it?'

'Isn't it obvious?' replied Ursula. 'He did it for the money that Philip left him.'

'What money?' demanded Donald. 'Grandfather didn't leave me anything as far as I know.'

'Oh, don't pretend,' snapped his aunt. 'The time for pretending is past, now. Philip told me all about it when he was still alive.'

'He *told* you?' said a voice in astonishment. It was John Haynes, who had entered the room unnoticed. He stepped forward. 'What did he tell you, exactly?'

'About the secret provision in his will, of course. Didn't anyone think it odd that he should leave his children only a life interest in half their inheritance, and that the money should revert to his solicitor after their deaths? Whoever heard of such a thing? Why, it's quite absurd. But what nobody except myself knew was that Mr. Faulkner had secretly agreed to hold the money in trust for another person—and that that person was Donald Haynes.'

'Nonsense!' said John. 'What in heaven's name gave you that idea?'

'I told you, I heard it from Philip. He said that he wanted to leave some money to his daughter Christina's illegitimate child without anybody else finding out.'

'What?' cried John, Louisa and Donald all at once.

'Don't try to claim that you didn't know,' said Ursula. 'You adopted Donald after Christina died. I remember it well, John—you brought him home one day and said that his mother was dead and that the two of you would bring him up as your own child. I admit I had no suspicion of the connection until Philip told me about the provision in his will. He did not name the person in question but I guessed whom he meant at once. As a matter of fact, I wondered that it had never occurred to me before.'

'But why should he tell *you* all this?' asked Louisa.

'Philip and I were fond of each other,' replied Ursula. 'He was very misunderstood, especially by his family, but I found him amusing at times. Occasionally he told me things that he had not told anybody else. This was one of them.'

'Now, Ursula,' began John, 'you have got hold of quite the wrong end of the stick.'

'Has she?' demanded Donald suddenly. He looked very pale, and there was a queer sort of smile on his face. 'Are you quite sure of that, Father? But of course, you're not really my father, are you? And Mother's not my mother. We all knew that, but we all went on, year after year, pretending it didn't matter.'

'Donald,' said Louisa in distress, 'of course it doesn't matter. We love you as our own child. You *are* our own child.'

'No I'm not!' he said fiercely. 'I am nobody. You heard what Aunt Ursula said. I am the bastard son of a disgraced woman.'

'Look here!' said Guy. 'You mustn't say that!'

Donald rounded on him.

'Shut up!' he exclaimed. 'Don't you think I know what you have been doing over these past few weeks, making love to Stella and trying to win her for yourself? Don't try and pretend to be my friend when what you really want is to take what is mine.' He drew himself up. 'Very well—so now Aunt Ursula has kindly told us all who my real mother is, perhaps the other thing is true too. Should I confess to it now and save the bother of a trial?'

'Don't talk like that, Donald,' said his mother. 'Ursula has got it all wrong. Of course we know you didn't do it.'

'*Do* you know it?' he said. 'Do *I* know it, in fact? Aunt Ursula believes me guilty, and so does Stella. So perhaps I did do it. Perhaps I lost my senses and killed all those people—my aunts and uncle and Mr. Faulkner—while in a sort of brainstorm that I have since forgotten about.'

Stella was gazing at him with a distraught expression.

'No!' she cried. 'I won't believe it. I *can't* believe it.'

'And yet you wanted to know where I was this afternoon,' he replied. 'It's perfectly obvious you don't trust me. I realize now why you have been avoiding me all these weeks: you think I did it. You think I put poison in Aunt Philippa's coffee, and pushed Aunt Winifred over the balustrade, and drowned Uncle Edward in the lake.'

He paused.

'*Did* you do it?' whispered Stella into the silence. Her eyes pleaded with him to say no.

'Oh, what's the use?' he cried, throwing up his hands, then turned and ran out of the room.

CHAPTER THIRTY-ONE

DONALD!' CRIED STELLA, jumping up and running after him.

John turned to Ursula.

'You interfering old hag,' he said angrily. 'Look what you have done. You have turned everything upside-down and driven Donald away with your ridiculous tale.'

Ursula drew herself up.

'It is not a ridiculous tale,' she said. 'I have kept quiet up to now for Louisa's sake, since she has always been kind to me, but this evening was the last straw. I cannot go on countenancing this murderous orgy.'

John snorted.

'You're mad,' he said.

'Do you deny that the deaths were deliberate? Do you suppose that Mr. Faulkner stuck that knife into himself?'

'No, of course I don't, but that's—now just you listen here—'

'He's gone!' cried Stella, bursting back into the room. 'He ran out of the house and wouldn't come back when I called after him. I'm so dreadfully afraid he's going to do something stupid.' She looked appealingly at Guy. 'Please, Guy, you must go after him and bring him back.'

Guy stood up.

'I'm not sure I'm the person he wants to see at the moment, old girl,' he said. 'But I shall try. Did you see which way he went?'

'I think he headed down towards the lake,' she replied.

'All right, then,' he said. 'I shall catch him and bring him back if I possibly can.' He took hold of her hand briefly. 'Never despair!' he said with a smile, and hurried out.

Despite the time of year the sky outside was lowering with the approaching storm. Angela thought of the last time she had taken that deserted path, and the fear she had felt as she tried to escape the unseen pursuer behind her. She rose and went into the hall, where she found William hovering.

'There's been a bit of a blow-up,' she said. 'No doubt you saw Donald leave the house in a hurry just now. Guy has gone after him.'

'Then he's going to need my help,' said William firmly.

'I know I can rely on you. Do you have the thing I gave you?'

The young man looked around carefully, put his hand into his inside pocket and drew out the handle of a revolver.

'Good,' said Angela. 'It's only small but it will do the job, and you might need it, so be sure and keep it with you at all times.'

'I will,' he promised.

'In the meantime I shall go into the attic and retrieve that box of papers. I only hope it's not too dark up there.'

He nodded and without further ado left the house, his jaw set in determination.

Angela returned to the drawing-room, and was about to excuse herself from dinner by pleading a headache, when Louisa announced that the meal would be delayed until Donald could be found. Angela withdrew again and hurried up the stairs. She found the door to the attic just as William had described it, and opened it slowly, wishing she had a torch. It was not as dark as she had expected, however, as a faint glow from some unknown source lit her way as she ascended.

As she reached the top a stair creaked loudly under her foot and she thought she heard a sudden rustle. She paused. Was it a rat? Or something else? Never mind—there was no time to worry about that now. The important thing was to get hold of those papers, as she had the feeling that all the proof she needed would be contained in that wooden box. She hoped its owner had not been up here in the last hour or two and seen the broken lock.

Angela moved forward cautiously. Her eyes had grown accustomed to the dim, flickering light now and she looked around for an old writing-desk. It was unlikely to be too far away, she reasoned, since the owner of the box presumably came up here regularly to put documents in it or take them out, and so would want to keep it nearby in order to be able to reach it easily. For some minutes she gazed about her fruitlessly, her eyes lighting on old bedsteads, chairs, tables and lamp-shades. A moth-eaten stag's head glared dourly at her from its undignified position next to a pile of chamber-pots, and everywhere she looked were trunks spilling over with the accumulated stuff of decades. William had been right when he described the attic as an Aladdin's cave. How many of these things would ever see the light of day again? Her gaze fell on a painting of some forget-me-nots in a vase, prettily done, and she wondered whether it had once belonged to Christina. Or had she even painted it herself?

At last Angela spotted what she was looking for: an old roll-top bureau, just off to her left. On top of it was a box with an in-laid lid, which looked just big enough to hold a few papers. She went over to it and shook her head as she saw the broken lock and splintered wood. It was obvious that it had been forced. Now it would be impossible to pretend, should the necessity arise, that it had been broken by accident. Well, it couldn't be helped—and did it matter, anyway? Things had gone too far to take a step back now.

She lifted the lid of the box. The first thing that met her eye was the photograph that had been stolen from her in London. She put it to one side and picked up the top one from the small sheaf of documents in the box. It was a letter, written through in a close, crabbed hand. She could just make out what it said, and she read it in increasing astonishment.

My dear boy (it said),

By now you ought to have grown quite accustomed to receiving these peculiar letters from beyond the grave, so I make no further apology for disturbing your peace—if indeed it is disturbed; the youth of today are quite hardened to the unpleasantnesses of life, I find. Mr. Faulkner made no comment when I gave him his original instructions, but his eyebrows rose at least an inch, and I could see he looked askance upon such unusual proceedings. How could I explain to him that it made an old man happy to think that, once he was dead and gone, he could still communicate in some way with his favourite, and yet unacknowledged grandchild?

So, then, if that old goat of a solicitor has indeed done as I instructed him, you will be reading this some time in early May. Spring was always your mother's favourite time of year, as you will no doubt remember—not just because May was her birth month, but also because, as she told me, she loved to run outside and feel the fresh air upon her face, breathe in the scent of the newly-blooming flowers and give thanks for the joys of the new season.

I beg your pardon—I had to pause for a few moments after writing the above. I had not thought that her death could still affect me so after all these years. Believe me, I still rue the terrible sequence of events that tore Christina so cruelly from her home here at Underwood House. Why, I have asked myself continually, was I not there to prevent her from being sent away in disgrace by the very mother, brothers and sisters who should have protected her against the dangers of the world? My dear boy, as I have repeated to you many times before, had I had the slightest idea of what they were planning, I should never in a thousand years have taken that trip to Manchester to visit my old friend who was gravely ill, thus allowing them to spirit her away in my absence. Time after time I tried to find her over the next eight years, but there was a conspiracy of silence against me. Try as I might, I was unable to discover her whereabouts, until it was too late and they told me she was dead.

But enough of the past. We are concerned only with the present, and I write once again to remind you of your pledge to me. Were I still in the land of the living, I should be able to help you attain our purpose of visiting retribution on my ungrateful children for the harm they did to my sweet, innocent daughter—but as things stand, I fear the burden will fall on you alone. Be not afraid, however: I trust you implicitly. I know you will avenge Christina's memory as only her true son could. I urge you to make them suffer as she did, and to ensure that their sins are returned tenfold upon their own heads. Remember also that by stripping their families of their inheritance you are regaining what is rightfully yours, and take it as a mark of my faith in you when I say that nobody could deserve his birthright more than you do.

Very well, then. I leave you to do your duty to your late mother and to me, the father who loved her. Do not let anybody turn you aside from your purpose, and remember the rewards that will be yours if you succeed.

I wish you all success in your endeavours.

Yours affectionately,

Philip

The letter left Angela quite breathless, and she stared at it blankly for a moment or two. Her hand was reaching out automatically to take the next document from the box when her attention was arrested by a noise to her right. Unconsciously she thrust the first letter into her pocket and raised her head, listening carefully. There it was again. It sounded like nothing so much as someone trying to shift position inaudibly.

Angela sighed.

'Very well, then,' she thought. 'It's about time someone smoked you out.'

There was an old wardrobe standing in a corner of the attic. The dim light seemed to issue from behind it. Angela picked her way round it and peered towards the source of the light, which turned out to be a burning candle. There, crouching on a makeshift bed with its back to her, was a figure.

'Hallo, Robin,' she said.

Chapter Thirty-two

ROBIN STARTED VIOLENTLY and whirled round to face her, terrified. He looked dreadful: unkempt and unshaven and under-fed. Angela regarded him not unsympathetically.

'Don't you think you should stop all this nonsense and turn yourself in?' she asked.

He shrank away from her. He appeared to have lost the power of speech.

'Surely you weren't planning to stay here forever?' Angela went on. 'You would have been discovered very soon, you know. Somebody would have noticed that food was being stolen, or you would have been heard, or seen.'

'I was only going to stay until the fuss had died down,' he said, regaining his voice with an effort, 'then I should have gone abroad somewhere.'

'And how did you propose to do that? They are looking out for you at all the ports. And even supposing you did manage to make it out of the country, how did you expect to live? The money you took from your mother wouldn't have lasted long. Really, Robin, I don't think you have quite thought this out. Speculating with other people's money is bad enough, but if you are going to do it you should at least be certain at first that you are going to make a decent fist of it. And then not even to have a proper escape route planned when it all went wrong—why, that looks very like incompetence to me.'

'I suppose you would have done it differently,' he said petulantly.

'I shouldn't have done it at all,' she said. 'But if I wanted to, I should do it better than you have. I thought you were supposed to be an expert in financial matters. You must have been aware of the risks you were running.'

'You're a woman, so I can't expect you to understand how the markets can turn against one at any moment. I was doing perfectly well—had been for months, as a matter of fact. Then that Anglo-Pretoria business happened and I was left completely exposed.'

'But why did you start doing it in the first place? Selling short is a dangerous thing to do at the best of times, but doing it with your clients' money is positively reckless.'

He looked sulky.

'I could hardly afford to do it with my own money, could I? I am not a rich man. I could have been, though—I had the chance to make thousands, and nobody would have been any the wiser had it all gone to plan. All I had to do was borrow the stock for a little while then give it back once I'd made the trade. What harm could it possibly do?'

'None, so long as the markets were going your way. Unfortunately for you, they didn't. Did you approach your Aunt Winifred after you got into difficulties following the Anglo-Pretoria business?'

'Yes. I needed money to cover my losses, and she had plenty. I thought I should have no trouble in making up the difference, and expected to provide a healthy return for her into the bargain, but things went from bad to worse and I was left stony-broke.'

'But how did you manage to cover it all up for so long?'

'They trusted me at Peake's,' he said. 'Or, at least, they did until recently. I gather that someone had lately got wind of what was happening and they had me watched. To tell the truth, it was almost a relief when it all came out. For over a year I had lived in fear of discovery. There was no possibility of getting money from anyone else—although I did ask everyone I could think of—so I sat on the losses for months and months, terrified that somebody was going to start asking awkward questions. When the police came I fully intended to face up to it all, but then they started hinting that I had murdered Aunt Winifred and I—well, I lost my nerve and ran away.'

'Yes, the police did suggest that you might have had a hand in her death.'

'I didn't kill her, I tell you!' he cried.

'But you did search her pockets when you found her lying dead on the floor, didn't you?'

He cast his eyes down.

'How did you know that?' he said.

'I didn't, until a few days ago. You and Donald both claimed that the other was first on the scene after she fell and it was impossible to say which of you was telling the truth. After you disappeared the police found a letter from you to Winifred, which you had tried to destroy, and they immediately concluded that you had retrieved it from her pocket after she fell.'

'You must think me an utter wretch,' he said.

'You have made rather a mess of things, certainly,' agreed Angela, 'but if it is of any comfort to you, I know you are not guilty of murder.'

'What am I to do?' he cried suddenly, and Angela was reminded of his mother's desperate outburst of a few days earlier.

'First, you must come down from the attic and have a wash and some dinner. After that, what you do is entirely up to you. Your mother is here, you know. She has been frantic with worry about you.'

'Has she? I thought she would be furious with me.'

'I imagine she is. But your father is dead and you are her only child—the only person she has left in the world. Naturally, she is anxious about you.'

For a second he looked forlorn, like a little boy who had been caught in the pantry eating sugar and was waiting to hear what his punishment would be.

'How—how long do you think they will put me in prison for?' he asked hesitantly.

'I don't know,' said Angela. 'I believe your mother has already engaged a good defence counsel, however. He will be able to advise you. Perhaps you will get off lightly.'

He sighed.

'I guess it was absurd of me to think I could hide up here for long without being caught,' he said. 'I was getting bored and that probably made me careless. And people keep coming up here. I think you're the fourth one today.'

'It can't be much fun living alone in an attic,' agreed Angela. 'Now, are you going to go down and face your mother?'

He winced at the thought.

'I suppose I must. Will you come with me, Mrs. Marchmont? I daren't face her on my own.'

Angela laughed.

'Don't worry—Louisa and the others are there and will protect you from her, then that will be the hardest part over and done with. After that, facing the police will seem like child's play.'

'That's true enough,' he said feelingly. He stood up and emerged from the den in which he had spent almost a week. 'Let's go, then,' he said.

'I have one or two things to do up here, then I shall come down,' said Angela.

He did not ask what the one or two things were, but nodded and went off. She heard his footsteps as he descended the stairs, then the sound of the door opening and closing. Her thoughts returned to the inlaid box and its astonishing contents and she moved over to the writing-desk, intending to read quickly through one or two more of the papers before removing the whole thing and taking it to her room to show to Inspector Jameson when he arrived. She had just lifted the lid of the box when she heard the attic door open again and the sound of footsteps climbing the stairs slowly.

'Back here already? I thought you were going to confess everything to your mother,' she said without turning round.

'My mother is dead,' said a voice behind her.

CHAPTER THIRTY-THREE

ANGELA'S HEART BEAT loudly in her breast and she turned round.

'I thought you had gone out into the woods,' she said.

'Yes, you did, didn't you?' said Guy. 'But here I am, as you see.'

He wore his usual insouciant smile, but now there was something chilling about it. Angela noticed for the first time how powerfully built he was, and remembered that he had once been an athlete.

'Where is Donald? Is he—is he all right?' she asked hesitantly.

He shrugged.

'I haven't the faintest idea. I should imagine your man has caught up with him by now—I saw him, by the way, as I was doubling back, looking terribly brave and firm of purpose. Perhaps he will shoot his quarry and save me the trouble. Or perhaps Don has returned of his own accord and is now being comforted by Stella. I'm sure he'll forgive her her temporary lapse in faith.' His expression hardened.

Angela said nothing and he looked at her thoughtfully.

'How silent you are, Angela. Don't you have anything to say for yourself? I thought you might at least apologize for breaking into my box and trying to steal my things.'

'You knew I should be up here, then?'

'I guessed, yes. You really ought to be more discreet when you confer with your young American, you know. I saw you both poring over my letter from Faulkner downstairs and knew the game was up, as they say. I came up here and saw what had happened. My first instinct was to take the box away, of course, but on reflection I thought it might be better to leave it here as bait. I knew you would want to read the other things.'

'Yes, I did,' replied Angela. 'I have just read your most recent letter from Philip and it makes me feel terribly sorry for you.'

He frowned.

'Sorry for me? Why on earth should you be sorry for me?'

'Because you are quite alone, and the only person you had to rely upon in your life—the person who should have protected you most of all—has been deceiving you cruelly, even from beyond the grave.'

'Deceiving me? Of course he hasn't been deceiving me. He told me the truth about my mother and her family when no-one else would. Finally, after all these years, I know why she was always so unhappy, and why she would never talk to me about it when she was alive. I have heard all about my so-called *father*,' he spat out the word, 'the farm-hand who attacked her. I know how her family spurned her after her disgrace and cast her out of the house without mercy when my grandfather's back was turned. And these are the people who congratulated themselves and grew fat on their new-found riches when Grandfather died—the brothers and sisters who treated my mother so wickedly that she died of a broken heart when I was only eight years old. What right had they to live when she was dead through their actions?'

'But Guy, your mother went of her own free will,' said Angela. 'Nobody cast her out. She hated her father and wanted to escape his influence, so she ran away.'

'It's not true, I tell you,' he snapped. 'That's what the Hayneses want everybody to think, but I know better.'

'Did your mother tell you the story?'

'I told you, she wouldn't talk about it.'

'Then all your information has come from your grandfather, and if I have learned anything in the past week or two, it is that he was not a man to be depended upon.'

'You are wrong,' he said. 'He was a good, kind man. After my mother died he sought me out and paid for my schooling. It is all thanks to him that I won my scholarship to Oxford. Then, when I came down, he gave me the post here at Underwood, and promised he should always provide for me. He was the only family I had—the only one who acknowledged me, at any rate. I know the rest of them would have shunned me had they known who I was.'

Angela had a sudden flash of realization.

'John knows,' she said. 'Did Philip tell him?'

'Does he know?' said Guy with mild interest. 'I've often wondered whether he did. He looks at me in an odd way, sometimes.'

'I think he has been protecting you, although I can't believe he knows the whole truth. Or perhaps he does know and has been trying to fool himself. Christina was his favourite sister, you know.'

'That's what he told *you*, I expect.'

Never one to argue uselessly, Angela was silent. He moved a little closer to her and she gazed at him warily.

'I mustn't take my eyes off him,' she thought.

'You've gone quiet again. Aren't you simply dying to tell me how clever you've been in working it all out?' he asked.

'Not especially,' she replied.

'No, you're not the type to boast about your triumphs, are you? I must admit I wasn't particularly impressed when I first met you. You seemed far too polite and reserved to do anything effectively. But then you immediately started looking at the thing logically and methodically, so I thought I had better watch my step. And then Louisa told me you had found the photograph, which I must have dropped when I was down at the lake in February, and I had to get it back at all costs.'

'So you thought you might as well try and put me out of the way while you were at it,' said Angela.

'Oh, that was quite on the spur of the moment,' he said. 'The opportunity was far too good to miss. It was a close thing, though—I nearly got caught thanks to the unfortunate public-spiritedness of an enthusiastic crowd of young lads.'

'The other day in the woods was premeditated, though.'

'Naturally,' he said lightly. 'I had already become somewhat concerned after I followed you one evening in London and saw that you were in league with Inspector Jameson—you kept that rather quiet, by the way. Then, when I overheard you talking about my mother to old Briggs, I realized you had somehow got on to the right track and thought I'd better do something about it sharpish. Unluckily for me I missed you first time and alerted you to the danger. Careless of me—I am generally a crack shot. But tell me, Angela, what put you on to me in the first place? I am curious to know.'

'Your mother's birthday,' said Angela. He looked at her, uncomprehending, and she went on, 'When I first met you, you said that on the day Winifred died you were away because it was your mother's birthday. I assumed you meant you had gone to lunch with her, but then later Stella told me that you were an orphan, and I realized you must have been visiting her grave.'

He nodded.

'In addition to that, something Susan said led me to believe that Philip had set up a secret trust to benefit an unknown person, and I wondered whether it might have some connection with Christina. Then John mentioned that her birthday was in May, and shortly afterwards I heard that she had had a child. Two dead mothers with birthdays in May and a connection to Underwood House might easily have been a coincidence, but I decided to look into it anyway. A trip to Somerset House confirmed the theory.'

'Didn't you suspect Donald, then? Everybody else seemed to.'

'I did look at his birth certificate just in case,' said Angela, 'but I thought he was too young to be Christina's son. Besides, you were the one with the broken watch.'

'Ah! I wondered whether that would give me away. Yes, drowning a man does tend to damage one's things, rather. I had to dispose of a perfectly good dinner suit, too.'

'And you had been up to London to try and get the watch repaired. Was it the same day you took the photograph from me?'

He nodded again.

'I thought it might be.' She paused for a second. 'So Philip left instructions that a family meeting was to be held on your mother's birthday every year,' she went on. 'But what about the other meeting, the one on the 16th of February?'

'It's the anniversary of the day she died,' he said. 'I asked Edward down by the lake whether he recognized the significance of the date, and he didn't—not even when I showed him the photograph. The date of his own sister's death, and he didn't even remember it! That is unforgivable.'

'Perhaps he didn't know when it was.'

'Then he ought to have found it out,' he said angrily. 'That was typical of them all—they cared for nobody but themselves. While they were living off Grandfather I don't suppose they ever spared a thought for the years of poverty and misery my mother and I had to suffer; all the times she went without so she could buy shoes and books and food for me. In the end it wore her out and she simply gave up. They deserved nothing, I tell you, except what they got from me.'

'Did you poison Philippa?

'No. That was Ursula's idea, wasn't it? Digitalin, or something. No, I didn't poison her—I went into her bedroom in the dead of night when she was fast asleep and held a pillow over her face until she suffocated. Nobody suspected a thing: after all, she'd been ill with heart trouble for years, and no-one would have been in the slightest bit surprised had she popped off at any moment.'

'When did Mr. Faulkner realize that you were responsible for the deaths of your aunts and uncle? Or was he in on the whole thing?'

'No, he wasn't in on it, but he received a nice, fat payment from Grandfather in return for keeping quiet about the secret trust. I think he started to suspect what was going on after I killed Winifred—it was after her death that he started to make excuses as to why I couldn't have my money immediately. I guess he was just testing things out a little, and looking to see how I would react. But I wasn't going to stand for that. I called his bluff and demanded payment and he gave in.'

'I take it he knew who your mother was.'

'Yes, he was in on that all right. It was his idea to set up the secret trust, as a matter of fact.'

'Then after Edward died you approached him for the five thousand pounds and this time he wrote back asking for a share of it in return for his silence.'

'That was the letter you saw, yes.' Guy shook his head slowly. 'Stupid old man. Did he really think I should let him get away with that kind of trick? And supposing I had given in to his demand, would that have been the end of it? Why, of course not! He would have left me alone for a little while, and then, just as I was beginning to breathe again and feel that all was safe, I should have received a terribly polite letter from him, telling me that he was unfortunately very embarrassed for funds at the moment and could I see my way clear etcetera etcetera? Once he had got his hooks into me I should never have been rid of him, and so I had to do something about it.'

'Blackmail is a risky enterprise,' said Angela. 'I wonder he didn't realize the danger he was putting himself in.'

'He was a conceited old fool who thought he was far too clever for me. Well, he was wrong. You don't happen to have his letter on you, by the way, do you?' he asked carelessly.

'No,' said Angela. 'I have put it in a safe place.'

'No matter,' he said. 'I'm quite resigned to being rumbled. Now I suppose everybody will find out what I've been up to. Not that that will help you, though.'

'What do you mean?'

He took a step forward. His manner was as carefree as ever.

'Why, I need to get away as quickly as possible,' he said lightly, 'and you're rather an obstacle in my path, I'm afraid.'

Chapter Thirty-Four

ANGELA MOVED BACK a step. He grinned.

'What's the use in killing me?' she asked. 'You've already admitted you've been found out. Another murder is hardly going to help your cause.'

'No, but it can't make things any worse either. I am already destined for the noose if they catch me, so one more dead body won't make any difference. I need time to get away, Mrs. Marchmont. I have plenty of money thanks to Philippa and Winifred—although I have had to give up on the idea of getting my hands on Edward's inheritance now that old Faulkner is dead. I can live a life of ease abroad somewhere, but I shall need a head start. If I let you go you'll run straight to your tame inspector, who will post look-outs at all the ports. Besides, you've escaped from me twice,' he went on, 'and I don't mind telling you I'm rather cross about that. I don't like to be beaten, you see, and certainly not by a woman.'

He rubbed his hands together absently. She looked at them: they were large, powerful hands. She pictured them, grasping Edward's neck and forcing him under the water until he ceased struggling, and unconsciously raised her own hand to her throat. It was growing warm in the attic, uncomfortably so, and the flickering light cast shadows on Guy's face, giving his smile a terrifying aspect.

'What will Stella think of you?' she asked.

'Stella is in love with that idiot, Don,' he said. 'I thought about killing him in the woods half an hour ago, just for the fun of it, but decided I had more urgent matters to attend to. A pity,' he said. 'Stella and I should have been happy together, I'm sure of it.' He took another step forward. 'Anyway,' he said, 'it's been simply enchanting to talk to you, and I should love to stay and chat, but I have a train to catch, so I fear I must say *au revoir*. Oh, how silly of me—naturally, I meant *adieu*.'

'Not so fast,' said Angela. 'I have something to show you.'

He laughed.

'Are you trying to play for time? I shouldn't bother, if I were you. Your young American is out in the woods looking for Don and no-one in the house can hear you. There's nothing you can do—unless, of course, you think you've got something else up your sleeve?'

'How funny you should say that,' said Angela. 'It's almost as though you knew.'

So occupied was Guy with his own cleverness in beating her that he had not noticed her hand creeping slowly and surreptitiously into the capacious sleeve of her evening jacket, but when she spoke, something in her voice brought him instantly to attention. He looked at the thing in her hand that had not been there before, then started to laugh.

'Put your hands up,' Angela said. There was no mistaking the deadly serious tone of her voice as she levelled the little revolver at him and cocked it in readiness.

'Is this the elegant Mrs. Marchmont? You wouldn't dare,' he said, still with a half-smile on his face. He made as if to move towards her, then yelled and leapt back as, with a steady hand, she fired. The bullet grazed his ear and he clutched at it then gaped at the blood on his hand.

'Perhaps I should mention that I, too, am a crack shot, Mr. Fisher,' she said. 'Try that again and next time I will aim for your heart instead of your ear. Now, put your hands up as I told you.'

She cocked the gun again and Guy held his hands up.

'You're rather magnificent when you mean business,' he said. He was pale and sweating. 'But whatever you've got planned for me, I should do it quickly if I were you, as we appear to be on fire.'

It was true. The faint scent of something that had been nagging at the back of Angela's mind for some minutes was now manifesting itself as drifting blue smoke, and she turned her head briefly and gasped as she saw flames licking hungrily at the sides of the armoire behind which Robin had made his bed. No wonder it was so hot in the attic: his burning candle must have caught something and set off quite a conflagration.

That one second of inattention was enough for Guy, and he threw himself at her, knocking her to the ground. She let out a shriek of surprise and pain as he pinned her down with his weight and reached for the revolver. Acting quickly, before he had managed to get hold of her right arm, she brought the gun round, panting, and fired. The shot went wide, but it gave him enough of a start to enable her to wriggle free from his grasp and stand up. Quick as a flash, he rolled over and threw himself at her ankles from behind as she tried to escape. Down she went again, and this time the gun flew out of her hand and skittered across the floor, disappearing into the very heart of the flames. Cursing to herself in frustration, she kicked out backwards with a high-heeled shoe and had the satisfaction of feeling her foot connect hard with his nose. He let out a yell of pain and she scrambled to her feet again, glancing about her. The rapidly-spreading blaze was behind her and Guy was between her and the stairs, blocking her way out. He stood up slowly, blood pouring from his nose to join the trail of blood already dripping from his ear. The careless grin had gone and his eyes were narrowed with deadly intent. He advanced step by step, pushing her inexorably towards the flames. She felt the heat at her back and coughed as the smoke began to drift insidiously into her nostrils. In a moment he would force her into the fire and all would be lost. She cast about desperately for something that could be used as a weapon against him, and her hand fell on an earthenware chamber-pot from the pile she had seen earlier. Picking it up, she hurled it at him with all her strength. It glanced off his shoulder and he gave a grunt and paused, breathing heavily through his mouth. That gave her enough time to grab at the next thing in the pile, which was the stag's head. She heaved it up with some difficulty and held it in front of her.

'Get back!' she cried, jabbing at him wildly with the sharp antlers.

He regarded them warily and paused, uncertain what do do next. They appeared to have reached a deadlock. She could hold him off with the stag's head and prevent him from pushing her into the fire, but soon the smoke and the flames would overcome them both. She had to act quickly. The stag's head was too heavy to throw so she stabbed its antlers at his face as hard as she could. He raised his hands to fend it off, then caught hold of it and wrenched it from her grasp. He cast it aside with a roar as she picked up another chamber-pot to throw, but before she could hurl it at him he was upon her, livid with fury. He twisted the chamber-pot out of her hand, and it fell to the floor with a clatter. His hands were on her neck now, and it was the end. She could feel the pressure of his fingers, choking her, squeezing the life out of her. A warm, calm feeling stole over her, and for one long second she closed her eyes and gave herself up to her fate. How easy it would be, she thought, to stop struggling and allow the delicious sleep to wash over her, enveloping her completely.

Then her eyes snapped open and, summoning up the last of her strength, she lifted her hand to her breast and plucked out a diamond pin from her jacket. He had relaxed his hold briefly, believing her to be unconscious, and in that split second her hand darted upwards and she thrust the pin as hard as she could into the fleshy part of his left thumb. He let out an exclamation and dropped his hold, clutching at his hand and staggering. Before Angela could move away, his foot caught on the dropped chamber-pot, and he lost his balance. For one terrible moment he seemed to hang, suspended by an invisible thread, his eyes fixed on hers in wordless horror. Then, with an awful inevitability, he plunged backwards into the flames.

For a second there was no sound apart from the crackling of the fire; then, with a terrible scream, he rose and turned towards her, arms raised, his hair and clothes afire, advancing upon her slowly like an avenging angel. Angela wanted to turn and run, but her feet seemed to have rooted themselves to the spot and she was transfixed by the sight before her.

'Run, you idiot, run!' she told herself. Instantly, the spell broke. She turned and dashed for the stairs as fast as her legs would carry her, just as the ghastly thing that had been Guy Fisher fell to the floor and lay still.

Angela half-ran, half-fell down the stairs and threw herself at the door, wrenching at the handle and pulling it open. She pitched out onto the landing, sobbing and coughing and gasping for air. All at once, she was surrounded by people and voices, exclaiming in consternation.

'Fire!' she croaked. Her knees gave way under her and she was about to sink to the floor when she was caught by a pair of strong arms and set down gently.

'Mrs. Marchmont! What on earth has happened?' said the concerned voice of Inspector Jameson.

'There's a fire in the attic, and Guy is dead,' was all she could say.

'Get everybody out,' said Jameson to someone, perhaps one of his men. 'Mrs. Marchmont, do you think you can walk?'

'Of course I can,' she said with dignity.

He helped her up and she stood, swaying slightly.

'Next time I shall carry *two* guns—one up each sleeve,' she said grimly, then fainted.

Chapter Thirty-Five

THE LATE MAY sunshine streamed in through a gap in the curtains with the promise of a beautiful new day. It shone gently on Angela Marchmont, waking her by degrees. She blinked a few times and lay where she was, enjoying the sensation of warmth on her face. After a while, she sat up and stretched, then yawned and coughed experimentally. She raised a hand to her throat. The aches and bruises were fading and she was definitely feeling much better. She reached over and rang the bell.

'Good morning, Marthe,' she said, when the girl arrived. 'I should like some tea, please.'

Marthe beamed.

'Ah, *madame*,' she said, 'you are better today.'

'Yes, I certainly feel as though I am on the mend,' replied Angela. Her voice was still a little hoarse. 'In fact, I believe I could manage some buttered toast as well.'

'*Mais oui*,' replied Marthe fondly. She went out and returned after a few minutes bearing the desired items on a silver tray. 'You have had many calls and messages from wish-wellers,' she said.

'Well-wishers,' said Angela.

'Those also. Mrs. Louisa Haynes sent flowers and a message. Mrs. *Ursula* Haynes,' (this said in disdain) 'telephoned yesterday. Then there are three or four messages from someone called Stella. Also, *Monsieur l'Inspecteur* called once and sent the most beautiful bouquet of blue irises.'

'Ah,' said Angela.

'And I think also there has been some mistake,' said Marthe, opening her eyes wide in puzzlement, 'because a man called Briggs has sent you some cabbages.'

'How delightful,' said Angela. 'We must have them for supper.'

'Me, I do not like the cabbage,' said Marthe indifferently.

Angela took a sip of tea and a bite of toast. They tasted delicious.

'I am sick of sitting in bed all day,' she announced. 'Today I shall get up and go out. I am quite recovered. It was only tiredness that made me stay in bed yesterday.'

'But no, *madame*, you cannot go out,' said Marthe firmly. 'I shall not permit it.'

'I assure you, I feel quite well,' said Angela.

'Maybe so, but you look a fright,' said the girl. 'See here!'

She picked up a hand-glass from the dressing table and held it out. Mrs. Marchmont took it from her and examined her reflection. The face that stared back at her was blotched, with red, swollen, watery eyes and singed hair.

'Good gracious, is that me?' she said. 'Perhaps you are right, Marthe. Very well, I shall not inflict myself on the good people of London today. You must see what can be done with my hair later. And now you had better bring me the newspaper and a cold compress.'

She settled back into her pillows and prepared to face another day of dullness, which was relieved only slightly by the amusement to be found in reading several different—and entirely inaccurate—descriptions of the recent events in the papers.

The next morning she felt better still and was quite firm in insisting she be allowed to get up, despite Marthe's protestations that she was not yet fit.

'I have many things to do,' she said, 'and I am hardly a delicate flower that needs protecting. 'Besides, I should like to speak to Inspector Jameson.'

Inspector Jameson was also anxious to speak to Mrs. Marchmont and sure enough, called in person at the earliest time that could be thought decent. He found Angela in her living-room, sitting at the little table by the window and watching the people pass by in the street below.

'I am glad to hear you have quite recovered,' he said.

'Yes,' she replied. 'A little sore and singed around the edges, but otherwise I am quite well.'

'You created quite a stir the other night, I don't mind telling you.'

'Yes, I'm afraid that events did run away with me rather, despite my precautions.'

'I suppose there's no use in my telling you that you should have waited for my return instead of going into the attic yourself.'

'None whatever,' said Angela firmly. 'Had I waited, then Guy would have removed the box and hidden it and we may never have found out the whole truth. As it is, I am only sorry that the papers were destroyed before I had the chance to read them all. I did manage to rescue one thing, though.'

She went to a little cabinet, brought out Philip's letter, which she had found in the pocket of her evening jacket, and handed it to the inspector. Jameson read it through then looked at her in astonishment.

'Good God!' he exclaimed. 'I had no idea of this.'

'Nor did I,' said Angela, 'and I should never have believed it had I not seen it with my own eyes.'

'Is it true, what he says about his daughter?'

'Not by all accounts. Everyone else is quite certain that Christina was so desperate to escape her father that she ran off of her own accord. I think this is a special version of events designed to dupe a susceptible young man.'

'What kind of person would do this?'

'I can't begin to imagine. But I think Philip Haynes must have had something very wrong with him to have behaved in such a cruel, callous fashion towards his orphaned grandchild.'

'But he must have had a reason for what he did,' said Jameson. 'Even the insane do not act totally at random. They always have some motive, even if it would not appear rational to the rest of us.'

'I can only assume that his—what shall I call it?—indoctrination of Guy was intended as some kind of posthumous revenge against Christina for having escaped his clutches all those years ago. Perhaps he even saw himself as the righteous one, visiting the sins of the mother upon the child. But why he went to all that trouble to persuade Guy to murder his aunts and uncles is beyond my understanding. Possibly it was another one of his twisted games. I have heard much of his mischievous love of causing strife, but this went further than mischief; indeed I can only describe it as pure evil. He must have lied and lied. And he must have been especially talented in manipulation to be able to drive a man to murder like that.'

'True,' said Jameson, 'but I think Fisher must have been a little unbalanced himself to start with. People don't generally go around murdering their relatives on someone else's say-so without having a screw loose somewhere.'

'Perhaps. But he fell under the influence of his grandfather at a very young and impressionable age. Who knows what poison was dripped into his ear throughout his youth?'

Jameson nodded assent.

'It's odd,' said Angela reflectively, 'but I had the feeling all along that we were being danced about like puppets—that there was someone behind the scenes pushing us in the direction he wanted us to go. But I never thought for a moment that it was all happening on the instructions of a dead man.'

'You have told me how Philippa Haynes was killed,' said the inspector, 'but what about Winifred Dennison?'

'It was quite simple,' said Angela. 'On that day, you remember, Guy was visiting his mother's grave and supposedly didn't arrive back until it was all over. In reality he returned to Underwood House much earlier than he claimed and went up to his room. He was looking out for an opportunity to kill Winifred or Edward or John. It didn't much matter to him which one—any of them would do. He got his chance when he heard Winifred come out of her bedroom, which was the one next door to his. He crept along the landing after her and then, when she paused for a second, picked her up and threw her over the balustrade. He then ran into Donald's room which, as you may recall, is just opposite that exact spot on the landing, opened the window and climbed down the same ivy that had provided his mother's escape route all those years ago. After that I imagine he went and hid somewhere for an hour or two, before turning up having apparently missed all the excitement.'

'As you say, very simple. But how did you deduce what happened?'

'When I was examining the scene of Winifred's death, I was wondering whether the murderer could have killed her and then dashed downstairs in order to give the impression that he had been nowhere near the landing when she fell. Guy helpfully ran down the stairs to test the theory for me and it looked as though it would have been possible but difficult to do without the killer drawing attention to himself. Then Stella turned up and pointed out that the most obvious means of escape would have been for him to hide in one of the bedrooms nearest the top of the stairs. The only person known to have been upstairs at the time was Winifred's daughter, Susan. She could have done it, of course, but I wondered whether someone else could have escaped through a window. I had a look outside and, sure enough, there was a convenient mass of ivy outside one of the rooms. In addition, Susan told me that she had heard her mother's bedroom door slam at about the same time as Winifred fell. I investigated and discovered that it couldn't have been Winifred's door as the sound doesn't carry that far. It seemed more likely that the noise came from someone slamming a door as he ran *into* a room, and who else would that be but the murderer?'

'I see what you mean. So, after some rather clever detective work on your part, you decided that Guy was our man, but how on earth did you know about the letter from Mr. Faulkner? Or was that a lucky guess?'

'It was partly luck, I admit. Once I had got the idea into my head that there was a secret trust involved, it made sense to assume that there must be something in writing somewhere that attested to its existence. But anything of that nature was likely to be in the hands of Mr. Faulkner and I had no idea how to go about getting hold of it. However, after I started suspecting Guy I remembered that I had seen him with a letter one day which seemed to have put him in a bad temper. I only caught a glimpse of it but I thought I recognized the handwriting. It was then that I made the connection and realized that it was Mr. Faulkner's.'

'That was the famous letter your man William took from the box.'

'Yes—and the letter that sent Mr. Faulkner to his death. In trying to blackmail Guy he misjudged his power rather badly, I'm afraid. He thought he was safe because he still held Edward's money in trust and Guy couldn't get it without his help. I suppose Guy decided to be satisfied with the ten thousand pounds he got after Philippa and Winifred's deaths, and preferred to get rid of the thorn in his side that Faulkner had undoubtedly become, rather than submit to blackmail in return for Edward's share of the money.'

'Yes, blackmail is always very dangerous,' said Jameson. 'But what of Ursula Haynes? What did she know, or think she knew?'

'From what I can gather, it appears that Philip told her something of the secret trust, but not whom it was intended to benefit. She thought he was talking about Donald and began to suspect that he might be behind the deaths, so she began to press Mr. Faulkner for information.'

'Why didn't she mention it to the police? She certainly kicked up enough of a fuss to make us think she wanted the murderer caught. Why not accuse Donald outright?'

'The other night she said that she had kept quiet out of affection for Louisa,' said Angela. 'That might be true, I suppose, but I'm not entirely convinced of it myself. Ursula is a queer, calculating sort of woman, and I think she may have had some idea of using the information to her own advantage.'

'In what way?'

'Let us look at it from her point of view. She suspects her husband has been murdered. She rather despised him, so it is not *his* loss she feels so much as the loss of five thousand pounds, which reverts to Philip's solicitor. She believes that the unknown beneficiary of the secret trust is the killer, and that Mr. Faulkner knows who it is, but she also knows that murder would be hard to prove. She wants to get the money back one way or another. What does she do, then? First, she reports her suspicions to the police. They can do all the hard work investigating the matter for her, and if they find a murderer then so much the better, since she will get the money back. However, she wants to hedge her bets and so she stops short of naming anyone in particular.'

'What do you mean, hedge her bets?'

'Why, if she gives Donald's name to the police immediately and they find no evidence against him, then the game is up and she has no other means of recovering the five thousand pounds. So what she does instead is to make a great show of implying that she knows who did it and is just waiting for the right moment to reveal all. This, she believes, will frighten Donald and Mr. Faulkner, and make it possible to reach some kind of financial settlement in private if the police fail to deliver the goods.'

'A kind of blackmail, you mean?'

'I doubt she saw it in that way, since the money was rightfully hers, but yes, I suppose one could call it that.'

'The Hayneses ought to be grateful to you for rescuing those two letters from the attic,' said Jameson. 'Had they got burnt then there would have been no evidence of a secret trust and the money would have gone to Mr. Faulkner's heirs instead of Philip's.'

'Was there nothing else in writing, then?'

'Nothing that we could find. But thanks to the letters there should be no difficulty now in returning the money to Ursula and Susan.'

'So Ursula's plan worked in the end,' said Angela. 'She will be glad of the money now that she has to fund her son's legal costs. Do you think they will be very hard on him?'

'Who knows?' said Jameson. 'Peake's seem to be rather embarrassed that they allowed a trusted employee to get away with stealing so much money, and so they are attempting to maintain a discreet distance. But that doesn't alter the fact that a crime has been committed.'

'True,' said Angela, 'and it's not as though there were any mitigating circumstances either—Robin simply got greedy and took what was not his. However, he has Ursula on his side.'

'Yes,' agreed Jameson. 'I shouldn't like to bet on the might of the law winning out against a Mrs. Ursula Haynes on the warpath.'

The inspector shortly afterwards took his leave and Angela was left to her own reflections. On the whole she was satisfied at the way things had turned out, although she was sincerely sorry that Guy had come to such an unfortunate end even if he had tried to murder her. He had been a most charming and clever young man. Who knew how he might have turned out had he been more fortunate in his family history?

But Philip Haynes: what kind of man must he have been, to have wanted to cause such chaos among his family even after his death? John had suggested half-jokingly that his father's will had been designed especially to set the Hayneses at each other's throats, and sure enough he had been right. Philip's malice had led to the untimely deaths of at least three of his children and one of his grandchildren, as well as his solicitor. John was the only child now; thank God he had turned out a sensible man, since he was the only one left to pick up the pieces after the destruction wrought by his father. It would be a long, hard task.

Chapter Thirty-six

A FEW DAYS later Angela received a visit from Louisa, who was dying to talk to her about the whole affair.

'I'm so glad you are much better, Angela,' she said as soon as she entered the room. 'I have been feeling quite dreadful, because of course it was all my fault. I ought never to have asked you to do it, but I assure you I never *dreamed* that you should be plunged into danger like that. Please say you will forgive me.'

'There's nothing to forgive, so you needn't worry in the slightest,' said Angela. 'I am only sorry the thing couldn't have been resolved without burning your house down.'

'It's not quite as bad as that,' said Louisa. 'Obviously there's been quite a bit of damage to the roof and some of the upstairs rooms will be uninhabitable for a while, but luckily the men managed to put the fire out before it took a proper hold.'

'That is a relief,' said Angela. 'John would never speak to me again if I destroyed his beloved Underwood House. How is he, by the way?'

'Exceedingly upset and ashamed, and doing his best to hide it by being as bad-tempered as possible.'

'Dear me. Poor Louisa—are you having to bear the brunt of it all yourself?'

'Don't worry about me. Had I been offended by John's manners I never should have married him in the first place. He has been truly distressed by the whole affair, so we are all being kind to him.'

'How did he know who Guy was?'

'He accidentally overheard Philip talking to Mr. Faulkner about it a couple of years ago, at about the time Philip was drawing up the final version of his will and creating the secret trust. He kept quiet about it because Guy hadn't mentioned it himself, so John thought he must be ashamed of it.'

Angela hesitated.

'Louisa, you don't suppose he knew that Guy—' she stopped.

Louisa sighed.

'Truly, I don't see how he could have known who Guy was and not have suspected that he was behind the deaths, but John is a stubborn old fool and, as they say, there are none so blind as those who will not see. Guy was the son of his favourite sister, so naturally John didn't want to believe he could have been guilty of anything so terrible. I know my husband very well, Angela, and I know that he wouldn't have let the murders continue had he been fully aware of who was behind them. I simply choose to think that he had shut his eyes to the truth.'

'Has he forgiven Ursula for her outburst the other night?'

'Oh, those two,' said Louisa in exasperation. 'Do you know, I believe they enjoy fighting. He knows she is highly-strung and yet he insists on goading her.'

'But you must admit she was wrong about Donald.'

'She was, and I don't imagine Don will ever forgive her. And yet, she was right about the will, wasn't she?'

'Yes,' said Angela. 'She knew about the secret trust, but had merely mistaken whom it was destined for.'

'It was an understandable error, I suppose. Donald's history wasn't generally known, and we had been vague about it even to him, as what good would it do him to hear the truth when we are the only parents he has ever known?'

'What is the truth?'

'Very prosaic, I'm afraid. His mother and father were tenants on the estate here, but she died giving birth to him and the father was quite unable to look after the baby alone, so we took him in and promised to look after him. Oddly enough, his mother had something of a reputation in the district for second sight, and I've always assumed that that is where he gets his occasional fey fits from. His father died a few years ago, so he has no real family left now.'

'It was an easy mistake for Ursula to make, then,' said Angela. 'I had considered the theory myself, but the dates were wrong. Donald is in his early twenties, but Christina's son was born more than thirty years ago. Guy was far more of an age to fit the description. I suppose they have removed his body by now.'

Louisa dabbed at a tear.

'Yes, poor boy,' she said. 'I wish I had known about him years ago, when he was a little boy. We should have been more than happy to take him in after Christina died and bring him up as we did Donald. What a dreadful end. I feel so terribly sorry for him. If only he had confided in John, then all this might have been avoided.'

Angela nodded but said nothing. Only Inspector Jameson knew the full truth about how Guy had met his death, and they had agreed that it would be better not to make the knowledge public. Angela was relieved: although she knew herself to be perfectly justified in what she had done, since she had been fighting for her life against a murderer, she felt the blood on her hands and was unwilling to have her actions and motives thrust into the spotlight. The official version of the story was that Guy had fallen into the flames accidentally while attempting to grab the document box, and as far as Angela was concerned the Hayneses were more than welcome to believe it.

'So, then, I suppose that's that,' said Louisa. 'Ursula was quite right when she said that there was a murderer among us. I can't thank you enough, Angela, for all you have done. The atmosphere at Underwood was growing quite poisonous, but now you have solved the mystery we can start to—not return to normal, perhaps, but at least return to living in some kind of peace.'

'There are one or two questions that I should still like to have answered,' said Angela. 'The first is: where was John when Winifred fell? He claimed to have been in his study, but Donald said he wasn't. Perhaps he was doing something quite innocent, but I am curious to know.'

'I know,' said Louisa. 'He told me. He was out walking in the grounds. He had seen Guy return earlier and thought nothing of it, but then when all the commotion began and Guy pretended he had turned up an hour or two later than he actually did, John didn't want Guy to know he had been seen, and so pretended he had been in his study all afternoon rather than outside.'

It sounded like a pretty thin story to Angela, and she wondered whether there was something more to it than that. Had John, in fact, seen Guy climbing down the ivy from Donald's bedroom and chosen to keep quiet about it? Naturally Louisa was reluctant to believe that John had known of Guy's guilt, but Angela was not so sure. However, there was no use in pursuing the point; Guy was dead now, and John was old enough to look after his own conscience, so she wisely resolved to remain silent on the subject.

'What of Stella and Donald?' she asked. 'I suppose it's too much to hope that they have made it up.'

'My dear, I shouldn't have expected it myself either, but strange to tell they seem to have done just that. I don't know quite how it happened, as the things that go on between young couples nowadays are quite beyond my comprehension, but

I shouldn't be at all surprised to hear that the engagement is back on.'

A day or two later Angela heard the whole story when she received a visit from the girl herself. Stella arrived looking at once embarrassed and pleased, in order (she said) to make certain that Mrs. Marchmont was quite all right after her adventure in the attic, and to thank her for solving the mystery and proving once and for all that Donald was not guilty of killing half his family.

'But how on earth did you get the idea into your head that he was the murderer?' asked Angela.

'Oh! Wasn't it ridiculous of me?' she replied. 'I hardly know how it started, but just after Philippa died we had one of our usual blow-ups about something or other, and things got rather heated and Don got one of his funny fits and started intoning portentously—idiot that he is—about how we should be careful about quarrelling at Underwood, since the house was susceptible to human emotions and might turn on us.'

'I have heard him in similar vein,' agreed Angela.

'I tell you, sometimes I think he's quite mad, but Aunt Louisa says he is just sensitive and needs a practical sort of girl to put him right. Anyhow, of course I told him not to be such a fathead, but that just made him worse and he started talking about how Philippa had disliked the house and had died as a result. Perhaps I was in an odd mood myself, but something about the way he said it made me see him suddenly in a new light and I started to wonder whether these fits of his were quite as harmless as they seemed, or whether there was something more serious behind them.

'Things went on as usual for a month or two, then one day Don started saying that he could feel something not quite right in the air. I didn't pay much attention to what he was saying to begin with, but he became quite insistent. He was worried, he said, that something terrible was about to happen, but he couldn't say what it was. Shortly after that, Winifred fell over the balustrade and died.'

Angela suddenly remembered something.

'Louisa said that when it happened, you ran over to Donald and cried, "Not another one!" or something like that.'

'Did I?'

'Perhaps you were thinking about what he had said about the house turning on those who disliked it.'

'That's quite likely,' agreed Stella. 'But I didn't suspect him of having had a hand in it—not then, at any rate.'

'When did you start to suspect him?'

'When Edward died. A week or two before the family meeting he went all funny again, and started saying that he could feel something wrong. It was just like when Winifred died, only this time I listened to what he was saying and began to be terribly afraid. That night, after Edward rushed out of the house, Don left the room and I didn't see him for the rest of the evening. The next day Edward was found in the lake, and people started asking questions and I didn't know what to think. The police wanted to know what we had all been doing that evening after the row, and Don told them that he'd gone to sit quite innocently in the library with a book, but by that time I didn't know whether I ought to believe him or not.

'Of course, I didn't think he had set out deliberately to murder his aunts and uncle, but he had behaved so oddly at around the time of each of the deaths that I thought he might have had some kind of brainstorm and killed them without knowing it. I thought that perhaps he had been working too hard and needed to see a doctor. I tried to ask him gently about it, but he just got cross every time I did and we ended up rowing again. By then I had fully convinced myself that he was the killer, and it was coming up to the date of the next family meeting and I was getting very scared. Oh, Mrs. Marchmont,' she said, 'What a fool I made of myself that evening! When Ursula started accusing Don I thought it *must* be true. I thought he would never forgive me after that night.'

'Then you never cared for Guy?' said Angela.

Stella shook her head, eyes wide.

'Of course not,' she said. 'He was amusing company, that's all. Of course, I'm sorry about what happened, but he was a murderer—there's no escaping the fact—and so he deserved it.'

'You don't feel sorry for him?'

'No,' she said with decision. 'I know one ought to feel sympathy for his difficult childhood and all that, but I don't. Lots of people have difficult childhoods and don't go about killing people. Murder is wrong and that's that.'

'That's that,' repeated Angela to herself later when Stella had left. She was a little surprised at the girl's uncompromising attitude, but supposed it was only to be expected given the resilience of young people these days to tragedy and disaster.

She sat for a while in thought, then stood up and looked about her. She was growing restless after several days indoors and determined to go out.

'What I need is a new hat,' she said, 'and perhaps a scarf and some gloves. Now, where did I see that darling little red silk cap the other day? Bond Street, I think it was.'

She rang the bell for Marthe, but it was William who answered.

'I beg your pardon, ma'am, but I was coming to return this,' he explained when he saw her look of surprise. He looked round, reached into his pocket and brought out the little revolver that she had lent him a few days earlier. 'I guess you need it more than I do,' he said.

'Thank you,' she said, taking it from him. 'It was one of a pair, but the other is no more so I suppose I ought to try and keep this one safe.'

He shuffled a little and looked sheepish.

'I'm sorry I failed you the other day, ma'am,' he said in a rush.

'You didn't fail me, William,' she said. 'It was a miscalculation on my part. I ought to have predicted that he would have doubled back into the house.'

'A whole hour I wasted searching through those woods for him,' he said angrily. 'When I got down to the little cove I wondered why the only person I could see there was Mr. Donald Haynes sitting on a tree trunk with his head in his hands. It took me far too long to realize I'd been tricked. You ought never to have had to face him alone.'

'It wasn't something I'd planned to happen, certainly,' she agreed, 'but rest assured it wasn't your fault. And besides, all's well that ends well. It's only a shame that he had to die in such a terrible accident.'

'An accident?' he said.

'Yes,' she said firmly.

He met her eyes for a moment.

'I see,' he said.

She looked away first, then coughed and waved her hand in a gesture of dismissal.

'That will be all, William,' she said. 'I am very grateful for all you have done in the past few days. Come to me next week and we shall see about that holiday of yours.'

He straightened up and beamed.

'It's a pleasure to work for you, ma'am,' he said, then turned on his heels and walked out.

New Releases

If you'd like to receive news of further releases by Clara Benson, you can sign up to my mailing list here: clarabenson.com/newsletter.

Books in This Series

- The Murder at Sissingham Hall
- The Mystery at Underwood House
- The Treasure at Poldarrow Point
- The Riddle at Gipsy's Mile
- The Incident at Fives Castle
- The Imbroglio at the Villa Pozzi
- The Problem at Two Tithes
- The Trouble at Wakeley Court
- The Scandal at 23 Mount Street
- The Shadow at Greystone Chase

Also by Clara Benson:

The Freddy Pilkington-Soames Adventures